UPROAR
and
HERESY

A.P. ANDES

UPROAR
and
HERESY

Volume II of The Latecoming West

This work, on occasion, ventures into moments beyond the boundaries encountered in traditional fiction. For this reason, any unusual images you experience on your reading device or see in your printed copy are neither in error nor accidental; rather, they were crafted to offer brief sensory events and an enhanced reading experience beyond the static black-and-white frame of the printed page or eBook. Likewise, as the series title, *The Latecoming West*, implies, this work embraces both the Old World of Africa and Eurasia and the New World of the Americas across many millennia, so the English employed, spelling of words, and phrasings of certain conventions will vary depending on the locale and time of the narrative.

Finally, the derivation of Pope Joan's name is one on which this story departs from the more widely cited versions. A few of the essential facts comprising the Pope Joan story contradict common sense; one of those is that someone who was born in Mainz, Germany and spent her childhood there should come to be known as "John the Englishman." Therefore, both in terms of logic and imagination, the earliest spellings of *Johannes Angelicus*, or "John the Angelic," found in several accounts of Martinus Polonus's narrative, felt the most authentic. Further searches revealed the much more common spelling of *Johannes Anglicus*, but, in harmony with the stance against consensus this novel embodies, the former has prevailed here, as a far more organic and plausible appellation. Surely, few would deny that John the Angelic seems far more evocative of Joan's actual nature and appearance.

Cover design by James T. Egan at Bookfly Design
Book interior design by Booknook.biz

ISBN 978-0-9863183-4-4 (paperback)
ISBN 978-0-9863183-5-1 (epub)

Acknowledgements

This book, and the series of which it is part, is the fruit of over forty years of labor and love, and I have many people to thank, without whom you would not be reading this; there is not room to thank everyone, but they must surely know how much their presence and encouragement in my life have helped. Several people deserve mention by dint of their extraordinary grace, timing and generosity, some for many years, at a time when I had little else in my corner to sustain me beyond the call of my imagination.

I must first thank Kellie Schruhl, a coworker back in the early 1980s, who passed on my interest in Pope Joan to a cleric friend of hers, who generously wrote back with key details and facts to get me started. Also, a huge debt of gratitude is owed to Dr. Matthew Lippman, a mentor and dear friend, who lent his expertise and critical sources on the Nuremberg Trials and the Holocaust to my development of the Rahel storyline as well as feedback on key scenes in this series at a most difficult time of his life. Thanks also to fellow lawyer Susan Russell, who provided the motivation for me to complete the work I'd started some four decades before. Susan has continued to be a great friend and supporter of my work even as her own literary career, especially in children's books, has taken off.

I will always be eternally grateful to my guiding lodestar, lover of literature and loving mother, Pat Andes, who died in 2017, and my sister, Alison McClaren, and brother-in-law, Bill McClaren, who have always supported my writing and creative life far beyond the level of polite endorsement you sometimes encounter in families. In countless ways, they kept me going and provided support in every way a person can. Alison and Bill even gave me a laptop to use when my old one self-destructed. Alison has been a tremendous and insightful yet enthusiastic beta reader for this work: the brunt of the most significant improvements to this volume came from her extensive feedback. She has also been a superb advocate for book sales of Volume I, *John the Angelic*; she attended my maiden Book Signing and Reading Event, and bought several copies for friends and loved ones, including Bill, who is currently reading *John the Angelic*.

I am also humbled by and grateful for the substantial support that Jack Knorps, whom I met through work, has taken out of his very full life to lend; he came to my Book Signing Event at Barnes & Noble, bought copies of Volume I, and wrote and posted on his superb book review blog, Flyinghouses (and then re-posted on Goodreads), the most impressive and nuanced review of *John the Angelic* I have ever read.

Two old and dear friends and fellow writers, Ulysses Smith and Chris Rabot, have contributed with their unconditional support in different ways, and their elation and words of deep praise and encouragement at the publication of *John the Angelic* were all by themselves worth the mountains of work that went into its creation and publication. Ulysses generously bought ten copies and gave them as gifts to friends and loved ones—a truly fabulous and brilliant act of promotion—and Chris has been there with encouragement and affirmation of my efforts in this process, every step of the way, and his insights into the critical Socrates chapter in *John the Angelic* were essential. A substantial debt of gratitude goes out to Sonya Kamell for being a fabulous beta reader for *John the Angelic*. Her enthusiasm and admiration for the writing, especially the more experimental elements in that volume, were extraordinary. Thanks also go to Kara Lang Guminski, Krista Harms (who tragically passed this year from cancer at only 59) and Maggie Kohls, friends and colleagues who have supported me from afar in this project, with various insights and contributions to Volume I, and to Daliah Saper, who generously donated her legal expertise back then on some questions I was working through.

I am blessed beyond words to have had the expertise and diligence of Christina M. Frey at pagetwoediting.com, who copyedited the book before you, as well as Volume I, with mastery and aplomb, yet always with humor, warmth, and tremendous patience, in spite of having to conform to the massive, voluminously detailed style sheet I provided, encompassing multiple time periods and both European/British and American spellings and styles throughout. As with the first volume, soaring panegyric must go to James T. Egan at Bookfly Design for yet another stunning cover design that far exceeded even my grandest expectations, as well as Bookfly's Kira Rubenthaler, whose expertise and queries on my tastes and preferences gave James a clear and detailed overview of what I was looking for. They are both a joy to work with, always, and James is immensely accommodating. Effusive thanks also go out to my conversion/IT guru, Kimberly Hitchens, and the fine folks at Booknook.biz big-time for their technical legerdemain and superb conversion services (and patience!), both to ebook and print on demand. Your seamless enjoyment of this volume—as well as *John the Angelic*—and its beautiful aesthetics are due to "Hitch" and her expert staff.

The preceding years have been difficult for my wife and me with the economy, and her parents, Bob (who has also now passed on) and Janet Takushi, provided financial and spiritual support without which the first volume would never have seen the light of day, and I am forever grateful. Janet has been not only hugely supportive financially in enabling *Uproar and Heresy* to go forward, she has had great suggestions regarding promotion of *John the Angelic* as well.

Most of all, I owe everything and more to my extraordinary wife and partner in life's adventure, Alicia. This entire process would have sent a lesser soul raving into the night, but her belief in me and in this project has been unwavering, and without it this work would not exist. Not only did she will my vision for my author's website apandes. com into reality, but she found a Barnes & Noble near us, in Algonquin, that was highly supportive of Book Signing Events for self-published writers, and designed fabulous posters advertising the event and put them up in a number of places around our general area. She has always been there with a word of encouragement and one more leap of faith that things would turn out in the end. Here's hoping, my love, that indeed they will! Last but not least, kisses to my two loving twin daughters, Micaela and Nila, who have for their daddy and his books the animation, voltage and adoration to resuscitate a walking cadaver back into an energized human being.

A.P. ANDES lives in the Chicago area with his wife and twin daughters. His writing has been published in *The Iowa Review* and is informed by his love of philosophy, postmodernism, and especially European literature, cinema, and history. His four books of historical literary fiction, *John the Angelic*, *Uproar and Heresy*, *Falling through the Roof of Hell*, and *The Annihilating Hero*, form the genre-bending quartet, *The Latecoming West*.

Death is at the center of everything:
Not because it is feared
but because it is not.

ONE

ON A LUSCIOUS, WARM and misty eve at the end of October 830, I arose in the dark of night from my pallet, picked up but did not put on my shoes so I could tiptoe out the dormitorium, and set out for a secret rendezvous with my Beloved, well past the hour when all the Brethren had fallen into slumber. I wore my monk's robes with a sash and just my hair shirt and stockings under it, since it was warm. I was going to see Clovis and expected to encounter no one at the abbey or anyone else on my journey at that hour. Scarce three months ago, Clovis had unbound my flesh and held me in his arms, but I felt a year's time at least had passed. We had arranged in advance through his messenger, Fabian, to meet at the boundary of a forest at the appointed hour, perhaps half a kilometre from the abbey. I slipt out Lorsch's back door without notice, distracted in my walk, for a full moon lit my way, even in the thick mist, and the humidity put its arms about me as I walked. I drank in the diaphanous, milky light tinging the trees and into which their tops vanished in a promise of some soon-to-be-revealed mystery.

As I drew near the rendezvous point—I had resolved to arrive ahead of time in the event he arrived in advance—I heard in the distance the faint calamity of a multitude of feminine voices, carrying on and erupting in laughter. After a couple hundred metres, I stopped and stood still in the heavy air, which did not transmit sound well. The voices were closer. As they advanced, I could smell smoke.

Chills brushed my arms and the back of my neck in cool tongues of fear. *Samhain.*

We were not in Celtic lands, but to the local pagans, this was of no moment. Samhain as practised by the pagans was an innocuous occasion, with offerings to pagan spirits at the end of Harvest to ensure livestock provisions and the like over the winter, but we had heard exotic rumours involving isolated bands of celebrants in orgy and animal sacrifice. They were not true adherents, but the pagan holiday was all these locals needed to inspire their festivities. *How could we not have seen this.* Aside from all else, I could ill afford anyone seeing me outside of Lorsch and identifying my true sex. My breath quickened.

And they were upon me. About a dozen pagan women, all of child-bearing age, some quite young, all naked with various paintings upon their bodies and faces, and all carrying torches, descended upon me, howling and dancing in ever-tightening circles about me.

'A young oblate in need of losing his virginity,' one of the celebrants said in a teasing, sing-song voice.

Another with flowing red hair approached and pulled down my hood. She laid her hand on my face and pressed her full lips to mine, but withdrew at once. 'What?' She studied my face. 'You are a woman.' I stood as a statue in front of her. I could not make my mouth work at all. Her hand brushed against my breast. 'You were so soft—I am right!' I was terrified. Her breath reeked of libations, and a smile broke out on her face. The commotion had settled into a hushed aura as she stood in front of me. 'Even better!' Upon this pronouncement, the joy resumed anew and redoubled.

'We shall enjoy you, and you shall enjoy us,' said the one who had spoken of my virginity. Queasiness intruded upon my belly, and I was feeling dizzy.

'Pray,' I implored, 'I am en route to meet someone. I mean you no harm—'

But the woman with the flowing red tresses and another blonde woman held me between them, one taking my left hand and the other my right, and the rest of the group chanted in song about us in a circle. As I stood between them, the one with the red hair who had kist me reached round and proceeded to undo my sash. She took off my robes, then directed me to raise my arms. I did so, and she pulled my hair shirt up over my head. I stood before all of them, my breasts naked. My heart pounded in my throat. So many locals had now seen me, once dressed in monk's garb, now a woman in her nakedness. A tear formed at the corner of my eye. Not since the raid in Mainz had I been so afraid. Yet, there, I had used one of the Norsemen's torches to club my mother's rapist to death. Here, amongst all these women, I could do nothing but observe events as they unfolded, as though I were outside my body, hovering above this frightening scene. The blonde woman directed me to remove my stockings. My mouth opened, but my power of speech betrayed me. I closed it, opened it once more and craned my neck forward in protestation, and still no words came out.

'You are a woman of the earth. You must celebrate with us in all your naked glory, just like the rest of us.' She said this with a welcoming smile, as if this would somehow dispense with any unease I might be feeling. As I stood in mute reluctance, I saw how intoxicated these women were. She stept forward even closer, mere centimetres from my face, her eyes wide with ecstasy, and waved her torch just beyond my bare flesh. 'Or we could just burn everything to Hell,' she whispered in a slow, deranged voice, still smiling, as others laughed behind her. Frantic, I reached down and grabbed at my stockings; a few moments later I stood naked from head to foot before a circle of women I had never seen before. Heart pounding, I allowed myself to be led by them far afield of our rendezvous point, in the opposite direction and deep into the forest. I fought back more tears. Deep within the wood, in a small clearing, we stopped; they made me stand on a small, raised mound, and I placed both my hands in front of my sex.

'She is shy,' the tall, dark-haired lass who liked to talk said, in a lilting, mocking tone, standing before me, her face close to mine. Looking up into my eyes, she cooed, 'But you have an ample garden of delights, full of thriving vegetation,' trying to feel my pubes. I wanted to kick her, punch her in the face, but the others had crowded in round us and overwhelmed me by their numbers and all those flaming clubs.

Breathless, I flashed back to that cruel assault in the wood by Garrick and his lads when I was but a girl of eleven and at their mercy.

'Let her drink,' one short blonde girl said, her voice so high she chirped, and handed the one in front of me a leather wineskin.

'Yea, Caelin, a splendid idea!' She took the vessel, opened it and proffered it up to my lips.

I shook my head, saying no in a quiet voice.

She stood back, holding the wineskin in one hand, her other hand resting on her hip. 'Why on earth are you wearing a monk's clothes in the first place?'

I knew at once I needed to distract them from this line of questioning before they could dwell upon it a moment longer, and reached out my hand, asking for the wineskin. I slipt into the spirit of someone else: no one whom I had ever met, but one of these women, as I imagined them in my mind, based on my impressions to that point. I tossed Joan—Johannes—off to the side in the dirt, and after several glugs of wine, I decided there was but one thing to do, and I reached out and drew my captor to me, pressing my mouth hard over her own and reaching down to finger her breast in my hand. I was nauseated kissing her but forced myself beyond it.

On the surface, it was a senseless choice, but desperate measures were needed in that moment, and I surmised, correctly, she would not enjoy being the one on the receiving end of a grope. She jerked back, and the wine spilt out. The taller redhead came at me, punching me flush in the nose, and I toppled to the ground. I screamed in pain and my nose bled, but for the first time, relief cascaded over me. The blonde woman who had threatened me came forward with several of the others, kicking me in the ribs and in the legs, a torrent of abusive words and epithets about my deranged sexuality raining down upon me as I lay there. One of them kicked me in the head twice. She held her torch down by her side, and the flames crackled within several centimetres of my face as she kicked me. This severed the air from my lungs and transported me yet again to my youth, when the Norsemen set my room on fire, but then the torch lifted, they all left, and there was nothing but silence. I lay crying, crumpled in a bloodied heap in the leaves.

I was cut, and my head, my nose, my legs and my ribs all hurt, and I wept where I lay, wept long after they had abandoned me there, as much for the poor decisions that had gone into this as for my wounds. When I at last arose after I had stopped crying, the blood in my nose and elsewhere, by good fortune, had dried, as I had to find my clothes and put them back on. This was no trivial task, for we had walked quite a distance after they disrobed me, and I retraced my steps in my battered, somewhat intoxicated state: once, twice, the third time at last took me to where my clothes had been pitched.

I cursed Clovis for not thinking better of the matter, as one so much older and more experienced than I, for it had been his idea to meet on this night. Yea, I was angered and disappointed to have missed this night with him we had planned, but my spirit was wracked anew with anxiety, as I would have to explain my appearance to the Brothers and Father Abbot. Plus, I smelt of alcohol, but I hoped I could at least sneak back to bed at this hour without detection. Somehow, stealing out for an amorous rendezvous with my Beloved and groping a young female celebrant to avoid an inquisition as to my garb did not seem as though it would meet with the Abbot's approval. I shook my head and laughed. My thoughts scurried off in an hundred directions as I imagined all the stories these local women could and might tell. And, because Lorsch was the sole monastery within proximity of the forest, they would of course connect me to the abbey. I had to leave off it altogether, comforted in the knowledge any such divulgence would implicate them in their improper activities in the forest.

No more than fifty steps later, the sound of thunder and a downpour of rain both hit in the same moment, soaking me from head to toe where I stood, water dripping from my bloodied, stinging nose.

'Perfect,' I said, fuming. 'Just what I needed.' I could not, after all, disrobe the way any other Brother would have in my position. By the time I got back to Lorsch, the rain had stopped, but I was shivering in heavy, soaked clothes that clung to my body. I crept round to the back door and found it ajar. I put my ear to the wood and listened for any sounds, and hearing none, I opened it; the door creaked at first, and of a sudden I heard footsteps and closed it again, hoping I had not been detected. My blood throbbed in my ears as I waited outside at the threshold for the door to open from the inside, but by the grace of God, this did not happen. After a little time had passed, and upon pressing my ear to the door again and hearing nothing, I eased it open once more. As I craned my head inside, I saw the hallway was empty and dark; I entered and tiptoed as fast as possible towards the dormitorium, which lay not far beyond the hallway. I had no idea of the hour, but to the best of my knowledge, it was still before Vigils, or Matins, when the Brethren arose at two in the morning for recitation of the Nocturnal Office. At most monasteries, and under the Rule of St Benedict, the monks retired after Vigils until Prime, at five o'clock, but not at Lorsch. Once Matins arrived, all the Brethren would be up for the entire day.

Once I made it into my pallet, I resolved to remain there for the duration, placing the burden upon Father Abbot to come and seek me out, which transpired sometime after three in the morning in the person of Brother Hasso, charged as always with the recitation of the Nocturnal Office. He was a tall and imposing man, a noble who reminded me more of Clovis than anyone else at Lorsch and with whom I felt at ease, because, like my Beloved, he was at once keen in intelligence and possessed of a most unpresuming air. By then I had fallen into a deep slumber, roused at last by his persistent shaking of my shoulder under the blanket. I may have been dreaming about my misadventure in the forest, for I started up wide-eyed and breathless in bed, though still covered by the blanket.

'All is well, Brother Johannes,' he said in a calming voice, his firm hand coaxing me back into a supine position, and I drew the blanket up to my neck. Even in the dark he could see by my nose and the area at the top of my forehead that there had been a mishap. He knelt down close to my face, and I closed my mouth, breathing through my nostrils to minimise the alcohol smell. 'Goodness, Brother, what has happened?'

I had worked out a story in advance, prior to sleep, and now explained the nature of my injuries. 'Sometime in the middle of the night, I awoke to a great deal of commotion, what sounded like heavy things being moved, coming from outside, and two voices below that window,' I said, gesturing. A trash receptacle and a small reserve of bricks and wood for burning stood near the back entrance. Hasso's brow furrowed. 'I know I shouldn't have, Brother Hasso, but I worried they were stealing from the abbey, and I slipt round the back way to see what they were doing—'

'Good Lord,' Brother Hasso exclaimed, clasping his hands together.

'Well, no sooner did I get outside than I was attacked; someone punched me hard in the nose, and I fell to the ground, and the other fellow kicked me in the head. And then they ran off.'

'We have never had such an incident before,' he said, shaking his head. 'This is most unsettling.' Without glaring, but with the slightest measure of admonishment, he smiled. 'You know you never should have done what you did; you are far too learned not to know it. We are blessed indeed you did not meet with a far graver end.'

'I know it.' My ribs and legs were aching, but I did not shew it. I had to ensure I would not be examined other than for my head wounds. By the grace of God, I had found a discarded nightshirt in the laundry hamper as I entered the dormitorium, and put it on, so my physical contours were not in evidence. I had to make certain I would not be examined below the neck. Because I had not got much sleep, I asked Hasso if I could sleep until Prime, and he assented but gave it upon condition I be examined by Brother Alberich, the monk at Lorsch trained in the medical arts, in the infirmary no later than Terce, the third hour, at nine in the morning. I told Hasso I was not injured anywhere else, and therefore Alberich needed to examine my head alone, and he agreed examination of any other part of my body would be unnecessary. All things considered, and the immense dread visited upon me by this mishap, I could not but feel God had a hand in my true identity remaining undiscovered by anyone at the abbey. I did not know when I would next have occasion to communicate with my Beloved, whether through another note passed to his estate or other-wise, but it would contain a harsh rebuke for the oversight responsible for the events of that night. For an erudite count in his thirties who had always lived in this area, I had hoped for far greater appreciation of the unique local history and dynamics of Samhain.

The gossamer bridge of the feminine in my own life had twisted in these events, both from within and without. Whilst I had made my best efforts in disguising my sex upon setting out for the forest, I had learnt a cruel lesson indeed on the relative ease of undoing all that in the world beyond the confines of Lorsch Abbey, given the right circumstances. Once they exposed me as a woman, the celebrants in whose company I found myself were masculine to a fault, forcing nudity and heathen practices upon me. In almost all respects, their actions were reminiscent of the worst qualities of the male sex: unrelenting ridicule, from the nature of my virginity as an oblate when they still thought me a man to the fullness of my pubes; imposing themselves upon me with kisses and groping my person against my will; and appealing to threats of force at the first sign of resistance on my part. Even before they threatened me with being burnt to death, my own role in those events in the forest was submissive and feminine, yea, out of character entire for me, though I'd no clear idea why at the time. Looking back, I suppose I hoped a more passive approach would keep me in good stead with them, for whatever reason, until their conduct shewed me antagonistic behaviour alone would land me clear of harm's way.

I was born in 814, the year of Charlemagne's death, and my privileged childhood in the quiet town of Mainz passed more or less without event—however brutal it might have seemed at the time—until I turned fourteen. After 820, tributary defences collapsed, and in 828, Norsemen, who had been coming up in their longships at dawn and sacking sleepy towns off major rivers, attacked Mainz one morning before dawn. They killed my father, raped my mother and burnt our dwelling to the ground, and life in our ruined town was never again the same. My father might have inherited his family's wealth and property, but he was a drunk and a brute who hit me and kicked me and my mother in fits of rage whenever the mood struck him, which happened far more often than I cared to remember; I did not mourn his passing. My mother was no better; she had always determined I should excel beyond all reasonable bounds in my studies, and her unrelenting cruelty, her demands and her criticisms of me in that regard for the year or so afterwards at last became unbearable. Though I had hoped the tragedy of my father's passing, the loss of our dwelling and our dependence upon one another would allow my mother and me at long last to have the loving relationship that had always eluded us, I found, alas, that I was mistaken. Perhaps because all else had been lost, my mother's investment in my studies grew even more unreasonable. After packing a satchel and taking a stash of money from my mother's till, I wrote her a letter detailing all the ways she had crushed my spirit, and on the twelfth of July, 830, at the age of sixteen, I left home, taking the ancient Roman Mogontiacum from Mainz to Frankfurt am Main, where I hoped to find a new home.

But I was a single young woman on the street and subject both to the physical perils such status invited and the considerable scorn and contempt directed at such women. I cut off all my hair to disguise myself as a lad of twelve or thirteen. I had imagined Frankfurt am Main to be a sprawling metropolis of art, culture and commerce, one of the great cities of Europa, and found I was most misinformed on all counts. Disappointed in the city's sparseness and unable to find suitable lodging or a monastery whereby I could acquire residence, I despaired of my situation and the poor judgment that had led me there, when I met up with a much older, charismatic count named Clovis with piercing blue eyes who captivated me at once. He took me on his horse to Lorsch Abbey, one of the most venerated abbeys in the realm, which, by a stunning, engineered coincidence, was less than a kilometre from his own estate. By then we had become lovers.

Though smitten with him straight away, I natheless became, as the weeks passed one into the next, more invested in the life of quiet contemplation and community I shared with the Brothers at Lorsch, even as I despaired of his absence in my time there. Whilst not fain to admit it, I knew my heart belonged to Clovis, but the rest of me, more and more, was Lorsch's. And so, by the grace of God, a scarce three weeks since arriving at the abbey, I declined Clovis's invitation to come live with him at his estate and resolved for the time being to stay on at Lorsch.

On reflexion, with the passage of time, I believe I hungered to some extent for the kind of structure and stability grounded in authority the abbey provided, else it is hard for me to fathom why I would have chosen the company of relative strangers over that of a man who excited me in all ways. Even as I questioned the Church's unflinching authority and rigidity in its silencing of women's voices, I strove to fill the immense void left in my life by the raid and my own act of running away. I may have borne deep resentment and contempt for both my father and my mother, but some vestige of filial love no doubt persisted, for they had given me the unquestioned assurance of hearth and home—until it burnt to the ground—come what may. In some sense I must have needed a new family or some equivalent following the catastrophe in Mainz and the loss of our dwelling and my family.

I had seen Clovis in the first days of August, at his estate and before completion of my postulancy, under circumstances not expected to repeat themselves. The cellarer, Brother Einhard, had sent me out into the neighbouring countryside in search of a certain rare, prized truffle, and I seized the opportunity for a side trip to Clovis's estate. After a fevered dalliance in the grass, we set out for our day trip, where I found several specimens which, alas, turned out to be poisonous and unusable. It was on that day he invited me to live with him, and I, with a torn heart, declined his offer, already guided by feelings I could not yet explain.

In the three months since then, no other opportunities to visit my Beloved, other than the mischance in the woods, presented themselves, and, in the midst of my year-long term as a novice, consumed in longing for Clovis's touch, I dwelt at length upon my future prospects. The thought of life without him was intolerable, yet I also harboured concerns about my own development beyond the metes and bounds of any man to whom I might give my heart. I regarded it as my mission, with singular purpose for someone of my sex, to contribute to the world's sum of knowledge, be it through Letters or through the Lord.

By November, as I entered my fifth month at Lorsch, a curious transformation took root in me. The transitory nature of the abbey and my place within it, until I could better figure out what I most wished to do with my life, was yielding to a more permanent vision: that I might indeed find sustaining fulfilment in the service of the Lord, amongst this community. I could not deny the level of my attraction to Clovis, nor the immense admiration and spiritual comfort he afforded me, but without his body, his voice and his touch, it was an unrequited hunger. Meanwhile, the satisfaction I derived from the hours and days spent amongst the Brethren grew into an ever-greater portion of each day's worth.

By far the highest measure of reward came from my work in the library and scriptorium, where my natural talents in Letters were transformed into powerful instruments of service in the name of the Lord. There were codices, sumptuous volumes with vivid colour illuminations and gilded with gold; translations of the realm's greatest works of religion, history and philosophy; and our glorious books for Mass: sacramentaries, which collected the priest-celebrant's texts, evangeliaries, excerpting those parts of the four Gospels to be read at Mass, and graduales, containing the Psalms. Until Lorsch, I had never in my life felt I served a useful purpose beyond the vexation of my parents. And so, I pondered in earnest whether I had not found my true calling.

With each passing week I had dwelt more upon this question, until at last I resolved to seek out the counsel of Brother Dieter. To that point, I had conversed the most with Brother Tomas, on issues regarding both the running of the library and my own compliance with the Rule of St Benedict. Still, in my heart I trusted Brother Dieter more, notwithstanding the fact he appeared to be in his mid-fifties and had been at Lorsch for decades longer than Brother Tomas, for it was Brother Dieter who had told me about the hidden copy of Acts of John within the library at his own risk, swearing me to secrecy on the matter. Acts of John, believed written by St John, is a non-canonical book rooted in Docetism, the heretical doctrine that Jesus's human body was of celestial substance and therefore not real. Hence, Acts states that while on the Cross, Jesus appeared to suffer, but in actuality He did not die on the Cross and suffered nothing. The Church had ordered all existing copies of Acts to be destroyed. Natheless, this book had transformed my perception of the relationship between Man and the Divine into the most intense emotional experience of my entire life up to then. Brother Dieter, in that respect, both as to the heretical work itself and his confidence in me regarding its whereabouts, struck me as someone more aligned with my own complex perspective of the Church and her overall trustworthiness than Brother Tomas, whose gentle admonitions to me about cheating the Rule by reading while at the library betrayed a uniform obeisance to the Church and all her policies I did not share, at least not yet.

I still had not seen or heard from Clovis, which was a difficult proposition, given the severe restrictions upon visits or leaving the abbey under the Rule, following my abduction that night in the forest. On the afternoon of the third of November, after assisting Brother Dieter alone in the scriptorium with codex layouts and while awaiting the arrival of vellum stock from another location to make into quires for the scribes, I decided I might never again have a better opportunity to ask him about his own path to monkhood.

'Brother Dieter, pray, if it be not untoward, I wonder if I might enquire when you realised your path was to serve the Lord.'

I could see at once my question had caught him unprepared, and for a moment or two, he gathered his thoughts for a proper reply.

'Well, Brother Johannes, you are so new here that I should not trouble myself too much if I were you over such ponderous matters if you are unable to answer them just yet…'

At this he left off, as if that should finish the subject, and I surmised my estimate of Brother Dieter as a more private soul even than most of the other men at Lorsch was in all likelihood correct.

I had, however, become obsessed with these matters and therefore pressed on in spite of his rebuff. 'Yea, I am sure you are right; natheless, I would still like to hear it, if you are willing, as I find myself lost at the moment.'

He fell silent for a bit. 'The answer will not be the same for any two people,' he said. 'But… for me, I suppose there came a time when all the specious arguments I had maintained against it in my youth, including even my arguments against the existence of God altogether, which I held in reserve from time to time, failed to make sense any longer.' He looked at me then, with a touch of apology in his expression. 'I know this is not the answer one in your position would hope for, but no magical moment or epiphany initiated this change in me. Christ never came to me in a dream or at my bedside.' He paused for a moment in reflexion, and continued: 'In many ways, starting when I was a small boy, I suppose I have been rational to a fault, and I surprised myself when that rationality abandoned me to the rationality of Christ, in especial once I became more familiar with other approaches to spirituality, to other religions or cults.

'See'—and for the first time, I sensed he was talking more to himself than to me—'I came to appreciate that, in ridiculing and finding fault with Christian doctrine and teachings, I was not armed with some superior truth against which Christianity lacked worth or merit, but rather just the opposite: I myself lacked any real spiritual centre outside of Christ's teachings, yet wanted to bring Christianity down to my level. It was a cheap ruse.'

I blushed at these remarks, for in truth he had described me and my own perspective with eerie precision. 'Yea, your words have more relevance for me than you can know,' I stammered. 'And yet… there are some texts and even some ideas I have read that have given me great pause—'

He smiled at me. 'Acts of John.'

Now I coloured deep red. 'Acts of John.' My heart pounded in my breast, as though we were about to kiss; the sensation was dizzying. '"For so long"…' I swallowed, trembling where I stood, and began again. '"For so long as thou callest not thyself Mine, I am not that which I am"—'

'"But if hearing thou hearkenest unto Me",' Dieter said, cutting me off, '"then shalt thou be as I am, and I shall be what I was, when I have thee as I am with Myself. For from this thou art."' These were the words that had transformed my understanding of Man's relationship to God: saying, in essence, that if Man does not believe in God's Word, God is not in full measure what He is, and neither are we, but if we believe in Him, then, forsooth, He is divine, and so are we in His eyes.

I stood before him as though I were naked from head to foot, having him recite back the most powerful—and apocryphal—words I had ever heard. 'It was you. You were the one who hid the volume.'

His eyes were fixed straight ahead, beyond me. 'I did.'

On the verge of coming apart in front of him, I had to remember my identity at Lorsch as Johannes, not Joan. I focused my gaze on a volume of Etruscan military history on a table, opened to a battle scene, to guide my thoughts back to a firm state of mind. 'But... but how did you resolve those words in your heart?'

Sadness filled his eyes, I suspect because he knew his words would crush my spirit. 'One day I came to that passage and saw nothing but another false prophet's words, something that could never be true, not about God the Father, who created all things.'

'You mean the notion He needs our belief in Him to be divine?'

'All of it. It is a passage you can read to mean anything you want if you are so motivated, as I was for quite a long time,' he said. 'But the irony of this is that even the doctrine of Docetism itself, which touches upon the most heretical aspects of Acts of John, is inconsistent. Marcion and other Gnostics couldn't agree on whether Jesus was mortal at all. There is but one true answer as to what the real nature of God, just like Christ, comprises, regardless of the protean ways we may perceive it. The beauty lies in the fact God allows us to perceive Him however we wish, but we are not permitted to fashion the most far-flung of those perceptions into the one true answer.'

I stood lost in thought, trying to sort through all his words in my mind and resolve them with those words in Acts, and at last looked up at him. 'Then why did you hide the volume?'

A faint smile formed at the corner of his mouth. 'You are nothing, Brother Johannes, if not astute for one so young.' He pursed his lips. 'That was almost thirty years ago. At that time, our collections were much smaller, and it had to be hidden with far more care.' He tossed his head to one side with a mild snicker. 'I suppose I wanted to ensure the Catholic Church did not have all the answers, or at least not all the right questions to ask.'

'Even when, in your own mind, all the right questions had already been asked.'

Brother Dieter fixed his gaze upon me, and his next words surprised me as much as anything I have heard spoken by anyone before or since.

'Are we at the end of history? I think not. Until that moment, your assertion is a factual and logical impossibility. And,' he said, leaning in, arms crossed, 'perhaps not even then.' I dwelt upon what he had said for a moment, and started to thank him, but when I looked up, he was gone.

There are not words for the queer sensation I was left with following that conversation. Most of what he had said lined up with traditional ecclesiastic doctrine, and in those moments, I felt a sense of loss and sorrow for someone who had once questioned the entirety of religion as I did but who had since surrendered that portion of his soul to the Church, once and for all. But I was also dogged by the persistent reminder that Dieter no doubt saw me as the one worthy of pity.

Dieter's explanation as to why he had hidden Acts of John left me wanting, and I had been unable to shake the feeling a more personal reason impelled this curious conduct. But his last words to me, as far afield as possible from the passage we had been discussing and the theological absolutes he had been expounding upon, transitioned from the curious or eccentric into the inscrutable. As I drank in the effect his words had upon me in my solitude, I understood with increasing clarity that he had divulged the blackest, most impenetrable secret, but one he dared not utter save through an occult language: that whatever I thought of him—and whatever I considered myself to be—was as meaningless and illusory as any difference I perceived between us. To this day I cannot say why I knew this, yet the passage of time has but revealed its truth with ever-increasing certainty. I have come to see that the question Brother Dieter's closing words posed *was* the answer, not a question with an answer behind it. Once I solved this puzzle, my gratitude for it was immense, and in its quiet, artless grandeur, it has visited me often in my life.

Rahel Buchwald met Patek Mroz for the first time outside Mueller's Market in Berlin on the twenty-seventh of January, 1933, three days before Hitler's appointment as Chancellor of Germany and one month to the day after she had turned twenty-three. It was a brutish, inclement moment of driving winds and sleet eating through her face in flawless depiction of the actual, physical depravity of her life—with no end in sight for either. She felt herself a chaos of frozen hair, despair and misery, able to see no more than a metre or two in front of her, when she was aware someone's eyes had been upon her for quite some time, and looked up to see him: bareheaded, unscarved and imperturbable, the left side of his face lit with the glow of an internal smile threatening to take his entire face hostage. He did not look away, and, if possible, his gaze burned even more into her where she stood. He stuck out his hand and introduced himself. A series of moments without thought held her back before she at last reciprocated.

'Do you believe you can be destined for someone?' he asked her in a grave voice. The smile had vanished.

'Oh, why not. There's nothing else left.'

They went through Mueller's together, picking over rotten cabbage and radishes and talking of unemployment, their faith in Hindenburg and what would happen to Chancellor von Schleicher. Like Rahel herself, Patek was a Polish Jew, an engineer whose family had moved to Germany in 1911 from Warsaw after he turned five, due to his father's promotion in the import-export business. She had to admit the cut of his jaw and the set of his mouth were much to her liking, and his dark, straight hair framed his face well. He was short—perhaps an inch taller than she—and even in his coat, his shoulders looked narrower than her own, but under it he wore a confidence that gave him bearing and heft. After a certain amount of time had passed discussing his own particulars, she picked a moment of awkward silence to go for the kill, a tactic she had developed in flushing out the vapid motives of men who had elevated to an art form the illusion of spiritual agony to dress up their pursuit of a beautiful, busty young woman they wished to bed as soon as possible. 'So, tell me about me.'

He stopped pushing the cart. 'Excuse me?'

'Tell me about myself. All the wonderful, amazing things you think you know about me.'

Patek's mouth opened wide, but nothing came out; he turned to the side, then stood to face her, hand on his hip, standing erect. 'First of all, you're a musician—I'd say the violin or the 'cello, given your hands and the way you use them. You've always resented you didn't possess the talent to be a true genius of your instrument, which you adore, and that explains in part why you're so poor now. My guess is you taught music at a school somewhere, but like the rest of us, not anymore. Once in a way you get thrown a bone for a performance—a wedding or a church service or such—but it isn't regular, and now you work at a menial job that just keeps the roof over your head, but it degrades your soul, which was put here to do so much more. You're not the *shiksa* everyone presumes you to be; as a young girl, you obeyed your father's wishes and studied the Torah in earnest, but the day came when you no longer believed what you read, and all the boys you had crushes on were Gentiles anyway. To a large extent, they still are. And you're a virtuous woman, in spite of your stunning beauty and constant suitors, but less because it's in your nature than because you had your heart shattered once upon a time—and, because you feel everything with such intensity, it almost destroyed you. Some nights you cry yourself to sleep hearing the strain of Mozart (or Wagner or Schubert, whatever it is) that for you is the sound of your life as it could be with the one man out there who could hear it and feel the same things you do.' A long pause. 'We are the same that way, you and I.'

She stood there colouring from head to toe, breathless, flushed in the crowded aisle and unable to speak. He was right about the 'cello, about her gift, about the teaching—and he was even right about her upbringing, though her father had died when she was a small child, and her mother had raised her. He'd been wrong about her faith as well, for last year she'd returned to it in some measure and started attending synagogue, more out of a need for some kind of spiritual balm in this foreboding climate of economic depravity and political crisis. Still, her heart was pounding; it was as though he'd reached inside her chest and squeezed it with his mind. Livid and embarrassed, she felt penetrated, violated—and yet she'd asked for it. She could not argue otherwise.

She stood back from him, her arms crossed in front of her chest. 'Do you know where I live?'

'No, of course not—'

'You've been following me, asking my neighbours about me?'

'Rahel, no, it's not like that—'

'I don't know what it's like. But I don't care for it.' She turned to leave.

'Please—'

'No, please—*you* please!' she snapped, wheeling round to face him. She forced back the knot threatening to break her voice. 'Please do not approach me again. Good day.' She left the store, abandoning the items she'd picked out, and walked the six blocks to her apartment, tears streaming down her face, unable at first when she reached the threshold to enter into the cold, empty room.

On the heels of my unsatisfying exchange with Brother Dieter, whose answers to my questions about his faith provoked more questions than they solved, I commenced my year-long term at Lorsch as a novice, after which time I could decide whether I wished to forswear my few belongings and enter into the monkhood. Having received no answers from Dieter or anyone else there that lent clarity to the wars being waged in my heart and in my mind concerning my sex and the place God saw for women in His Church, I redoubled my vigour towards reading as many texts, Gnostic as well as canonical, as I could lay hold of. As I had during my postulancy, I steeped myself in Lorsch's illimitable stores of ecclesiastical knowledge; having already plumbed the works of Eusebius of Caesarea, Clement of Alexandria and Tertullian, amongst other Church Fathers, I discovered all roads to understanding —and disillusionment—passed through Irenaeus, as significant and influential a Church Father as any who existed in the first centuries of Christianity.

More than anything else, Irenaeus represents the notion of Christian unity through obeisance—to episcopal councils. His doctrine's sole authority appeared to be its own existence, and this antagonised me towards an institution built from the ground up, it appeared, on a similar self-perpetuating logic.

Born around AD 130, Irenaeus was in all likelihood Greek and a student of Polycarp, who was in turn a disciple of John the Apostle. His connexion to the Apostolic Age is thus closer in time than the other Church Fathers discussed to this point. Irenaeus was born but thirty years after the heretic Marcion of Sinope—and thus as contemporary to seminal developments within the first centuries of the Christian Church as any Church Father. I hoped this proximity to Jesus's Twelve Apostles would transmit a verity that would strengthen my faith in the scaffolding of ecclesiastic doctrine. I soon discovered quite the opposite.

Irenaeus's *Adversus Haereses*, an attack on Gnosticism in general and in particular on the teachings of the influential Gnostic Valentinus, remains his most important and well-known work. A model for all future apologetic works on heresy, *Adversus Haereses* is the single greatest source in existence on Gnosticism in the formative centuries of Christianity. I had intense curiosity about the Gnostics and most of all Valentinus, whose ideas I did not yet know well at that point, and was drawn to *Adversus Haereses* for that reason as well. I hoped to find great merit in Valentinus's work and was impressed with the degree of influence Valentinianism had garnered at large.

In some aspects, my feelings towards Irenaeus were akin to those I had for St Benedict: someone whose spirituality was built, brick by brick, upon the comfort, refuge and atomist function of structure, rules and the state of consensus such structure fostered. Like Benedict's, it did not move my soul; it was a vision of the world remote from the human—and therefore from me.

Tertullian, I had learnt, was rigid in his conservatism yet beset by paradoxes at the end of his life. His affiliation with the Montanists— the most influential Gnostics at that time—made him all too human, too complex, for one line of thought, one pigment of colour, to define him outright. A certain humidity, a warmth, a fragrant fermentation, rose off the page out of his words, and underneath it all, even in light of his views on women and Jews, I found, to my surprise, a certain comfort in them, a sense they sprang from a soul as divided and troubled as my own. Irenaeus, on the other hand, afforded not a moment's comfort; his writings were cold, contained and untouchable, with an abstract, inhuman materiality I could not access—and which would not admit of me or anyone of my sensibility within it.

Valentinus, Irenaeus's principal combatant, lived from about AD 100 to 160. He was educated in Alexandria, a major cultural and strategic centre for Christianity. He formed his school of the Valentinians in Rome after being passed over as a candidate for bishop of Rome.

In essence, nothing of Valentinus's actual writings survives; whilst believed to be a pupil of Paul, Valentinus intermarried Christian doctrine with a deep grounding in Platonism, which formed a spiritual nexus to much of the Gnostic's teachings.

I had become far more curious about Gnosticism after reading earlier through the works of Tertullian and Clement of Alexandria, both influential Church Fathers whose harsh appraisals of the female sex left much to be desired. My mistrust of and resentment towards the dominant ecclesiastic doctrines of the Church and its banishment of women had plunged me into a state of deepening despair over the fate of my spiritual future. Knowing little about the Gnostics' actual doctrines and beliefs, I had nonetheless cultivated a certain infatuation with them; the Montanists, for example, had two women, Prisca and Maximilla, who were high-ranking priestesses in the religion. And even Simon Magus, the very first Gnostic, had his Helena, whom he venerated as 'the mother of all things'. I had phantasies of what I would have done to the hateful Tertullian, had I lived in his time and were I able to attain to such a position of clerical power and authority. I pictured myself performing incantations about him, conjuring forth some Gnostic deity, dancing with the strength of a cyclone and stretching my fingers out towards his face in a spell on his mouth so he would be struck dumb forever.

Such were the images these stories of the second-century Gnostics set my brain afire with, and whilst my lower instincts feared I was in store for a harsh crash to earth, the strong influence of Platonism intrigued me, and I held out hope for a new version of God that celebrated women in their magnificence. I would, in the end, be as disillusioned with Valentinus's teachings as I was with Irenaeus's—if not more so.

The key figure in Gnosticism, modelled on Plato's *Timaeus*, is the demiurge, but is more evil in the Gnostic texts. That same month, as Providence would have it, I came upon a copy of *Timaeus*, the one major secular Greek work available in the realm, owing to the philosopher and scholar Calcidius and his translation of the work from Greek into Latin in the 300s.

Clovis, who in his twenties had spent several years in Athens and was a fluent reader and speaker of Greek, had introduced me to the ideas of Plutarch, who came after Plato, teaching that God, the Creator of the world, had transformed matter as the vessel for evil into a divine World-Soul, which was, however, the source of all evil. Plutarch's cosmos thus exists both as good and evil, in what was called the Dyad.

'You might think Plutarch's World-Soul inspired the malevolent demiurge of Valentinus,' Clovis had cautioned me. 'But Plutarch, just like Plato, has a virtuous World-Soul and its dark side co-governing the universe in concert. Both Plato's and Plutarch's visions are distinct entire from the Gnostic view of a faulty Creator fashioning the world as the inherent source of all evil.'

In Plato's soaring original, the Sophist Timaeus of Locri recounts how the demiurge gives order to this chaos:

Now that which is created is of necessity corporeal, and also visible and tangible. And nothing is visible where there is no fire, or tangible which has no solidity, and nothing is solid without earth. Wherefore also God in the beginning of creation made the body of the universe to consist of fire and earth... now, as the world must be solid, and solid bodies are always compacted not by one mean but by two, God placed water and air in the mean between fire and earth, and made them to have the same proportion so far as was possible (as fire is to air so is air to water, and as air is to water so is water to earth); and thus he bound and put together a visible and tangible heaven.

Now the creation took up the whole of each of the four elements[,] leaving no part of any of them nor any power of them outside... And he gave to the world the figure which was suit-

able and also natural. Now to the animal which was to comprehend all animals, that figure was suitable which comprehends
within itself all other figures. Wherefore he made the world in
the form of a globe, round as from a lathe, having its extremes
in every direction equidistant from the centre, the most perfect
and the most like itself of all figures; for he considered that the
like is infinitely fairer than the unlike.

Through the several Latin-Greek lexicons lying about at Lorsch,
which I thumbed through often out of curiosity while reading Latin texts,
I discovered the word *demiurge* was rooted in the Greek δημιουργός, or
'public worker', in Plato's time: a skilled artisan who refashioned what
was already in existence. The demiurge ordered the universe, that is all.

As I would soon discover, Valentinus's appropriation of Platonic
thought and Plutarch's demiurge in all the worst ways fashions a
vision of a Creator so impotent and feckless as to offend all my dearest
notions of what God—not to mention the Word of God—embodies. At bottom the Valentinian system is a nonsensical quilt of others'
ideas, lacking a single original contribution of its own, other than this
concept of an evil demiurge creating a flawed world. The writings of
Valentinus, rather than affirming a God and a doctrine more accepting
of women's voices in the Church, would, in the end, do nothing save
permit the conclusion that religions and doctrines different from those
of mainstream Christianity were not, on that account, any better.

At the beginning of the second week of November, a visitor came to
Lorsch, a tall, dark-haired man of strong build and penetrating, light
eyes; this was Clovis, but with shorn hair and a clean-shaven face.
He requested me by name, stating he had 'news of a personal nature
regarding Brother Johannes's family' he needed to confer with me in
private about. He gave us his real name, explaining he lived near Mainz
and, whilst he had not yet made my acquaintance, was an old friend of

my mother's. I had never seen Clovis without a beard, and I feared I had an odd, distracted look on my face.

Brother Peer, in charge of any Lorsch business conducted within the chapter room, and, I suspected, Adelung's assistant, led us into a small room off the chapter room, where we were able to close the door and confer in private.

We had not yet sat down after Peer had closed the door behind him, when Clovis seized hard at my shoulders, so that I gasped in pain, whispering at me but in a strident tone, his face close to mine. 'Where in Hell were you? I waited over an hour, and you never appeared.'

I slapped him across the face. 'Unhand me.' It took every milli-metre of my resolve not to order him out of my sight. His expression changed, and he saw at once that my state was worse than what he thought.

'My love?'

'I will tell you "where in Hell" I was,' I snapped, struggling to keep my words to a whisper. 'You suggested with sanguine calm the night of the thirty-first of October.'

'And with sanguine calm you agreed,' he said in a cheery voice. It stopped me cold.

'Well, I-I presumed you—'

'Owned you outright like property, and you had no mind or will of your own?'

'Oh, all right, very well,' I snapped; he was of course in the right. 'I do suppose I could have thought of it myself, had I the presence of mind. At any rate, the thirty-first of October it was.' I stopped. My eyes burnt holes through his, and I flashed a brittle smile, arching my eyebrows upwards. 'Any ideas, anything at all come to mind?'

I watched the astonishment drain from his features, giving way to despair. 'Samhain.'

'Samhain.'

'Oh Lord, my dearest, what happened?' He took a seat on the bench against the near wall, and I sat down beside him.

'Well,' I said, my voice still ice cold, 'to begin with, I arrived a bit in advance so we might enjoy more time in the event you arrived ahead of schedule. Alas, a band of naked women celebrants chanced upon me in my monk's garb, and when one of them kist me—'

He put his hands up to his mouth. 'No!'

'They discovered I was a woman in monk's clothes, and stripped me naked, danced round me in song and led me far, far away from our meeting place. They said they were going to "enjoy me", and I would "enjoy them".'

Clovis could not speak at first. 'What did you do?'

I explained my bold exploits to avoid further enquiries from them, and their brutal response.

'Oh, my poor, poor Joan.' He hugged me and stroked my head, and for the first time I felt tender in his arms. 'I am so sorry for all of this and that I was not there to rescue you from those wicked souls.'

I looked up into his eyes. 'I had expected to hear from you,' I said, 'or at least from Fabian, well before now.'

'I know, I know; I feared it, but I felt I could not risk shewing up so soon after that night and arousing further suspicion, when you had snuck out in the first place. I thought you had been found out, and did not wish to create more difficulties for you. I see now the error of my ways. And then, I am sorry to say, someone called me away on pressing business for a short time; it was unavoidable, but this is not acceptable. I should have come sooner or had Fabian get you a message. Can you ever forgive me?'

I worked my face up into the best sneer I could muster. 'And, pray, what else am I going to do? I suppose you were sound in your logic, not knowing the truth—just that I had them so fooled...'

His countenance changed yet again to one of excitement, and he asked after the night's events upon my return to Lorsch. I explained my various creative fabrications, and he sat dumbfounded, shaking his head and laughing. 'Your gift for truth in all its spontaneous forms is a miracle to behold.' We embraced in quiet but passionate kissing until at last we both grasped at the same moment that the time had come for him to go. My soul, my body ached for so much more, but alas, it was impossible, and we both knew it. We arose, and he had started for the door when I tapped him on the shoulder.

I leaned in close until my lips touched his ear, and whispered in as quiet a voice as I could, 'And, pray, what was the news about my family you came to tell me, good sir?'

He smiled, shaking his head. 'Nothing gets past you, Joan.' He put his hand on my cheek. 'I regret to inform you your dear uncle Fontenot has died.' I could tell from the seamlessness of his words from the first sentence to the next that he had worked it all out in advance but forgot.

'Very well.' I bit my lip to keep from laughing. 'I didn't care for him much anyway.'

Clovis withdrew a small leather pouch and produced a libra—worth twenty solidii—which he pressed into my hand. 'Be that as it may, you must have held some small esteem in his heart, for he left you this modest bequest. I recommend you shew this to Father Abbot upon my departure and enquire if he needs to hold it for you. It will lend an indicium of authentication to my visit.'

'Well done, my love, as always.' I gave him one last full kiss, and with that we opened the door out into the empty chapter room and embraced the day awaiting us in musty tones of brown wood.

Rahel had just sat down to her dinner of creamed chipped beef on toast, the soles of her feet still aching from standing at the pharmacy register and stocking shelves all day, when the telephone rang at the other end of the apartment. It was just past seven, the time when she always ate her dinner, and, as it happened, about a half hour after her mother always finished hers. Her mother never called, it seemed, save in the middle of dinner, in spite of being reminded on repeated occasions Rahel took her supper at this hour.

'Hello?'

'Rahel, my dear, this is your mother.'

'I know.' She took the telephone and sank into a nearby chair. 'No one else calls in the middle of dinner.'

A pause. 'Oh, I'm sorry... The radio broadcast starts at seven thirty—'

'Yes, I know—it always does.' She laughed. 'So, you always call now.' It was one of those days when the exhaustion and disappointment of life left her with no reserve of patience or charity. More than a week later, she was still angry with the world and furious with herself for having spurned the wonderful man HaShem had eased into her loveless life. She had not spoken with her mother since it happened.

'How are you, Rahel? How was your day?'

'The same as yesterday,' she answered in a tired voice. 'Bleak, hard, exhausting. My feet are killing me.' She paused and heard silence on the other end of the line. Her mother had listened to these complaints many times in the past. 'But at least I'm being paid a king's ransom.'

'I know it is hard, my dear. But I read in the paper yesterday there are now over six million unemployed in Germany. Six million! I thank HaShem that my daughter has a job and worry the pharmacy will cut back your hours or let you go, as happened to Herr Schiff from our old neighbourhood just last month. And he's a chemist!'

Rahel drew in a long breath and exhaled. *It is of no use*, she thought to herself. *This woman woke up after ten this morning, settled in to reading her* Berliner Tageblatt, *took Fifi out for a walk and did a crossword puzzle.* Trying to reason with her mother about the stress of working in these times would accomplish nothing but making Rahel more upset. The *Tageblatt* was the most liberal daily in Germany, but since Hitler's rise to power, it had been taken over by the Nazi Party; its Jewish publishers, the Mosse family, had fled Germany the day after he became chancellor. While Rahel had heard this three days later, she imagined her mother had no idea the Nazi Party published the newspaper she read each morning.

'How are you doing, Mama? How is your arthritis?'

'It's been much worse, I'm afraid—it has been so cold and damp these past couple weeks.'

'It sure has. I'm sorry, Mama. I know you have a lot of pain with your knees when it gets like this. Are you still getting gold salt injections from Dr Jacob?'

'Yes, dear; in fact, I'm supposed to receive another one next week. He also mentioned some new treatment, an intramuscular sulphur injection, I think; I guess some people have been having success with that. So... anyone new in your life?'

'Oh, Mama...' Her mother asked this question far more often than she would like, and Rahel resisted the temptation to call her on it now. 'Maybe.'

'Maybe? What does that mean? Maybe there's someone? Maybe it's a man, you're not sure—'

Rahel burst out laughing. 'No, no, he's very much a man. I—I just am not sure I will hear from him. It—it's strange; we met at Mueller's.'

'Sure, sure. You know, I met your father at the *Post*, sending a package. It happens.'

Rahel figured the safest move was keeping it vague; she had not yet given up hope of running across him again but did not share the details of their encounter with her mother, knowing she would never hear the end of it if she did. The day she rebuked him, Rahel had looked up his name in the phone directory, despondent to find nothing but the following four entries:

Paul Morse
P. Morz
Pavel Morz
Pawel Mrot

In that moment she had conceded she would in all likelihood never see him again. But she resolved to tempt fate, if indeed fate had designs upon them, by trying to duplicate their chance encounter, coming up against the implacable fact that their meeting was just that: a chance encounter. She had pledged not to give up. Not yet.

Rahel fielded a few more well-intentioned questions about Patek: where he grew up and lived now, his age, what he did, but beyond that, she was just not up to it.

'Is he attractive?'

'Yes, Mother, except for the fist-sized hairy eye in the middle of his forehead.' She welled up even as she spoke these words. 'Listen,

Mama, my dinner is getting cold, and chipped beef is disgusting when it's cold, so I'm going to say good night.'

'Oh, okay, sure.'

'But thanks for calling, and I love you.'

'Love you too, dear. Good night.'

Rahel hung up the telephone and collapsed into sobs in her chair. It was the kind of long, convulsive sobbing that was timeless; it could have been thirty seconds or it could have been five minutes. Rahel had no idea. She pictured his strong face and those soulful eyes, and for a moment a fleeting vision of the life she might have had with him flashed before her. The sobbing yielded to an anger that boiled over; she wrung her hands and punched the arms of the chair before dragging herself in a benumbed state over to the couch and picking up her dinner plate. The cold chipped beef in her mouth stunned her, and she flung the plate on the floor, cursing her mother's rotten memory and her own poverty.

Against the philosophical backdrop mentioned earlier, Valentinus emerges around that time as one of the foundational Gnostics, though not by any means the first. Irenaeus and Clement of Alexandria both identify Simon Magus ('the magician') as the first Gnostic around AD 50, who wandered from town to town performing various 'miracles', accompanied by Helena, a prostitute whom he had redeemed and married. Simon appears in Acts, bewitching people in Samaria with alleged magical practices. But he revealed his true mercenary, commonplace nature when he witnessed the apostles Peter and John receiving the Holy Ghost, offering them money that he might also have such power, whereupon Peter told him to keep his money, for his heart was not right with God.

We have already seen the divers and concerted efforts of the earliest writers after Simon to discredit Marcion. But Valentinus, the man who was almost pope, wielded immense influence and popularity in the first century of Christianity, and it is to him Irenaeus devotes the lion's share of his efforts in discrediting the Gnostics.

For Valentinus, God consisted of some thirty *aeons*, or 'emanations'. The absurd complexity and massive numerology of the Valentinian God and its endless array of male-female couplings induced an explosive laughing fit in me that would not abate, such that I had to muzzle myself, as people were turning to face me. In truth his writings, as described by Irenaeus, were the silliest words I had ever read.

In the midst of his labyrinthine intricacies, one could miss that Sophia, the 'mother' who gives birth to Christ, is 'excluded' from the Pleroma, an odd analogy to Mary and the 'begotten' nature of the Son.

But Sophia's entrance brings eternal imbalance and evil to the world, just as Eve precipitates Man's fallen state. Already I was assailed, even by the Gnostics, with the universal construct of Woman embodying Man's most ruinous instincts.

Irenaeus relates what at first appears as an eccentric feature of the figure of Christ, whereby He is brought forth by the mother, but 'with a kind of shadow'. More extraordinary still is the next sentence in Irenaeus's narrative, quoting Valentinus's description of Christ in that moment:

And that He indeed, as being male, severed the shadow from Him, and hastened back to the Pleroma[.]

Irenaeus explains the shadow as 'matter', saying Christ separated Himself from that substance and ascended to the divine Pleroma. But, since Gnosticism embraces a docetic Christ, with no physical, human body, I reasoned a more logical rendering of this passage might be that Valentinus was describing the figure of Christ shedding His 'mortal life' on earth, the 'shadow', as it were, of His genesis through a mortal vessel. The sentence may be the most astounding in the entire work for its active, rather than passive, construction.

For, if Christ 'severed the shadow from Him[self]', that shadow being Christ's life on earth, a shocking and unspeakable revelation would follow: that Christ willed His own Crucifixion. The language is so unmistakable in action and intent, it cannot be construed in any other wise. A few amongst us, two to whom I myself have spoken, maintain this is unremarkable, as Christ in fact submitted to crucifixion to take on all our sins. Such statements from the mouths of contemporaries angered me even more than these writings themselves. In rebuttal, Matthew 27:46 gleans Christ's heart at the moment of Crucifixion as he cries to God: '[W]hy hast thou forsaken me?'

The much older gentleman with whom I debated this point was an ecclesiastic cut from Irenaeus's cloth; for him these distinctions were of no moment and mere hair splitting. To his mind, Christ took on all our sins on the Cross in pure deliberation: an ultimate truth any further discussion debased.

'In other words, you are an intellectual coward,' I retorted, 'and your primitive, untested beliefs are as poor at serving the advancement of an enlightened faith as are your words in this discussion.' As I would later learn, this cleric's views on women's voices within the Church were as callous and provincial as Tertullian's.

Valentinus's writings have not survived, so the scandalous meaning of his words cannot be confirmed in the text. But the common-sense reading of these words alone was enough for me to dismiss him out of hand going forward.

If anything, I had expected a more inclusive, more accessible creed, in which men as well as women, of all professions and all classes, of all backgrounds and nations, could share and bond through faith. Instead I found an impenetrable labyrinth, towering in height and kilometres deep, which no man or woman hewn of mortal flesh could hope to solve. At the forefront of these inscrutable mysteries lay one clarion figure: a Christ who did not take on the sins of Man in Crucifixion as the ultimate sacrifice but wished to be rid of his mortal form—and, according to at least one Gnostic sect, the Cainites, in a work known as *The Gospel of Judas* cited by Irenaeus, enlisted Judas in accomplishing that aim in collusion, not betrayal.

However, for me in this time, as a sitting pope, these progressions of hidden truths and the betrayal of Christ admit of an additional complexity, one not easily reconciled in the heart of this writer. As a young girl at Lorsch, I saw the obscurantism of Valentinus and the Gnostics, and the elitism of a movement based on spiritual knowledge reserved for two or three people but denied to the rest of humanity, as an absurdity I did not need to examine further. But if one agrees, as it seems I must, that secrecy and privilege is not the path of the Lord, and acts in the service of God must reveal and not obscure His Word for us in our lives, how is one to explain the reign of a pope whom the world knows as a man, when that person is not? How is such a fact to be reconciled when doctrine is clear a pope who is female cannot reign?

In some measure I must concede my own circumstances are no different from those of the worst Judas, with whom Christians and non-Christians alike are familiar. Like Judas, I gained the Church's trust after long and studied efforts to conceal my true nature and identity from her while being honoured, as Christ did His apostle, with the gravest of duties and confidences. And, like Judas, I would never have gained such a position of authority and influence had I revealed my true identity, and were I to be discovered in my deceit this day, I would be thrown out with all my effects before sundown, if not jailed.

These are the facts, and they cannot be disputed. The question arises: how does my ascension to the papal throne not dishonour the fundamental precepts of openness and disclosure Christian doctrine requires of the Church in administering to the needs of its flock? The inevitable answer is that such ascension dishonours those beliefs. When Charlemagne initiated the rite of papal coronation as emperor of the Romans on Christmas Day, 800, he intended to instil across all parts of the realm a universal faith in a ruler who had the pope's blessing—and by implication, God's—to govern.

But what if Pope Leo himself had attained to his office by improper and deceitful means, so that any such blessing was not his to give: by say, concealing the fact that in reality the pontiff was a Sodomite? And whilst the Church's stance on women in positions of pastorship or teaching, in contrast to her views on *peccatum contra naturam* or sins against nature, have shewn conflicting evidence, as we have seen, her current stance on this issue is not open to interpretation, least of all as to the permissibility of a female as the sitting bishop of Rome.

So, the question becomes: how do I answer to this charge, brought as it is by and before my own conscience? First and foremost, it must be answered by a penitent soul; I have sinned and must seek forgiveness. This is painful beyond words to my spirit, for what began as the sole practical means for survival as a girl on my own in the world became over time my new identity. I cannot and will not repent of the initial deceptions practised in my encounters with strangers, based upon a currency of iniquity at force in the world, which reckons a girl on the streets as a prostitute or reprobate and a boy possessed of the same circumstances and attributes as a noble emissary to the communion of God's creatures. I find such a burden onerous in light of the necessity of my flight from my previous situation, where, in all ways, my mother degraded my spirit and identity. I shall never believe God would have had me abide those conditions.

Still, I need not have chosen the path of free room and board at the expense of Lorsch Abbey and on deceit as to my person and my gender. The point at which my shame and my rightful sense of sin begins is marked upon the date I entered Lorsch. Most damning of all, Clovis offered me his own home as a place to take up permanent residence after I had been at Lorsch but a short time, and I refused, electing to continue my life as a lie in the company of the Brothers.

And yet I cannot say all those deliberate choices were in their entirety irredeemable. The reason, for which to this day I can offer no proof, is that the hand of God guided me to Lorsch and coaxed me back into its fold upon Clovis's invitation. I have always felt this to be so, and had I left Lorsch on that day, I know in my heart I would have turned away from God forever. Upon reflexion, I understood that the decision to stay kept God in my life, but also had a profound effect on Clovis's presence in my life, which an acceptance of his invitation might have changed.

I have turned these questions over many times in my own heart, each time hoping for some epiphany in which the righteousness and order of the world would establish once and for all the unassailable good or evil of my actions—an epiphany which never came. In the end I feel I must reckon my actions much the way I reckoned those of Judith's in concealing her plot against Holofernes to liberate her people through God's Will, albeit on much humbler terms. Yea, I have sinned, but I prefer to think that, in the main, I have sinned not against God but against the lower nature of Man, in an effort to redeem that nature and to admit of the fairer sex—not unlike Judith—in ways men have not considered, and which I hope and pray have elevated that nature closer to the Creator's.

In the last week of November, we had yet another unexpected visitor concerning 'Brother Johannes' at Lorsch, a far more sinister one.

As it so happened, I was crossing by the chapter room en route to the calefactory when I heard voices and saw Brother Peer engrossed in conversation with someone at the conference table. I looked over at the other person and saw, to my utter horror, the young and impudent dark-haired woman from the forest whom I had wound up groping. My heart caught in my throat, and I walked fast with my head down into the empty hallway to avoid detection, lingering nearby just behind the corner wall so I could still see them and catch the substance of their conversation.

'So... you are saying there is a young woman in our midst, disguising herself as a man?'

My blood boiled.

'Yes. That is what I am saying.'

'What is her—ah, that is, what is the individual's name?'

'I do not know.'

'And when was this, and where were you?'

'That... that is nothing I can speak to, as I was with someone else whose confidences would be revealed were I to disclose them to you now—'

'Then there is very little I can do,' Brother Peer interjected, straightening in his seat and resting his hands upon his knees. 'These are most serious charges you make, and we have a great many men here who have given their lives over to God in the service of their community, many for a number of years, and we cannot turn all of that upside down and subject these good souls to humiliating enquiries on account of someone whose reliability we cannot vouch for coming forth with the vaguest of innuendos. If you are so intractable in keeping the pertinent details of this matter concealed, then my hands are tied; I hope you can understand.' This progression astonished me, and I could not help but imagine Abbot Adelung might well have another view in mind.

Vexed, she leaned forward and said in a softer voice, 'Then, pray, would it make a difference were I to tell you this woman, on her own initiative, fondled my breast?'

I gnashed my teeth in rage at these words, whispering under my breath, 'You mean, as you stood naked before me, after trying to grope my sex?'

Brother Peer, taken aback at her words, sat in reflexion for a time. He gestured for her to stand up, and he stood as well, saying something in a hushed voice to her, and she brought up her right forearm, bent at a right angle to her upper arm, her hand extended flat in front of her, palm down, perhaps seven or eight centimetres higher than the top of her own head—a gesture indicating the height of her 'assailant'.

This was a colossal piece of good fortune. This woman stood a good two or three centimetres taller than I, but she had remembered me as I stood upon the mound in the forest—the lion's share of the time she was standing before me, and the last impression of me she had before they knocked me to the ground and attacked me. Peer asked her something else, and she nodded in response, then sat back down.

He left her sitting at the table and returned before too long with Brother Achim beside him, a man close to ten centimetres taller than I, someone whose height I could not ever be mistaken for. She arose and stood before him and nodded again in assent. Achim, a much older man with thick, angular features and stubble, could not be a suspect; rather, Peer used him as a reference point for the alleged height of the 'perpetrator'.

He dismissed Achim, thanking him, and turned to the woman. 'I must tell you, I am most confused and troubled by this entire matter, but because you have at least provided me her height and there are not many men here of such stature, and even fewer women of such height in this town, I will talk to Father Abbot and look into this. Thank you for taking the time to come in.'

The young woman, not leaving but standing silent before Peer for a long moment, then said: 'Begging your pardon, but in part I came forward, difficult as it was, because I find myself in a state of penury, owing to the loss of my income at the beginning of the year. And I must care for my mother, who is at death's door.' Here, she looked down at the floor and then into Peer's eyes. 'Of course, I don't mean to seek restitution against the abbey—but a reward for the information, should it prove useful, would not seem untoward.'

Peer cleared his throat, as if searching his mind for how to respond. He coloured. 'Of course, I can, ah, broach the subject with Father Abbot should the investigation yield a result.' My assailant and accuser nodded with a smile, they shook hands and she turned to leave.

As I watched her walking towards the door, I wished with all my soul I could bolt round to the entrance and pound her into submission with my fists, feeling her facial bones break under the force of my hands. I had known despair, defeat, tragedy, yea, even fury in my life, as after the entire Garrick incident, but never the sort of daemonic rage that possessed me in that moment. My heart pounded in my ears, and I had to restrain my legs from carrying me forth into her. She might have been taller, although slighter in build than I, but the sheer fervour and pitch of my spirit would have demolished her and all her bones.

Whilst I was relieved beyond words over the woman's gross error of recollection, natheless there were but the barest handful of men at Lorsch with the sort of smooth, whiskerless visage that could be confused with a woman's, my own of course included in that category. For that reason, the next weeks passed in considerable anxiety, for neither Father Abbot nor Brother Hasso made any mention of it to the Brethren as a group. Any enquiries, if made at all, must have been in private, for nothing ever came of it; I was never called in for questioning, and none of the Brothers breathed a word of it to me.

But well into March, whenever anyone asked after me or requested my presence before anyone in the monastery, I was beclouded with terror until the purpose of the request was made plain. At some point I did at last let go my anxieties.

Rahel thought of Patek's observation to her that 'you feel everything with such intensity', and wondered where on earth he had pulled that out of with someone he had just met, because nothing could be truer and always had been with her. Perhaps losing her father at such a tender age and having no brothers or sisters to moderate her emotional experience of the world had left a palpable impress on her bearing; she could not say. In love she was by far the most vulnerable woman of anyone she knew, and he had been right too about having her heart broken and how that had altered her approach to men going forward.

When Hugo Berglund first came to take 'cello lessons from her three years ago as a beginning student, he was twenty-six and Rahel but twenty. Tall—1.95 metres—with dashing Nordic looks, long, flowing blond hair and a powerful physique, Hugo had an appreciation for the German Romanticists, Brahms most of all, and this combination left her powerless to resist his flirtations, which began a couple months after he had commenced his lessons with her. At one point, when he had made successive comments about her beauty and her exquisite taste in clothes, she stopped using her bow and rested it on her leg.

'Do I take it, Hugo, you are less interested in learning your instrument than you are in flattering me?'

He looked deep into her eyes, drawing closer to her than he ever had before. 'No, I would say that is not altogether true. I am far less interested in flattering you than in learning whether my remarks are having their desired effect upon you.'

Despite being born and raised in Sweden, he spoke flawless, sophisticated German and perfect French as well, all of which seduced her even more; Rahel had always been much more drawn to intellectual men than to athletes or similar types. But Hugo played ice hockey and was a polyglot with refined tastes in music; he had the physique of an athlete and one of the most gorgeous faces she'd ever seen. It was overwhelming to the point where she had fantasised about him two nights before, and despite her best efforts to conceal her attraction, Hugo sensed his power over her.

She coloured at his bold response to her enquiry, offended he had been so direct and at the same time flushed and breathless with excitement. In her own heart, she knew she was falling in love with him, and she let him kiss her that first time in the studio, both of them still holding their instruments. The kiss continued for so long, she initiated opening her mouth and using her tongue, becoming so aroused and inflamed with emotion that she broke it off.

'We are in a music studio,' she hissed, and commanded them to return to the business at hand. But when the lesson ended, he asked if he could take her out that Friday night, which she accepted without hesitation.

'The music you have played for me this day is as intoxicating as any I can recall,' he whispered, with a final brush of his lips against her cheek as they parted. 'I look forward to a full reprise.'

Hugo was a skilled factory worker and still employed, doing well enough to maintain the small old car he owned, which he picked her up in at the front of her apartment building. The night progressed in rapid fashion from there, and at the end of the evening, after a wonderful programme at the theatre, as with all the men she had ever been out on a date with, his kisses and embraces moved in short order to fondling her bosom, which she submitted to with far more desire than usual on a first date. She made a small protestation when he went in under her sweater and put his hands on the cups of her bra, but they were deep-kissing, and she'd never in her life been so aroused; before she even realised it, he had her nipples between his fingers.

'God, you've got magnificent breasts,' he said, and asked her if they could go upstairs.

'*You're inviting yourself up to my place?*' She was laughing, her eyes wide with astonishment. She pulled him down onto the seat and kissed him as long and as hard as she'd ever kissed anyone. She put her hand over the crotch of his pants and jumped at what she found. 'Oh my.

Well—it would be cruel of me to leave you in such an excited state to your own devices. So, yes!'

She had never given herself to a man on a first date and had progressed beyond kissing and petting but twice in her life; in spite of her apprehension, she found herself enraptured by the host of physical and emotional sensations flowing out of such boldness. Rahel had always been a strong-willed, prideful woman who thought nothing of asserting herself and imposing her opinions in social situations where other young women would sit back and defer to the men. Yet in matters of sexual seduction, she was more withdrawn, more passive—even more so than the same wallflowers who looked on in silence as she engaged the men in animated dialogue—in large part because, in plain terms, it was what was done. Her aggressiveness and participation in the blossoming of her and Hugo's sexual relationship felt like spiritual emancipation, a belief that she could permit and even direct the most important actions in her life, up to and including congress with the man with whom she chose to share that life. And yet, even in the face of her own ardent passions, Rahel, ever the cynic, believed in secret that romantic love was an invention of natural selection intended to facilitate procreation.

Somehow, Hugo seemed perfect, and after less than a month's time together, happier and more smitten than she'd ever been in her life, she confessed her deep love for him—an admission which, to her great disappointment and confusion, went unacknowledged. When she pressed him on it a second time, he nodded with a stiff smile, saying he liked her very much too. Her heart plunged so deep in her chest, it caused physical pain, but she banished that from her mind. As time went on, she noticed he worshipped her breasts, lingering over them and spending more time on that part of her body than the entire rest of her, not even kissing her but in passing, or doing anything else with her, and after he had his climax, he did nothing to bring her to arousal before rolling over and falling asleep.

And then one day, at the end of a lesson some six months after she had confessed her love for him, with her next student and his mother seated in the adjoining room, Hugo mentioned in the most casual, quiet voice that he had begun a serious romance with someone else and would need to break off their relationship.

She blinked in silence several times in disbelief and bent in close to him, glaring at him and whispering in a soft voice, 'So, you liked me for my tits, do I take that right? Does this girl have bigger ones?'

For the first time in their relationship, Hugo was the one blushing from head to toe, and Rahel, serene in her chair, was not embarrassed in the least. Fumbling for words, he explained his new girlfriend was a virgin and intended to stay a virgin until their wedding day.

'That is the kind of woman I want to marry,' he said, staring down at the floor, 'a woman who believes she is too special to be passed from one man to the next: a woman who holds herself in high esteem.'

Gasping, and mindful of the young boy and his mother in the next room, Rahel forced the string of manic profanities dancing on the tip of her tongue down into the bowels of her inner self. In all her life, she had never heard such a mountain of shit. 'Does she know about me?' she asked, staring up at him.

'That is none of your affair,' he said, refusing to meet her gaze.

'Or hers, I'm quite sure—you pathetic hypocrite.' Wiping away a tear, she told him to leave and never to come back.

The following lesson was an anarchy of missed instructions, dissociative thoughts and emotional fissures threatening rupture; three times she could not recall the student's name, and on multiple occasions she neglected to stop him when he played the wrong note or was improper in his bowing technique. After a half-dozen such incidents in less than ten minutes, his mother enquired if anything was wrong.

'No, just life,' she said with a sigh, and as she began to cry, she apologised, explaining she would reschedule the lesson free of charge. For the first time in her young life, she had opened her entire heart and soul to a man she never imagined could make her so joyous to be alive, only to discover she had been nothing but a passing amusement. Most ludicrous of all, by giving herself over to him as he commanded, she had lowered herself in his esteem to little more than a prostitute.

She went home and wept most of the day and night for over a week, from when she first woke up to the time she went to bed. As a consequence and poignant reminder of her heartbreak, she awoke one morning and discovered under her right eye a permanent crease, which nothing would get rid of and no passage of time would erase.

None of the universal gifts of compassion and salvation given to the race of Man would have been possible in a Christ who made secret pacts with select individuals at the expense and exclusion of all others. Nor would His love have circled the earth and made believers of men in all nations, were His true nature or the nature of the Father unknowable save to a few chosen mortals, as Valentinus asserts.

And yet, the intolerable hypocrisy of the first Christians right up to the present is well documented. Constantine the Great, like Tertullian before him, expressed his unflinching contempt for the Hebrews, calling them 'such wicked people' and 'the murderers of our Lord', and their practices 'evil designs of the devil' in the Easter Letter he circulated after the First Council of Nicaea.

In our own era, Charlemagne's response to paganism, for example, was unambiguous, brutal and anything but Christian. In 780, he decreed cremation of the dead, failure to maintain Christian festivals and failure to be baptised punishable by death. After the Saxon leader Duke Widukind led a revolt against the formal institution of these laws in 782, Charlemagne in response 'baptised' in the River Aller over forty-five hundred Saxon leaders known to be practising paganism following their conversion to Christianity—by beheading them. Beyond the horrific nature of the act and the loss of life, the massacre was devastating to the Saxons in that it left them bereft of tribal leadership. This was known as the Bloody Verdict, or Blutgericht, and the river ran red with their blood.

For all these reasons and more, I had been open to discovering a gentler, nobler God in the Gnostics, for whom at least their women appeared to have more value and status than for the Christians—that is, if Montanus's female acolytes, Priscilla and Maximilla, were any reliable measure. But this enquiry brought me more incredulity and exasperation. Like Marcion, Valentinus attributes the evil materiality of the cosmos to the flawed creation of a lesser deity who acted outside the scope of God's Will and knowledge, trivialising God's power.

Valentinus's Gnosticism is a narrative of divine rather than mortal transgression, by both God and Christ. God's secret knowledge is beyond Man except Valentinus himself and his chosen acolytes; the rest of humanity, unworthy, will stumble in blind ignorance through their time on earth. The sixteen-year-old whose spirit was a new work in progress in her time at Lorsch came to the same conclusions about Valentinian doctrine, without pause, though with grave disappointment.

At that point in my spiritual development, I stood at a crossroads, one I did not recognise then but see with clarity now. As time passed, I understood the idea of serving God and serving God's people—not the Church—appealed to me as a long-term mission worth striving for, but I am not at all certain I appreciated this at the time.

I already harboured antipathy towards Catholicism from the Church Fathers' writings condemning both women and Jews, but after the Gnostics and Valentinus most of all, my view of the Church was, if anything, softened. Marcion and the Valentinians were worse in their invalidation of the Jewish people and their religion. Valentinus may not have gone quite so far as Montanus, who proclaimed himself the Paraclete, but the difference was meaningless, for Valentinus had rendered an unknowable scripture. This was the antithesis of the Word embodied in the spirit and words of Christ.

As regards my deep contempt for Valentinus's ecclesiastic authority, compared even with the bishops, this is not to say the episcopal councils did not commit grievous error in certain doctrinal matters. They decreed the Acts of John heretical, a text with amongst the most profound revelations in the canon as to the nature of God and the nature of Man as being both human and divine when in communion with God—an inexplicable and tragic exclusion.

Yet, even now in my position of sovereign authority, despite my utmost concentration upon the subject, I am thus far powerless to devise a plan for Acts' inclusion that is practical, given the Church's—and the king's—current provincialism on these issues. The bishops, with blithe dullness, dismissed Docetism—one of the lone elements of the Gnostic teachings with an aspect of merit—*in toto* without consideration of the term in any complexity whatsoever.

Forsooth, if the Holy Saviour is divine by nature, His ability to transform His appearance to various mortals in the interest of communing with their spirits cannot be disputed amongst rational minds. If Christ is divine as well as human, capable of walking on water, transcending death and performing miracles such as the feeding of the five thousand and countless other preternatural acts, He can transcend the form He took in the flesh. Yea, such acts are unassailable in their rejection of the flesh as His sole form of being.

I was surprised to discover that Irenaeus's primary anxiety concerned not the Valentinians themselves, but Christians' inability to distinguish the followers of Valentinus as heretics, as the Valentinians in public professed faith in one God. Around this same time, the followers of Marcion declared one gospel, Marcion's version of the Gospel of Luke—gutted of all Jewish texts—canonical, rejecting all other writings save ten Pauline epistles.

Suspect as his doctrines were, Marcion was the first theologian to propose a Biblical canon and define a New Testament to support the texts of the Old Testament, and his teachings enjoyed great influence and popularity. I imagined the terror this must have struck into the hearts of all serious Christians. In an act of supreme courage and initiative, Irenaeus took witness in his writings to the Gospels of John, Mark, Matthew and Luke, and in particular to the Gospel of John as the one Gospel where Jesus speaks of His own divinity, proving He was God incarnate, and thus supplanting Marcion's ambitions. There is in all likelihood no act by any Church Father of greater consequence for the future of Christianity.

Even the Nicene Creed bears the impress of Irenaeus's influence. The Third Council of Toledo, in 589, added the single word *Filioque* (meaning 'of the Son') after the phrase 'who proceedeth from the Father', instigating one of the most divisive and enduring rifts in the history of Christianity, one that persists to this day. The council added the word to the Creed without consulting the Eastern Orthodox Church. The Greek text had always embodied the concept of God the Father as a single person.

But the Latin Church, not unlike Irenaeus's race against Marcion to author the world's first Biblical canon, was intent on closing the doors of doctrinal legitimacy to Arianism's contention that the Son, unlike God, had a beginning. Therefore, the council added *Filioque* to clarify God and Son were a 'double procession': coeval and prior to the existence of the universe. Still, the Creed today mirrors what Irenaeus envisioned in his *Haereses*—a rule of faith and affirmation of God, grounded in the canon of truth.

Irenaeus's presence and influence within Church history is overwhelming, yet, in the end, for the young girl struggling to find the nature of God—and herself—he moved through a world too simple in form and spirit for me to accept. But so too did all the second-century Church's greatest thinkers.

Valentinianism was too inscrutable and too elite to be of any use whatsoever. Yet the God of Irenaeus, whilst less absurd, matched Valentinus's in His oppressiveness, or so it seemed to me, trapped as I was in a young woman's body. And the age through which I myself now make my way bears witness to a brutishness that clutches at my heart with the talons of some monstrous wingèd wraith.

Even as Rahel stood out in the cold in front of Mueller's for over an hour, hoping Patek, who had approached her with such bravado three weeks ago, would reappear, she cursed herself and the entire situation, that she should be reduced to such pathetic, fatuous behaviour. Most galling of all, she had no one to blame but herself. She had made sure to arrive at just about one thirty in the afternoon, a good half hour before they had met on the previous occasion, just in case he were to set out earlier than usual. She had assumed Patek was a man of routines, when this could not be further from the truth. For the third successive Saturday, she had staked out the market in hopes of catching him during his shopping—but the object of her affections, unlike herself, was no creature of habit. She thought she might spot him on one of the sidewalks in front of the market, a busy intersection where people passed en route to other places even if they did not stop to do any shopping. Alas, Patek never appeared. However, a harsh and cutting wind gouged her bare cheeks, and with a tear forming at the corner of her eye, she turned away at last in dejection.

HaShem had sent her a handsome, soulful man, someone who adored her on sight and a real thinker to boot—a genuine chance for happiness, someone who could have warmed her spirit and her bones through these brutal winter months and beyond. And Rahel, genius that she was, had thrown it all away. And why? Because he had called her bluff and beat her at her own game. Come to think of it, he had not played her game at all but had rejected the entire premise of it and played his hand straight up; he showed her his perspicacity and how much he already knew about her—or, better put, what a transparent read she was—and it infuriated her a complete stranger could see into her in ways she herself could not. So, she had banished him.

Rahel had made a point of taking multiple trips to Mueller's each week since their meeting, in addition to the stake-out each Saturday, in the hope of running into him there, but all her efforts had gone for naught. Although, to the best of her recollection, Patek lived in the neighbourhood, Rahel had to face the prospect his visit to Mueller's on that fateful day would never be repeated—that in fact he did the bulk of his shopping at some other market. She also considered the possibility Patek, having watched her from afar for some time before being rebuffed with such disdain, might have taken his shopping elsewhere to spare himself the torment and discomfiture of seeing her there. That sounded more like the fevered romantic who had introduced himself to her and asked her if she believed she could be destined for someone. This progression made her queasy, for if it were true, any real chance of rectifying the consequences of her bad actions was gone as well. But when she thought about it, Mueller's was the mainstay large market for the entire neighbourhood, and Patek's arrogance—for that was a prominent aspect of his personality, without doubt—would not suffer such passive resignation and sacrifice of an essential activity, not for someone who would never be in his life. Still, she failed to see him again in the store.

Another time she ran for two blocks to catch up to a man she swore was him—but when he turned round, it was someone else. Inconsolable over her bad judgment and worse luck, Rahel stopped looking for him in doorways, in the street, at the *Reichspost* or coming out of synagogue, and the brutal chill of February turned into the warmer, wetter chill of March. But Patek's words about her musicianship and love of music had not been without their effect, and she found herself reconnecting with some of her favourite recordings, including the Verdi *Requiem* and most of all the breathless '*Hostias et preces*' within it, which always gave her gooseflesh and tears in the same moment. It was the one passage she had ever heard which she imagined forced even the composer to curtail all activity and be hushed into listening by its ineffable spirit and glorious yet humbling sense of the supernal: *If you miss this, you will miss the secret of what it is you seek in your life.* These were the sentiments that held her heart fluttering in her breast whenever she heard those strains, and the almost erotic grieving which seized at her throat as her eyes welled up with tears: a connection to her crushing loneliness so intense that the man for whom she ached, who would feel and understand these precise emotions, seemed, as it were, seated next to her. Not until she sat alone in her apartment, listening to this passage on her gramophone for the first time—by now, some four years past, long before she met Hugo—did she discover this was the secret of her life: the desire for a man who would be just like her in this one way, a man transformed in his understanding of himself and of the nature of the object of his innermost desire. In that moment she understood what she connected with most in music, the inexpressible beauty of this one figure, this ecstatic mourning for what was lost to her—but not yet to the world and therefore not in truth to her.

Patek had gleaned this from their simple conversation in Mueller's and announced to her, *We are alike in that way,* the most powerful herald she had ever experienced of something being destined rather than a function of her own choices, a notion she had never accorded much credence to in the past. But that one act of penetration into her psyche, her very being, into the ultimate desideratum of her life, which she had never confessed aloud to a soul—it was all too much and now whelmed her into action, into setting aside her petty pride and finding this man whom she had rebuffed with such contempt. Now, all these weeks later, as she sat listening to this beloved piece which Patek had reintroduced into her days, her face wet with tears, she condemned herself, cursing all her fruitless efforts to find him, cursing the proud, mistrustful nature of hers that had compelled her to strike out against this man who had shown her such wisdom and elegance on that day which could have—should have—ended on such a different note.

But one early April morning, long after the deep scar within her heart had ceased to be her first thought upon arising, Rahel, having just picked up the paper, turned a corner not three doors down from her apartment and bumped into him. It was drizzling and brisk enough to require a light coat with a hood, and Patek, staring down at the ground, did not see her.

'Patek!'

He looked up, and his eyes drank her in with apprehension, for he saw at once the hugeness in her eyes, a cascade of anxiety and dread that reminded him of his own on that January afternoon. He lowered his umbrella.

'Rahel—'

'How can you ever—I mean, can you...' She wanted to apologise, she wanted to say ten things, but not one would come out proper. She threw her arms round him, put her hands on his face and kissed him full on the mouth. She fought to keep the tears at bay but did not succeed. 'You were right about the kind of girl I am—you were right about everything—well, almost everything!'

This dreary, lifeless day was now as joyous as any she could remember, and his own obvious delight at her finding him on the street gave her great relief. Patek, thunderstruck at her initiative, at the boldness with which she had taken matters into her own hands, but far from being put off by it, found himself under her spell all the more. Rahel was nothing if not proud and wilful, but under all that lay a smouldering, tender vulnerability which was irresistible.

The two of them played hooky from their respective lives and spent the entire day and night in one another's company, arm locked in arm, discussing the myriad thoughts they had each had in the intervening period about the other: regret, contempt, rage, pity, hatred, ridicule, pretence towards not caring—and inevitable heartache and misery. Both of them, within a week of one another, had abandoned all hope of ever meeting again. At first Patek had indeed stayed away from Mueller's, not wishing to give her the satisfaction—but in the end he could not justify doing his shopping elsewhere, since the other market he trusted required a bus ride and a transfer to get there.

Needing a rest from their long walk in the park, they sat down on a damp bench. After some giddy laughter on topics that would have sounded anarchic and the product of intoxication to an outsider, the jollity subsided. After a long and pregnant silence between them built up some tension, she blurted out, 'So tell me, please, Patek, you must; how did you come up with all those facts about me, my music, my upbringing and so forth?'

'Oh, that.' He stared down at his hands. 'You were right; I asked your neighbour.'

'Nooo! I don't believe you.' Rahel sat up straight, her hands on her thighs, perched at the edge of madness. 'After all that—you can't have…' And then she remembered: she had never told a soul about the Verdi *'Hostias'*, as she was far too embarrassed to have shared that with anybody. 'You're having me on again.'

He covered his mouth, for he was exploding with laughter. He gazed up at the sky and all about him, holding out his hands and intoning in a slow, grave voice, 'I just… said… *abracadabraaa*.'

She reached out and punched him on the shoulder, not a glancing blow, and he winced from the shot.

'Ow!' He rubbed his shoulder. 'You're a regular Jack Dempsey.'

'Just you try making yourself scarce like that again—then you'll see the wallop I can pack,' she said, half joking. They talked at length about music and their respective loves and dislikes. Patek's greatest passion lay in solo piano, a form he could listen to for hours on end: the Liszt Sonata in B Minor and his *Transcendental Études*, most solo pieces by Scriabin and Chopin, though he far preferred the former to the latter, Ravel's virtuosic *Miroirs* and several more minor composers Rahel did not know, including a most obscure Lithuanian contemporary composer in the machinist school, by the daunting name of Vytautas Bacevičius. A few months back he had learned a young composer named Olivier Messiaen had written some revolutionary preludes for piano back in 1929, but he had not yet been able to locate a recording. From what he had read on the subject, Patek felt they might well be the most exciting compositions he had ever heard.

When he waxed lyrical over the Liszt sonata and its scope of grandeur and complexity, Rahel, after listening with patience at some length to his paeans, which he interrupted with three separate melodic excerpts—each of which he first sang note for note and then analysed in terms of their thematic figures—at last submitted, 'You know, Brahms fell asleep while Liszt performed it for him at his home.'

'Yes, I know,' Patek responded in a dry tone, familiar with the story. 'Sounds about right, don't you think? I'm not sure there's a Brahms piece I am able to stay awake through.'

'Interesting, then, that the world equates Brahms with the greatest composers in history—Bach, Mozart, Beethoven—and as for Liszt, well, what would you say the world—'

'I don't give a damn what the stupid world thinks,' he snapped, exasperated. 'Poor Archduke Ferdinand may be the one person who can't attest to the world's wholesale spiritual and moral stupidity these past couple decades. Please.'

The trouble was, Patek had employed just the sort of argument she often used herself when people resorted to merits based on consensus and popular opinion: that judging an artist's work and staying power on mere popularity constituted the most banal dismissal of serious aesthetics a sentient being could ever engage in. A smile turned up the corner of her mouth. 'You can judge the entire human race brainless, for all I care—and go bowling somewhere in America with the globe.' Here she leaned in close to him, fixing her huge brown eyes on him.

'But your boy Franz will still be a second-rate show-off, and Brahms will still have more musical genius and substance in one of his caesuras than Liszt has in his entire family tree.'

Their breath was hot enough to feel on one another's faces, and Patek seized at the back of her head and pulled her into him, kissing her deep. 'You have no idea how much I want to bed you—right at this moment.'

'Oh, but I do,' she shot back, flashing him the points of her white teeth. 'I know what I'm doing.' The baring winds caught in the poplars like fire, spreading the hard, nutty scent of wood gone too long without bud, just on the verge of sprout.

'You know, I believe you do.'

When I laid down the last book at Lorsch, inconsolable over the flood of exasperations and half truths I had absorbed, I retreated into the familiar, protective walls of Augustine, my first teacher, who afforded more fundamental comfort in the credibility of the knowable than anything else. For, more than any of the earlier Church Fathers, Augustine held to a view of scriptural meaning grounded more in metaphor and in the likelihood of multiple interpretations than in the view of writers like Irenaeus, who treated the Bible as a statute to be read in the black letter of the law. Augustine writes in his *Confessiones* that what an author of Scripture understood may differ from what a reader may take from it, but that God admits of both truths, if they be truths indeed.

Such a philosophical stance towards the interpretation of Scripture admits of its human as well as its divine origins and in that regard would be a more faithful rendering of the true nature and spirit of Christ. If Tertullian imposed the most rigid prohibitions on the conduct and speech of a woman living in Christ, while in private and in public endorsing the views of a sect which by his own definitions was heretical, something must be in place to expose and crush such arrogance. Augustine brought to the Church a non-literal reading of the Bible in practice that was liberal in comparison with that of his predecessors.

Augustine posits God created the world, in sum, out of nothing, through His own free Will. The God of Augustine is not the neglectful, ignorant God of Valentinus, unaware of the actions of the demiurge in fashioning an organised but evil material realm. Augustine declares God to be immutable, eternal, omnipotent, Trinitarian and devoid of composition or potentiality.

In the fevered brew of my own tenuous existence in those early days, the dawn of my erotic life and interminable hours spent in hapless aching and longing to be enfolded once again in Clovis's thick, strong arms, I took to pleasuring myself at night in breathless silence in the great room and falling asleep with those singular words out of *Confessiones* in my head, words that spoke to the exact colour and shade of my own feelings and desires in my days and nights there:

To Carthage I came, where there sang all around me in my ears a cauldron of unholy loves. I loved not yet, yet I loved to love, and out of a deep-seated want, I hated myself for wanting not. I sought what I might love, in love with loving, and safety I hated, and a way without snares... To love then, and to be beloved, was sweet to me; but more, when I obtained to enjoy the person I loved. I defiled the spring of friendship with the filth of concupiscence, and I beclouded its brightness with the hell of lustfulness[.]

# ❖ Two ❖

Y FIRST CRISIS AT Lorsch, which I had been long dread-
ing, came, by the Lord's mercy, in the late-night hours after
Compline and before Matins, on the night of the third of
December, 830, in the absence of prying eyes. The two months of my
postulancy and my first three months as a novice, perhaps due to the
profound upheaval in my life, had transpired without event, but at last,
not to be forestalled any longer, the feared ritual struck with a vengeance. A few fleeting abdominal cramps had nibbled at me during supper, bringing some anxiety to the hour, but appeared to pass without
incident. Sometime round midnight, upon turning onto my left side
in the pallet, an unmistakable warmth between my thighs roused me
out of my state of drowse and into immediate panic. After first confirming no one in the great room was awake, I wrapt my sheet about
me and tiptoed out to a closeted room, taking a candle with me. With
the door closed behind me, I threw off the sheet and, upon disrobing,
discovered a stain—a bit larger than the size of two fingers—on the
lower portion of my monk's robes, deep red in colour, not as conspicuous as I had feared but still more than noticeable. I searched the room
for something I might use to plug up the bleeding. Finding nothing
about that would suffice, I tore off a small section of my under-tunic
that would not shew—notwithstanding the sacrilege to which I subjected this garment—and stuffed it as well as I could up there. The
more I looked at the stain on my robes, the more I could not glance at

myself even in passing without my eye being drawn to it, until at last I felt I presented to the world the image of a stain dressed in monk's robes. But as I glanced in resignation about the small room, my gaze fell upon an inkwell on a small table, and a chair upon which rested a ledger of some sort. This was perfect. Given my recent appointment to the scriptorium and my penchant for writing, I had asked if I might be permitted a quill and inkwell for use outside the library, which had been granted. Eyeing the inkwell and remembering also its pungent, sweet scent, I went over and held the stained portion of my robe up to it, tipping the ink onto the fabric by candlelight, taking care not to spill an amount that would be noticed, and creating a much larger stain with two or three drip marks that looked spontaneous. Holding the candle, I examined the floor to ensure nothing had spilt, and, having satisfied myself, took my leave. Pleased with my handiwork, I resolved to go to the launderer after Matins and explain my 'mishap' in the course of using my inkwell, so I might obtain new robes. I also recalled the utility of yarrow to stem the bleeding—a plant which was indeed grown on Lorsch grounds and cultivated for medicinal purposes. In line with Benedictine doctrine, the tending of the sick constituted the abbey's primary mission of mercy, so Lorsch's infirmarian had access to amongst the most impressive medicinal stores in the realm. From that time forward, I made certain I had generous quantities of yarrow leaves at my disposal, and as soon as I felt the onset of discomfort, I would prepare and drink a tea made of its leaves—a ritual I have maintained to the present day. The whole leaves themselves, whilst not comfortable, could be inserted as a plug which staunched the bleeding to good effect and permitted me to function, more or less, amongst the Brothers. Baths at Lorsch were forbidden for monks, except for the ill, for exposure of the body was a threat to chastity—which was helpful in the sense offensive odours were the order of the day, harmful in the sense the feminine odour of old and festering blood from the sex possesses an appreciable, powerful otherness. In the winter months, the coldness of the monastery suppressed odours, as opposed to magnifying them in the thick, sweat-inducing torpor of summer, the sole saving grace for me at that time. This helped suppress the odour emanating from my issue; however, if the Brethren were sweating less, my own distinct odour might for that reason be more noticeable. I had no idea where the truth lay.

Due in large part to the lingering effect of Charlemagne's capitulary in chapter LXX mandating the cultivation of some ninety plants, herbs and fruit trees he saw fit to make staples of the empire, cyminum was in amplitude at Lorsch, as elsewhere. While eating a dish one Compline with cyminum, I noticed by chance its pungent scent, striking in its resemblance to body odour. To the extent I could on occasion cleanse the area in the small hours of the night or at other times when no one was about, I found that by rubbing cyminum on my body and ingesting small amounts of it, I gave off the same general odour as the Brothers. Placement of the spice above my clavicles, just centimetres beneath the line of my robes, where the fragrance could emanate up into open air, proved most effective. Under the heavy robes, my own natural body heat activated the fragrance of cyminum and maintained its distinct aroma. Whilst these precautions did not remove the potential for disaster always suspended Damocles-like over these physical trials, they natheless managed them well. I disposed of the old plugs in discreet fashion, and when I presented my ink-stained robes to the launderer, he issued me new ones without question. Going forward, I became so vigilant in my attention to dress and my progressions each month, I avoided any repeat incidents of soiling my robes.

The status of a woman's issuance as an object of doctrinal condemnation, scorn and sequestration from human contact is as unquestioned today as when it was first written of in Leviticus 15:19-30:

The woman, who at the return of the month, hath her issue of blood, shall be separated seven days. Every one that toucheth her, shall be unclean until the evening. And every thing that she sleepeth on, or that she sitteth on in the days of her separation, shall be defiled. He that toucheth her bed shall wash his clothes: and himself being washed with water, shall be defiled until the evening. Whosoever shall toucheth any vessel on which she sitteth, shall wash his clothes: and himself being washed with water, shall be defiled until the evening. If a man copulateth with her in the time of her flowers, he shall be unclean seven days: and every bed on which he shall sleep shall be defiled.

Almost identical language appears in the sections preceding this upon the subject of a man's seed that has gone forth from him—with the key distinction between the two being that the issue of a woman's blood from her sex is an involuntary biological function over which the woman herself has no control, whereas the man's act is one of wanton and wilful sexual conduct. Biblical treatment of the two, however, is indistinguishable, so that the virtuous woman's involuntary issue of blood out of her sex is as vilifying and impure in essence and in deed as a man's seed of copulation—and most damning to the unfortunate innocent who should by any means come into contact with that blood. For this reason, the spiritual terror engendered by its appearance within the monastery walls rendered it akin to wildfire. The discovery of a woman residing at Lorsch in such a state of spiritual and physical contamination would have been met with shock and outrage, along with my immediate eviction from the premises, whatever the hour of day or night, not to mention possible criminal charges. That discovery could not be risked. Sometimes, beholding my tonsured skull in reflexion with its gracile features and lines, I was certain my femininity was plain as day upon sight and had to convince myself my own knowledge was key. As time went on, the most daunting aspect of this regular ritual, to my mind, became managing the odour, which persisted however much I stemmed the bleeding—though in terms of changing the yarrow plugs, that occurred less often—and which to my keen sense of smell was distinct in the extreme from the anonymous odour of unwashed filth worn by all. The cyminum was my godsend; the long, formless robes and leaf plugs may have been in fact what saved me from detection, but the cyminum afforded me equanimity in my movements amongst the Brothers, as it masked the distinct alterity to which I was bound from head to toe. On the rare occasions that for one reason or another I did not have access to the spice, in lieu of that I chewed as much raw garlic as I could find, which functioned as an adequate substitute, since human beings are constructed to encounter one another at face level rather than at the level of their groins.

Natheless, my facial features were not on this account lost on the Brothers; first at Lorsch, by way of Brother Dieter, of whom I was more fond than anyone else, and later at other monasteries, I came to be known as Johannes Angelicus—John the Angelic—which, according to Brother Dieter, evoked both my softer appearance and the gentle, assiduous nature upon which he had come to rely in substantial measure. The name stuck, and I took it with me wherever I went. Whilst my appearance no doubt typified that of a sixteen-year-old young lady, for the male sex it placed me closer to that of an older boy of, say, thirteen, and this would prove most useful in playing upon Father Abbot Adelung's sympathies when it came to delaying my solemn vows.

In the meantime, starting in December of 830, having already become acquainted with the abbey by way of his visit in November, Clovis ingratiated himself to Lorsch by coming to Abbot Adelung with the proposal of deeding lands to the abbey, for which in return he wished to be permitted a room at Lorsch for half the year once they completed the transaction, and at times following that as lodging permitted, a request they found unusual but granted with pleasure, as there were already a couple such rooms which had fallen into disuse. He explained he was penning a memoir with a more historical bent and wished to live amongst us to better inform his portrayal of these times and counties. Deciding which lands to deed to Lorsch, drawing up the proper instruments and tending to various other pressing matters regarding the lands in question all took time, and the balance of the winter and early spring passed in interminable solitude and despair before the documents were sworn to and sealed in completion of the transaction. But Clovis was a man of title, with vision, ambition and a deft, lawless flair for the creation of his own identity, with access to some of the highest circles of power and influence in the kingdom. Moreover, he exercised the highest degree of caution in avoiding any and all contact with me during this time.

As he had told me on the ride to Lorsch, he had a gift for seeing potential in others and drawing that potential to its highest level of accomplishment, and in time I would come to see the extent of this gift as he brought it to bear in the service of other disciplines of which I was as yet unaware. For the time being, all I knew was that I was alone in my bed in the dormitorium for many months while he kept arranging logistics which on their face I had hoped would have taken far less time than they did. Much later the reasons for these delays would come to light.

A curious development transpired upon the commencement of Clovis's first residency at Lorsch, which took place in mid-April, 831: the continual ache for his companionship and most of all for his hands on my flesh ebbed in dramatic fashion. To be sure, those first few dalliances were as glorious as anything I had ever experienced up to that time, the sheer animal need of his touch having come to such a point, I could no longer bear to be in my own skin, as images and memories of his lips suckling at my breasts, or his fingers slipping into my fruit and making it swell and drip with the desire for his animal bore me aloft and just shy of the eaves of the scriptorium as I struggled to ground myself in Latin declensions. The cathartic release I experienced with Clovis behind closed doors had to be muffled and closed up into stifled sighs and inaudible whimpers on the bed—his status as a major benefactor warranted the replacement of the narrow pallet of straw with a full-sized bed—as he made love to me. My emotions, too, were at a fever pitch for this man in whose absence I had been miserable all those many months, and there as well I had to restrict my confessions to a mere whisper. On our first night together, before he bedded me, I took his face between my hands and said to him, 'My dearest Clovis, I must needs confess a thing I cannot withhold a moment longer, for I have had many months alone with this thought, and I swear it has eaten the flesh right off my bones—'

'Then, pray—' His brow was furrowed with concern.

'I am in love with you, Clovis—helpless in my love for you. For entire days I am unable to think of anything else—'

'And I with you, dear Joan, it could not be more true,' he whispered. 'Your tender beauty, your soaring mind and all the noble mischief behind it, your fortitude of heart and will so lacking in your sex—I cannot be without it.' Our union was ineffable on that account, and on that bed in his room, all sense of walled dimension in space and time fell away from our embrace, as though we were floating upon the air, upon the boundless bed of our desires.

And yet, in spite of all this, my unassuageable ache for him, for his sex inside me, subsided after about ten nights, and I cannot even recall the moment at which this possession left me—just that, in time, the fever was gone. Both a puzzle and a relief, in the end I presumed my lower instincts required its flight for me to function within my station at Lorsch. Sex with my Beloved never quite hit the same pinnacle after that, and in all these years, the reason for it—as well as the fact I seemed not bothered by it in the least—has remained an unfathomable mystery. Perhaps in the end, I no longer needed what always lay close at hand, however essential or cherished.

This notwithstanding, the notion of eventual marriage and a life together occupied both our minds and arose often in our talks behind closed doors. My commitment to and investment in my work at Lorsch Abbey was increasing day by day, but the thought of forswearing marriage and all my belongings in the space of three months' time terrified me. Clovis struck upon the shrewd stratagem of letting my tender age—which, as a lad with a cherubic face, I had represented as but thirteen upon entering Lorsch—work to my greatest benefit. When I approached Father Abbot in a tearful state, imploring him to extend my novitiate until my 'twentieth birthday', which would not be until the eighth of September, 837, some seven years hence (when I would, in fact, be twenty-three), he assented after giving the matter a long moment of contemplation. In a single stroke of genius, the most daunting aspect of my life at that time, deciding such monumental issues by July 831, dissolved into the spring air.

Except for Clovis, I was the newest resident at Lorsch, and in a bit of Providential good fortune, they gave him the room next to a kind of storage room, never used, at the end of the west hall, a hall not often traversed. Although by no means a daily indulgence, or it would have come to Abbot Adelung's attention, a couple times a week after Compline, I slipt away to Clovis's quarters for a brief visit before retiring to my reading and a good night's slumber. With his quarters positioned at the end of the hall and nothing but an empty storage room in proximity, we had the benefit of luxurious privacy. Because he would be staying there for six months at a time, it was easier to make it a permanent assignment rather than hope another room would be available in six months' time; hence the isolation and convenience afforded by its location would be ongoing. His benefactorship, a substantial gifting of lands, commanded accommodation by Father Abbot far in excess of normal circumstances, and the trifling value of a room which might or might not have been otherwise occupied in the intervening period would not have entered into consideration, although the luxury of its provisions would need to approximate those to which a count would have been accustomed.

And so it was that Count Clovis of Basinsheim and Brother Johannes, whose difference in years more resembled father and son, became fast friends in altogether unremarkable fashion. Natheless, our conduct needed to be altogether circumspect amongst the Brothers, for Charlemagne's capitulary punishing monks for sodomy—as such practices had become commonplace—predisposed the monastic community and its leadership towards suspicion and vigilance in observation. Already, with the alarming rate of cultural erosion taking place under Louis in the wake of his father's death, the level of distrust as regards all matters of the flesh had been raised, and monks were more vulnerable than others to such charges. There was also the difference in our ages and my own more cherubic appearance. This notwithstanding, his noble status and initial visit upon the premises as a contemporary and old friend of my mother's, entrusted with the provision of my dear uncle Fontenot's bequest, dispensed with any such concerns. Still, we did not speak, and when we did, it was with the utmost formality in front of others. I would make my way to the west hall at the prearranged hour, on the pretext of going into the storage room, and finding no one about—as was most times the case—I would knock at his door once so he knew right away to let me in. It worked well, save the rare incident of a longer wait if someone was in the storage room.

Clovis asked to be put to work the first two days of each week so he could write from experience about the labour itself as well as its effect upon the person at day's end. He rose to the challenge, being the most able-bodied man in the abbey during his residency. Once I watched him carry into the calefactory a load of stone at least twice the weight of the others' without the slightest effort. His physical strength and stamina seemed illimitable. I, on the other hand, had no appetite for physical labour and was grateful for my transition to the library and scriptorium, where I spent most but not all my days. More than anything else, I was anxious about my physical limitations; not at all diminutive, even for a man, I had a larger-than-average frame for a woman yet was incapable of lifting the kind of weight other men who were my height or shorter and slighter of build could manage. I worried it would raise suspicions, but this never came to pass.

It did not take long for the Brothers to recognise my Clovis's mastery of Letters, and although he connected with physical labour, he enjoyed his intellectual duties in the library, and on the days they assigned him there, I savoured his proximity, albeit in silence. In time I came to learn we shared another legacy: a strong insistence by the woman of the household upon a mastery of Letters.

Clovis's mother had been taught Letters and passed on to her son all she knew, whilst his father, much like Charlemagne himself, grew up illiterate, but with a preference for being read to. However, whilst I had always considered such instruction an imposition, young Clovis had taken to it apace, and his irrepressible curiosity as regards all disciplines in life had guided him the rest of the way. Unlike many nobles, he could read and write, and his appetite for women ran to a type most men would flee from: educated, well read, articulate, self-assured and possessed of a quick, penetrating mind. A woman who was content with her station in life extinguished any flame he might feel for her flesh. He could not suffer the stupidity and submissiveness of most women, with whom he craved as intense and fortifying a communion on the spiritual and rational planes as on the physical one. I might have been tender in years, but, at least according to him, I possessed a mind and a will of my own he found lacking entire in his contemporaries of the fairer sex as well as in younger women. And there was no chance of me being satisfied with my own lot. We were an excellent match to one another in all those ways weighing most upon us both.

As the weeks passed into months, even with the occasional secret rendezvous with Clovis, I found the cultus of monastic life an isolating yet settling influence upon my soul and the focus and direction I wished to bring to my life. Why this should be so, I had not the faintest idea; I could not then have explained the mysticism of its effect to anyone, not even myself. For I had brought an inexhaustible capacity for energy to Lorsch when I first arrived there, most of all for those forms of discipline and beliefs driven by a desire to subvert the general order. For in a very real sense, I had been violated by the world, and wanted to do to it back what had been done to me. One day I arose to discover this reserve within me had been transformed, not into listlessness or satiety but into a kind of animated preparation, for want of a better word. I now recall that for the second time in as many years, I thought of Adolfo, impressed by a certain prescience to his words in my early childhood, warning of how ill prepared my life on earth had made me for real adversity. Without ever saying it, for he never needed to, his words of ridicule on that unforgettable afternoon were a challenge: how would I meet such adversity? My connexion and susceptibility to those early memories were a mystery to Clovis—not just the memories of Adolfo and our friendship but of that entire period, of the years when I was an object of ridicule and contempt, along with the anxiety and dread taking root in me under the roof of my own home. Clovis only ever saw the confident, daunting firebrand of a thinker starting to flower at Lorsch and could not see into the frightened girl who could feel her strength tested by her own shadow. There is nothing more terrible than the sound of one's own silence in the face of attack, and this remained the single defining image of my childhood until the age of ten. From then on, I developed the ferocity of vengeance and made amends for all I had permitted myself to suffer. That vengeance lit a fire in my belly, but for what or for whom it burnt I could not say. Before Lorsch, I knew it was the successor in interest to the guardianship of my identity, and that was all. Young men and women need such voices to feel alive and visible in the talking world, which was about as far as I could take it. In truth, with the advantage of hindsight, it was another skin, another appearance untested by adversity, swollen with the turgor of hubris, to be torn open by the first wind with teeth that fell upon it. Lorsch was that wind.

But the storm came in quiet, as calming as a walk in the meadow on a summer day with a gentle breeze that brings the nearness of a bird's warbling in a tree, or a song in flight. This voice summoned me to its side—a guide, wed as it were to the steps I took in the glade, one placed in front of the next, my feet slowing at their approach of my awareness of myself, the deliciousness of it, of my soul as a globe of fruit warming in the light and suspended in wind, ripening and coming to myself while doing other activities in an effortless vein, accompanied by another but without touch or gaze or the need of conversation, which magnified the beauty of nature round us—yes, us. The guide walked beside me in witness to the changes I knew were there but could not voice—and did not need to. A sure rhythm held the measure of life in place; it clouded skies, mixed our shapes into the dusk and put me to bed without dreams. This was how God entered into me in those vast, momentary fields of my reckonings.

On a warm and sunny late Friday morning in early April of 1934, just before lunch hour, Rahel turned the corner on a sidewalk not far from the pharmacy—she was on her break—and saw a Mourning Cloak flit about and land on a bush in front of her. One of the larger species of butterfly in Germany, the Mourning Cloak was a herald of spring's return, and throughout her childhood, it had been a happy sight, as the appearance of its gorgeous deep burgundy-purple wings with French vanilla borders lined with rows of iridescent blue dots foretold an end to snow, ice and freezing winter days. To her it looked like some delicious blackberry and ice cream dessert in flight.

After attending the *Volksschule* ('people's school') for four years as a small girl, Rahel tested into the School for Higher Daughters. In her last years there, when her heart took to fancying boys, the butterfly's appearance was one of those rituals that turned her mind to thoughts of romance, and it continued to have that pleasurable association well into adulthood. She excelled in the liberal arts and at the 'cello, although it was there she also learned she lacked the gift of genius or true talent on her instrument she had always presumed she possessed and might access, if she applied herself in earnest—another truth Patek had plucked out of thin air.

While pursuing her own studies at the School for Higher Daughters, Rahel became friends over time with a quiet, withdrawn lad named Jürgen Mueller, a neighbour down the street, who attended the prestigious Gymnasium zum Grauen Kloster, with the most gruelling academics in all Germany. The Gymnasium, erected in 1574 and centred in the historic early Gothic monastery of Franziskaner-Klosterkirche, which dated from 1250, housed Berlin's first printing press. Rahel played hooky from her own studies one day and walked up to it with Jürgen—to her great dismay, they barred her from entering the grounds or the buildings on account of her sex—and its storied legacy bounced and reverberated off the steep walls themselves of the magnificent Gothic structure.

Jürgen, with a face more beautiful than any woman's, with his bee-stung lips, and his hair and eyes the same light gold colour, was frail and timid around others except when he spoke upon subjects he had knowledge of or with people he knew well and among whom he felt comfortable. He had an IQ of 184, and Rahel never had met a more daunting intellect in her life, either before or since; his mind moved at velocities and through planes of reality in apparent defiance of the laws of physics and well beyond the grasp of other mortals. Rahel's fiery, free-thinking personality and predilection for engaging others and confronting their assertions had blossomed during her time at the School for Higher Daughters, even while segregated among the company of other girls, and she discovered through her friendship with Jürgen she was made weak in the knees by a big brain rather than by muscles and brawn or physical prowess.

He knew more about the humanities, history, mathematics and languages than any human being she had ever met. At fifteen years of age, he had already mastered ancient Greek, Latin, Hebrew, Mandarin, Japanese, German, French, English and Sanskrit. She became smitten with him in that saccharine, hollow way endemic to young schoolgirls who are in love with a single imago they hold always before them but could never explain or articulate, and she strove to be round him, to his great discomfiture, like a child. Not until she got him to open up one day in anxious, fatuous tones about a classmate, Joséf, did she understand he was not the least bit interested in girls.

Now, all these years later, just over a year to the day since that rainy morning when she and Patek had rediscovered one another on the street by sheer happenstance, a far more wonderful man blessed her life each day. Seeing the butterfly, a harbinger of romance, remembering her childhood and her unrequited feelings for Jürgen and contemplating the protean other events of unhappiness in her life—such as her tortured dalliance with Hugo—all of which now made Patek's presence in her life possible, Rahel shook her head in wonderment and laughed. In those first few months with Hugo, she had been happy beyond anything she'd ever known, but it was illusory happiness, based on the affections of a cad who saw her as nothing more than a sexual plaything. In contrast, her love with Patek was real and certain, and even after they had been together for more than a year, his acts of kindness and sacrifice towards her each week made it clear beyond all doubt he put her interests above his own.

Just this past winter, on a bitter, cold night with a piercing wind, she had caught the *Autobus* to his apartment for the night and for once neglected to bring her old, flat night pillow, which prevented her from getting a neckache. He insisted on going back to her apartment by himself (and had walked most of the way there before the bus came) and retrieving it for her, despite her repeated entreaties to accompany him there.

Moreover, since Hitler had taken power, her life had improved; she made more money per hour now than when she met Patek and more when she met him than in 1932.

She loved Patek as she had never loved anyone before, like someone she had known for years and years; she felt safe in his arms and knew from his words and his actions he would die to protect her. Even if she did not experience the white-hot erotic spark with him she'd had with Hugo—so big and strong he could toss her about like a rag doll—Patek was attractive enough, and what he lacked in raw sexual power, he more than made up for in passion, for she had never been so adored and worshipped in all her life.

In ways great and small, the two of them were made for each other, and the trifles that often came between her and other men she had been with were of no moment with Patek. The lack of interest in sustained conversation she observed in many men never existed for Patek, even after spending days together; he could talk with her for an entire day without stopping for anything more than food and sex. Their proclivities were so well aligned, they were even at ease sitting in silence and enjoying one another's company. In every regard, Patek's views were as one mind with her own.

A breeze kicked up and ran its hand through Rahel's hair, blowing a long wisp across the front of her face. She brushed it aside, dispelling her thoughts. After passing the shoelace vendor who always set up on the sidewalk two doors up from her favourite café, she turned into the shop for her late-morning cup of coffee, which she enjoyed for the walk and for the opportunity to stretch her legs. Rahel walked in on a heated exchange between an old woman and two younger men in line. The taller man in front, a blond, Aryan-looking gentleman, had passed in front of the old woman, who had put her arm out to halt his progress.

'Excuse me, you are cutting in front of me,' she said in a raised voice. 'I am in front of you.'

'Aryans before Jews,' he snapped back, brushing past her.

'How do you know I am Jewish?' she asked.

The man turned round. 'You're Jewish; I see you in the neighbourhood. I know where you go. You're telling me you're not?'

His friend nudged him and whispered something, trying to convince him to let it go.

'No!' he snapped, knocking his friend's hand away. 'I'm sick of this shit. These goddamned Yids have worn out their welcome, and I'm tired of it.' He stepped up and shook his finger at the woman, less than ten centimetres from her face. 'Your day of reckoning is coming, old lady, mark my words, and our chancellor is going to see to it you Yids are sent away and don't come back.'

'You're a stupid, ignorant man,' she shot back with a dismissive wave. Raising her head and locking eyes with Ursula, the woman who always worked behind the counter, she shouted, 'Tell us, please, young lady, who was first in line?'

Ursula looked ill at ease for a moment; then, to Rahel's chagrin, she gestured to the men. 'These gentlemen were in line ahead of you.'

'Oh, for goodness' sake, I've never in all my life...' With that, the woman snapped her purse shut and stormed out.

Rahel had known Ursula for years and had always considered her a fair and generous woman in a job that was not easy. Rahel had entered too late to see for sure if the old woman was right, but in her heart she found it implausible a lady her age would have made it up if the men were in line first.

While the men put in their orders, Rahel stood in a state of mild bewilderment, unable to focus her mind away from the itch tickling her brain. Her break now all but over, she could ill afford the time to go elsewhere for her coffee. And she knew this place; she liked their coffee and the proximity to her job—close but not too close, giving her the short walk she needed to stretch her legs—and she'd always enjoyed talking to Ursula, who in general had few customers at this hour. Yet, in spite of all this, a small voice persisted in the back of her head, leaving her wondering, *Why am I still here?* She had in fact arrived too late to know if the woman was lying.

'Next?' A brief pause. 'Ahh, Rahel, *guten Morgen!* The usual?'

She hesitated and stepped up to the counter. 'Yes. The usual, please.'

And so, with the subtlety and grace of the day's dawn, in which the fixed gaze of an observer will note no discernible change between one moment and the next until the passage of an hour has brought forth the momentous event, so did the Lord—and my own conviction to follow His path—forge a gentle but firm insinuation of His way into my life. All at once I saw, in the midst of a hushed conversation with Clovis one June night before heading off to the dormitorium, that I was both content at Lorsch and identified with the life I had there, with what was happening to me and round me. At the end of each night, I thanked the Lord for the day I had had. This couldn't be put into words, but its effect upon my spirit and my soul could not have been more elegant. For the first time ever, I belonged somewhere. Yes, I would have no doubt belonged with Clovis too, had I chosen to take up his offer and live with him on his estate, but as I was discovering, I needed not just to belong but to have a purpose, and more than in a private, personal sense, but one with a larger social mission.

This did not surprise Clovis in the least—yea, far from it. 'I keep telling you, you are destined for greatness.'

'Yes, yes, that is your gift, is it not?' On this night I was somewhere between disbelieving of and amused at this ongoing theme of his.

He nodded, reaching up and fondling my earlobe. 'But some people make my calling far easier than most.'

'So, pray, what is it you see me destined for?'

'If I knew that, I would be a far more famous soul than I am,' he quipped. Looking at me, thoughtful, he said, 'I should imagine it will be in some sphere of influence—knowledge, the law—even here in the Church—'

'In other words, you haven't a clue.' I laughed.

'Quite.' There was silence, and he ventured into the subject I guessed was occupying his mind. 'Natheless, I dare say, with your education as well as your facility with Letters and languages, you could leave quite an impress upon the monastic world, were you so inclined—assuming, of course, you were able to maintain this new identity of yours. You are all of sixteen and already surpass the men here in terms of your skills and abilities, in the library and scriptorium in particular. At this pace, it is not beyond the realm of possibility you could find yourself in the position of assistant abbot somewhere in the span of several years— once you have taken your vows, of course. There is plenty of room in the Church for advancement for a young man of your gifts and abilities.' His voice and expression were bereft of all traces of irony.

'Quite. A young man.' I was seated upon his bed and grabbed the edges with my hands. I met his gaze with my own, sighing before I spoke. 'It is all so exhausting; you've no idea.'

Clovis stroked the side of my face. 'I am sure of it. But that will not always be so. In a year or so's time, I dare say you will be unaware of it—which carries its own risks and duties of vigilance. But the exhaustion of it all—that will fade over time, like learning a language you must converse and write in at all times. It will become another aspect of who you are. You must believe this.'

'Yes, I know you are right.' In truth, the transformation taking place within me was fundamental and untroubled concerning my newfound place within Lorsch. For the first time in my young life, I arose each morning without the need to confront those familiar daemons which beset me round on the nature of my purpose here on earth—of what I would accomplish, what I wished to accomplish. All of this already existed as a settled matter within my heart and mind, requiring no further attention on my part. The issue of my disguise as a man constituted the sole distraction, the one element which did not fit into the serene effortlessness of those days. That burden, truth be told, was one I would never be rid of, one that would plague me all the rest of my days. But I also knew my continued status as a man was prerequisite to my ascendancy within the ranks—and I had no desire whatever to become a nun. I knew Clovis's assertions regarding the passage of time were correct, yet, if anything, even nearer the truth regarding the need for heightened vigilance once it did become more second nature, as the tendency towards carelessness could otherwise imperil and bring down the entire illusion, leaving me scandalled and condemned for all time.

The monastic life within Lorsch, in the end, whilst fortifying to the spirit, also lent terrible and at times unbearable isolation to my days for all of that. This would be even more true later on, after Clovis had finished out his first six-month residence at Lorsch and left to resume his life outside the abbey. The Code demanded silence in almost all endeavours, and those issues I dwelt upon and cared about with the greatest passion were all taken from the books I had read, and many of the Brothers outside the library and scriptorium were illiterate. In my youth, when so little of what I knew or expected I knew was grounded in actual experience, this fact never failed to disappoint and astonish. And whilst much has been made of the savagery of our world prior to the emergence of Charles Martellus and his rout of the Arab Hagarians at the Battle of Tours in 732, the fact remains a wealth of documents demonstrate at least a significant presence of literacy amongst the Christian clergy well in advance of that date.

Around 633, Archbishop Isidore of Ishbiliya, one of the last great lights of the ancient world, set forth in his two-book work on ecclesiastical offices, in a chapter on rules governing the clergy, that they should be occupied foremost with teaching, with reading, of Psalms, hymns and spiritual songs. The obvious presumption follows that the monks must, as a group, have been literate, or Isidore's rules requiring an emphasis on reading would have been of no moment. If anything, the moral desuetude and descent into sexual debauchery and predation—even, so the rumours went, upon female penitents from whom they might withhold absolution until certain sexual favours were granted—has spiralled downwards into the present time. Still, whilst the credo *Laborare est orare* continued to hold a prominent place within the monastic cultus even in the world of Lorsch Abbey in the year 831, the sweeping changes initiated by another Benedict, Benedict of Aniane, starting in 817 at Aix-la-Chapelle, were having their effect in monasteries throughout the realm. The ordained class in all probability knew how to read, and in fact at Lorsch, given its unique status in the realm as a repository of knowledge, a higher proportion of the Brothers there were literate. Moreover, the post-Aix-la-Chapelle emphasis on spiritual contemplation over pure manual labour—which relied more and more on paid servants rather than on the monks themselves—hastened more formal discussions of the Gospel within the abbey's walls.

Whilst I was a mere novitiate, the issues most dear to my own heart were ones centred on the Church's view of women and the roles they could fulfil, as well as a growing disharmony with Augustinian Original Sin and the lack of free will. All of these were topics which were already established in the Lorsch cultus as irrelevant, and my own views would have been perceived as heretical. I also suspected my inordinate preoccupation with women might well invite closer scrutiny of me as a person if not of the person itself, given that debacle with the visitor from the night in the forest—a development I could ill afford. Therefore, whilst discussions were had amongst the Brothers both in assembly and on less formal occasions as to their understanding of the Gospel, none of it touched on any of my questions, and on the balance I suffered the condign punishment, as for certain they would have deemed it, of open-mouthed silence and agony. From the beginning, I shared a certain inexplicable bond with Brother Dieter, and his admission to the concealment of Acts of John affirmed that bond of acceptance and even unspoken knowledge of my own haunted perspective, but I still dared not voice certain thoughts, even to him. Dieter might have brought a more complex grounding in the literature to his understanding of Christianity with regard to its early history, but his views still fell, for all his prior personal struggles, within the metes and bounds of traditional ecclesiastical doctrine, and my own quandaries as to the narrow, circumscribed territory reserved for women in the Church would have been met, even by him, with consternation.

Once, for a moment, I had a word from Father Abbot near the chapter room. He caught my ear with a 'Brother Johannes' in a quiet voice, and I turned round to face him. 'I am hearing from Brother Dieter and Brother Tomas you are doing excellent work in the library and scriptorium. I am glad of it.'

These were some of the kindest words anyone in a position of authority, including my parents, had ever spoken to me to that point in my life. Yet Abbot Adelung had a curious manner about him in the dispensing of praise, for the tone in his words all but obliterated any laudatory sense conveyed in the words themselves; he might just as well have been instructing me to carry a load of firewood somewhere, for all the coldness and precision in his tone. It acknowledged commendable conduct yet confined the praise to the context where it belonged, work performed in the service of the Lord, rather than offering congratulatory or otherwise boastful praise of the individual responsible for the conduct.

Natheless, I welcomed the compliment, which elevated my spirits well into the next day. However, the following day an event transpired which provided a sharp rebuttal to the previous day's mood. Brother Chlodwig, an older, simple man who could not read and whom the Abbot always assigned to work in the guest house, the garden or the bakery, was singled out before the entire assembly in the chapter room.

Father Abbot gestured to the Brother, ordering him to rise. 'Brother Chlodwig, it has come to my attention that on the twelfth day of this month of July in the year 831, you did enter upon the threshold of a female guest staying at Lorsch Abbey, and in flagrant and unconscionable violation of your vows and of the rules under this house of God, did close the door to her room, with both of you therein and sequestered in privacy from the eyes of your Brethren. The guest informed us that after a brief exchange, you did therein attempt to fondle her bosom.' Chlodwig's face turned crimson as Father Abbot spoke to him in loud but calm, measured tones. Chlodwig stood silent and still, his arms motionless at his sides.

'On the twenty-third day of September in the year 830, you were censured in private and excluded from prayers for touching a female guest about her waist upon her departure, a gesture you explained as an overfamiliar form of farewell, which was, however, inappropriate in its entirety and a violation of your vows as well as the duties with which you are entrusted in the care of the public as an innkeeper.' Focusing his gaze upon Chlodwig, Father Abbot leaned forward from the podium. 'Do you deny these events?'

Chlodwig shook his head. 'No, I do not, Father Abbot.'

'This is too grievous an offence—against the woman in question, yes, but moreover against this abbey and against God Himself—to let pass with a light sentence. For just these sorts of transgressions, the idyllic figure of the monk, so long held in such high esteem in Frankish society, has become of late a target of denigration and mean-spirited rumour. It cannot be permitted to flourish, and the sole method for ensuring it does not is to root out all sources of such blasphemy. Forthwith, you are to be flogged thirty times in the misericord, and you shall be excommunicated.' A muffled shriek went up out of the poor wretch, at which Father Abbot silenced him, holding up a finger. 'But that is not all.' He turned and looked about the room to all of us.

'All your Brothers here are to be punished as well for your transgression, Brother Chlodwig: myself and all the Brothers, for we are all responsible for one another and bear the shame of your actions just as sure as if we had done the deed ourselves. It cannot but be so, for when the community hears of this, it will judge not you alone; it will judge all of us. Therefore, we shall all sit in silence and listen to every lash you suffer and each cry that issues from your mouth, so that the very blood which courses through the beating hearts in this room is affixed to the blood drawn from your flesh by the lash, in order that we are convicted to the memory of the horror and torment of your punishment this day before God, the better to arm us against the possibility of any such temptation to our own souls. God's Will be done.'

We lived in silence, day and night. But it was an appalling silence that attended the next several minutes of poor Chlodwig's wretched existence. Not one cough, not a sneeze, not a single heavy sigh issued from anyone. There were creatures crawling on the walls whose feet could be heard, one in front of the other. With a slow solemnity more appropriate to a papal funeral, Father Abbot led Brother Chlodwig out of the chapter room into the narrow passageway connecting to the misericord, and, the door kept open, Chlodwig disrobed, the whip was brought and the punishment administered. For the first five or so lashes, Chlodwig's cries were muffled, but he was older and his skin loose and more fragile, and as the tails of the whip reached bone and tore the flesh open, his screams filled the rooms and bored into my ears like knifepoints. Each lash chiselled the experience into my very soul for eternity—and it has informed the horror and dread which has since accompanied every slip, careless error or ill-attended detail that has threatened to expose my true identity, for as long as I have lived.

The severity of Chlodwig's transgression notwithstanding, I took issue with Father Abbot's punishment. Under the Rule, as I understood it, two such incidents must occur that result in discipline by way of private censure before public punishment is permitted. Moreover, the Rule favoured flogging for intractable offenders, with excommunication as a last resort if corporal punishment was unavailing. Administering a whipping for the first time after a single admonishment in private, accompanied by excommunication, was in clear violation of the Rule. I had the utmost respect for Abbot Adelung and the moral nobility he endeavoured to restore to the monastic cultus, at least in the small—if important—corner of the world over which he held sway, but in this instance his methods disgusted me. Most disconcerting of all, Father Abbot's own words, that Chlodwig had 'attempted' to fondle her bosom, gave me pause. Did we know what that meant? Had he requested it of her or made a motion to that part of her person with his hand, which she blocked before anything could happen? Granted, it seemed odd for him to close the door to her room, but no less odd than the fact Father Abbot could just as well have said Chlodwig 'fondled her bosom', which would have been more accurate if that had happened. On principle, for an offence of such a serious nature, most of all a repeat offence, I was not opposed to the flogging in public, given the burgeoning problem of sexual misconduct amongst the clergy in those times. But the excommunication on top of the flogging without proper precedent struck me as unconscionable.

In the end I could not but reason the prestigious status of Lorsch within the realm was at issue, demanding more drastic measures, along with complete disassociation of the abbey from anyone engaging in such debauchery. Lorsch's prominence in the public eye, and the elite personages who both frequented the abbey and were its benefactors, no doubt demanded it. But it left a sour taste in my mouth, and from that day forward, I knew no one there—myself least of all—was promised tomorrow, in especial if the monastery's political ends would be served by a quick and unjust end to a monk's career when the circumstances warranted it for the sake of convenience and the 'greater good'. I tried, as best I could, to serve well and, to the greatest extent possible, make myself indispensable.

July dissolved into August, the hottest I had ever lived through to that point, and with it came temperatures and humidity that made life itself unbearable. Worst of all, the heat magnified both the stench and the intensity of flow from between my legs. The Brothers' body odours intensified to the choking point, but it was the same smell common to all the Brothers except me. I lived in terror, convinced someone would figure out the specific biological function behind my odour at my next issuance, but Clovis, through Providence, bless his soul, still under his term of residency, secured the special provisions and materials I needed and provided a private room outside the dormitorium, where I could change to clean myself. This was most fortuitous, given the stricter-than-usual codes governing cleanliness implemented at Lorsch by Abbot Adelung—in spite of the increasing latitude evolving canons were providing at that time. The Aachen Synod of 816, for example, girded by the aforementioned ambitions of Benedict of Aniane for a more rigorous code of conduct, decreed bathing was for the infirm and not to be practised by healthy monks. Baths were permitted at Christmas and Easter alone, and even then any bathing had to take place in separate tubs. Bloodletting was no longer to be done at specific, fixed times of the year but on an individual basis of need. Yet the forty-three canons published but one year later in 817, also at Aix-la-Chapelle (the West Francian name for Aachen), relaxed the Code's grip upon those same rituals of cleanliness, decreeing the number of baths monks were to take per year could be set by the Prior. These changes notwithstanding, Father Abbot refused to depart from the inflexible earlier standard, forbidding baths to monks except the infirm and oblates of a tender age and continuing to limit baths for the healthy to Christmas and Easter. I would have qualified as an oblate of a tender age, being a fourteen-year-old boy, but with Clovis's assistance I stayed clean and had no need of a bath, which, given everything else, was for the best.

Father Abbot's strong antipathy towards the increased reports of monastic debauchery and sexual perversion were well known, and his conviction that nudity undermined efforts to stem such behaviour and threatened the monk's ability to maintain modesty and celibacy allowed no place for regular bathing. Whilst the vows undertaken by Benedictine monks under the Code are limited to obedience, stability and conversion of manners, both poverty and celibacy are understood to inform monastic life. Chlodwig's transgressions had not helped in the least to relieve Father Abbot of this preoccupation with sins of the flesh.

But Abbot Adelung's conformity to the capitularies was not uniform. For example, the earlier Aachen Synod had decreed healthy monks should not consume the flesh of animals, including fowl. In the canons of the following year, the rules carved out an allowance for fowl—on the holidays of Christmas and Easter. However, Lorsch Abbey served soups and dishes made from beef stock on a regular basis, which Father Abbot permitted on account of its derivation from bone marrow and not the flesh of the cow itself. Whilst not forbidden beyond a doubt, such an item seemed in the main an object of excluded fare. But Father Abbot was convinced some introduction of red meat—or at the least red meat derivatives—was an essential staple, in especial for lay priests for whom manual labour comprised a significant and visible portion of their day's work. Forsooth, meat and bread alone provided the sort of fortification needed to sustain a body through the exertions required of it in the course of a day's labours, and Father Abbot, with good reason, took advantage of a lack of express exclusion of certain comestibles to better enhance the health of his monks.

The Rule required fresh fruits and vegetables to be served at every meal, along with two cooked dishes, one of them fish, more often than not. Still, the prominence in our age of cheese and bread at meals prevailed at Lorsch, evinced by the continual belching and flatulence during Compline. Our Abbot found the balance of various staples essential to good health. Given his quiet rectitude and piety in all other matters, the few minor liberties he took with the Code in preparing the monastery's menu were of no concern to him—nor, for that matter, to any of us. The Old Testament forbids the eating of unclean meats such as pork and shellfish, and 1 Corinthians condemns the eating of meats sacrificed to idols, but Jesus Himself shared in the eating of fish in John 21:9-13. As a Jew He would also have eaten mutton.

Whilst Father Abbot's lack of adherence to the literal letter of the 817 edicts regarding the eating of meat were of no moment in my life at Lorsch, his dismissal of their more liberal provisions regarding bathing were of a different order. His insistence on reserving baths for those highest and holiest occasions invited greater peril as regards my own unique hygienic situation than I would have been subjected to at another abbey. The oppressive heat aggravated both the condition itself and the magnitude of its assault upon the senses, such that I feared anyone in my general vicinity could not but have been struck blind with revulsion. And yet, bathing was not an activity at Lorsch where absolute privacy would have been vouchsafed to anyone, so, in fact, not bathing might have avoided catastrophe.

Now a major benefactor of the monastery, Clovis, like the duke with his affection for truffles from earlier on, who had also resided at Lorsch for extended periods in exchange for his grants, could request and receive any item he wished, and so long as the item requested existed in inventory or could be found in the general territory, the request was granted without question. A bowl of fresh, drawn water, washrags and soap were amongst the easiest items for a monastery to provide. I was happy to endure a stench under my armpits for purposes of camouflage, but the distinctive rancour of old blood flow from my sex in humid heat overpowered any other odour on the premises. Regular washings of my sex, however, courtesy of Clovis, permitted my movements amongst the Brethren without suspicion.

We had made love very little that summer, and in late July and August not at all, as the torpor drained us of our vitality and predisposed us towards sleep and satiety in all aspects of life. The stifling heat and humidity made it difficult for the older Brothers, and some suffered laboured breathing even when under no exertion. The youngest oblates had it the easiest of all and at times appeared to all but frolic in the heat—at least in comparison with the rest of the monks. By the grace of God and the nature of my gifts, I spent most of the summer in the library and scriptorium—where I most wished to be and where in fact both my physical limitations and my aversion to gruelling labour in such stultifying heat were least in evidence.

One night in early August, the state of life at Lorsch culminated in one of the most terrifying storms I have ever experienced. As always, I was the last to fall asleep, and on this particular night, what began as soft, distant flickers of light at the edges of the small windows progressed to intense flashes and powerful, reverberating earthquakes of thunder. Before long, the flashes of lightning were constant, and a fearful wind had kicked up, slamming the thunder right into the stone wall on the other side of my pallet. The wind hurled deafening curtains of rain into the windows, but by then fatigue had started to overtake me, along with the hypnotic fingers of the rain's repetition; and the violent weather went down in me with such force of darkness, my senses themselves broke apart into things unspeakable in nature and of ineffable evil. A throng of countless voices but which gave off a frightful vibration, as of dozens of bees as large as small birds, lived in my mouth and snaked down my gullet; I could feel it contracting and expanding like an animal within the walls of my stomach, tormenting me with the hopeless, horrifying knowledge of being trapped with some monstrosity that could not be banished without banishing myself along with it. Of course, I could not speak or make a human sound to anyone; whenever I tried to speak, some tender and beautiful strain decanted the air of its darkness and terror, and the murderous din was long departed—as if it had never existed. The instant I stopped trying to speak, it all returned with renewed vigour and vengeance. Shut up in impenetrable darkness, as in a crypt, I still felt the eyes of all humanity upon me, wide with horror and overflowing with the judgment of condemnation, though I was as trapped and innocent as a fly which had by sheer misfortune found the fatal stealth and invisible lure of the spider's lair. My monk's robes were soiled and in shreds, and as I twisted in vain to wrest myself free of this harrowing vision, I saw that all those eyes upon me beheld something more terrible than their mortal consciousness could bear. I looked down, and as though the light of their collective horror were trained on my body, I could see my flesh. My robes were open, and my naked body, my breasts and my sex were exposed, but the rest of my body was a corpse, eaten through to rotted adipose and bone and covered in squirming maggots. I screamed louder than I had ever known anyone could scream, a deafening echo in empty space, the fetor of my putrefaction unbearable. Into this hideous purgatory a sound emerged, faint at first, which built into something stronger and closer in distance until at last it was an assault upon my very flesh. Though it was painless, I felt intense shame and grief; over what I knew not, but it was grounded in judgment absolute and inevitable to the narrative of my life, something I had earned through my actions, through my conduct over years and years. I needed that sound to stop—it traumatised my ears, and with each repetition it tore deeper into my soul and severed it from whatever memory of my previous life on earth remained—and steeped me in this irretrievable crypt of time from which I could not escape and in the same breath in which I seemed not to exist. I was lost to myself—in every way a woman hewn of mortal flesh can be lost—and knew that the world and God judged me lost to God. Then the sound rent my ears apart in a single hammer blow from which I awoke drenched in sweat: a thunderclap so close, the glass in the windows almost broke.

Chlodwig!

And in that moment, I understood all of it: what the sound had been, where the shame it brought in its striking came from and the monstrous transformation of my body in front of humanity, except for my sexual organs, which were bared to everyone—the entirety of it all. In those spectral visions of shame, punishment and public disgrace came cascading down upon me everything I lived with—and denied—every day, in both mortal fear and fear for my eternal soul. And if it were true God brought me to Lorsch and kept me there instead of choosing a life for me with Clovis outside the Church, it might have also been true He called me to renounce my stealth and deception within the walls of His own house. However, I did not heed Him this time.

I was young and careless and should not be surprised at my stupidity and arrogance. Although I did not avail myself, as justification for my actions, of any detailed and informed argument grounded in the doctrine of necessary evil or examine the complex morass of free will and God's Will as represented in Augustinian theology, I fell back upon the most facile, glancing recitations of both as an expedient means of resolving my inner tension. In the decades since, I have felt the impress of these doctrines, in their full consideration, upon my own thoughts often. Still, in all that time, I have yet to fashion any rational, comprehensible system of God, morality and free will that resonates with my lower instincts, beyond necessary evil—which strikes me as pure self-justification in its worst form at this distant remove, although I was more than happy to appropriate it in my youth for convenience.

Natheless, after that terrifying dream, confronted with mounting anxiety over my repeated acts of deception, I took shelter in Augustine for succour, skimming just across the surface of his views to justify my own actions. The relationship between God and Man is a complex and difficult one in Augustine. His writings characterise Man as dependent upon God for grace and the ability not to sin. Man could cooperate in maintaining himself on that path, but the Prime Mover was God. Man, on his own, could choose sin alone, not good.

In my youth and in my first years at Lorsch, this view comported well enough with my own beliefs, inasmuch as I scarce believed God gave us any thought at all—and between my father, my mother, poor Adolfo, the few other unmoored souls with whom I had come into contact prior to that point in time, and my own self-absorbed meanderings, I was all too willing to believe Man was little else save the most wicked and oblivious, destructive animal to creep across the earth. And so, I accepted God as the Prime Mover without reservation, feeling myself a chess piece pushed from one square to the next—or not, as His Will dictated. If I continued to sin but did not disclose it, that was a consequence of some necessity deemed warranted by God's Will.

But with each passing year I outgrew in increasing leaps and bounds my unblinking trust in Augustine's portrayal of Man as a creature devoid of the faculty of initiative and bound without hope to sin and the basest evil instincts. In the course of my studies at Lorsch Abbey and beyond, in the academy of life, I found too many high-minded souls who chose grace over sin when the path before them pointed to the latter.

To such claims one might well retort: How do you know those acts were not the product of divine intervention? For not one amongst us may know the mysterious ways of the Lord. But I must believe I know myself, and in the simplest matters, there was no intervention, yea, not even time for nor necessity of an Aristotelian Prime Mover to impel me towards grace. It is implausible an unremarkable soul such as I should have so often chosen the path of good in magnificent exception to her race.

Unlike Irenaeus and others who argue for evil as a necessary means to achieving good, and therefore God-created, Augustine contends evil is neither necessary nor God-created but rather the function of Man's fall from grace and the absence of good. Even floods and natural disasters are the work of fallen angels, in Augustine's view.

Instead, evil arises *ex nihilo*, in defiance of God's perfect creation in Genesis. This is unknowable in human terms, little better than the opacities of Valentinianism. Moreover, if we alone, not God, are the source of evil, then God does not move us to choose evil as a necessity on the path to good.

If I choose to intervene and prevent the rape of Lucretia by Sextus Tarquinius, hearing nothing under his threat by sword but bursting upon the threshold quite by accident into a room I believed to be empty, to see the deed being done, thus ingressing and throwing myself between them in the same seamless movement, where is the moral paralysis Augustine reckons as the condition of Man? I dare submit one would need to search far and wide for a soul so incarcerated in his own sin, he would need to be moved first by God to such action.

Most compelling of all, I have a powerful and vivid memory of one of the times in my life when in truth I was moved by God towards a certain action: that is, of coming to Lorsch in the first instance and of remaining there and refusing Clovis's invitation to come live with him on his land in the second. I could feel its stir within me, for my own will was urging me in the opposite direction. Far from believing Man is never so bound up in his own sin that he must rely on the Lord to move him in the direction of good, I natheless cannot abide the permanence of such a state at all times on account of Adam's fall from Paradise. In the end, I read Augustine's *Confessiones* as the key to his stark view of the whole of human existence as a product of Man's will: slavish, filthy and paralysed, a vision of the world as an older man's fearful hopes for the boy's absolution—an absolution that would never come, for certain not from Augustine himself, even if from God.

But it does mean that for me, the final judgment of my actions takes one of two paths: either I have sinned as a product of my own free will, and that is the end of the matter, in which case, my papacy as well is the fruit of mortal sin and an irredeemable blasphemy; or, in the alternative, my continued deception was a necessary evil, and one God Himself created for the greater good in order to raise up the nature of Man. The former was too brutal for me, even at sixteen without a papacy to defend, and in most respects, it is still. But the latter felt too easy, too convenient and self-serving a conclusion. God alone knows how I am to be judged in the Hereafter.

Regardless, the fact I did not heed the nightmare and its meaning for me would not put an end to the matter.

The following years were ones of subtle achievement and glaring short-comings. Despite my youth—for, so far as they knew, I was but a lad of fourteen—Father Abbot handed me increasing responsibility and authority within the scriptorium, until by 834, I was second to none save Brother Dieter, the man accountable to Father Abbot himself for all work done there and who had overseen the compilation of the *Codex Aureus Laurensius* some years back, one of the world's most magnificent Gospel books. I also had an eye for visual detail and approved much of the illuminated leaves which the abbey produced from 833 to 836. This detail work encompassed anything from verifying all the correct colours were used in the right places in a historiated initial (which on rare occasions could consume an entire page) to identifying transcription errors in the text to correcting art elements not perfect in alignment or symmetry within the page layout. The abbey used vellum for all its illuminations, the finest, most supple grade of unsplit calfskin, and the application of gold and silver to these pages meant any errors requiring correction were expensive indeed. I possessed such keen visual acuity that on rare occasions Dieter overruled my recommendations. A lavish page with ornate, heavy illumination and perfection in execution save a minute variation in the vertical centring of a miniature, undetectable to all trained eyes but mine, for example, would be allowed to stand. The scribes were superlative artisans, and this work gave me tremendous satisfaction for many reasons, not just for the beauty and glory of the finished works themselves. Father Abbot and Brother Dieter placed a high value on the skills I brought to the monastery in terms of its larger presence within the realm—both with its reputation and prestige and with its accumulation of wealth through the production of commissioned works for royals and nobles. This latter pursuit most of all was becoming a significant means to monastic affluence and position, one for which, even after Charlemagne, Lorsch was predisposed for strategic ascension. Between Clovis's endowments of land to the abbey and my own stalwart service in the scriptorium, we were contributing much to the monastery's growth, my uneasiness over my own methods of assimilating into the monastic community notwithstanding.

But my shortfallings were more noticeable to me than the accomplishments for which Lorsch recognised me. To begin with, a certain difficulty in keeping my dreams to myself at night became a reported subject about which I found myself in private audience with Abbot Adelung. He called me in one morning and, dispensing with all pretence of niceties, sat me down and said, 'I must enquire as to the nature of your relationship with the nobleman Clovis, who has been residing with us here again these past months.'

So shocking to me was this topic of conversation that for some time I sat in front of Father Abbot, blinking and holding my hands together in front of myself, my mouth open. My mind also flashed upon the incident back in 830 of the Samhain reveller reporting a woman in our midst disguised as a monk, impressing upon me the magnitude of the stakes at this juncture, relating less to that incident than to any connexion the Abbot might draw between those accusations and the current difficulty. This was in November of 835, during Clovis's fourth such stay at the abbey, and by then our amorous activity had trailed off to the occasional congress, and we were always vigilant in the extreme in ensuring there were no witnesses, even to my knocking upon his door. There were many aspects of my secret life as a woman I feared, more often than I would have liked, coming to light, but at this particular time, our physical intimacy was not amongst them. I shook my head in disbelief and laughed.

'Begging your pardon, Father Abbot; I am trying to fathom the nature of your question. Are you suggesting I am engaged in some kind of improper relationship with that man?' I still smiled as I spoke, looking at him but yet somewhat past him—the smile of someone in genuine assistance to another in coming to an understanding about something that was beyond doubt a false impression.

Father Abbot's posture and demeanour changed somewhat. 'I apologise for the intrusion, Brother Johannes, but I have been told by one of the Brothers that for the past two nights, you have spoken the nobleman's name several times in your sleep, in rather frank language, it appears. He heard you say, "You know I love you, Clovis." He also'— and here the Abbot coloured and drew his forefinger down his left cheek and round his chin—'he also said your voice was very high, almost feminine, like a young girl's voice. He found it quite disturbing, and I cannot say I disagree.' He looked down at the floor for a moment—more for my own benefit—and then at me again with those large, icy eyes. 'Is there anything I need to know about?'

Immense relief flooded my thoughts; this had nothing whatever to do with someone having seen or heard the two of us together. 'Clovis is a noble name, after all,' I murmured. 'It has been the name of multiple Frankish kings, and I too am of noble birth. I had a little brother named Clovis, who died when I was quite young, and I sometimes dream about him.'

The Abbot's head tilted to one side in understanding, his facial expression changing from scepticism to sympathy. 'God have mercy.' He paused long enough to betray the lower instincts of a seasoned mind too well versed in the subtleties of fabrication to leave off without further questioning. 'May I enquire, in case I am asked, of the circumstances leading to your brother's unfortunate end?'

'Of course. We were engaged in a rather perilous variation of blind man's buff,' I replied, for I had already thought ahead. 'I say perilous because we were playing at a high altitude, by a cliff where such young boys have no business running about with their eyes closed, and our game led poor Clovis too far astray. As his elder brother, I was responsible for him. It is a tragedy from which, for reasons that are no doubt obvious, I have never been able to free myself entire, and on occasion I have dreams, well, nightmares about it or dream I am back in my childhood with him...' Here I tried to fumble for the right words, as best I could: 'Perhaps I—could that account for the high voice?'

'Quite. Please forgive the intrusion upon so private a matter; these days an abbot cannot be too careful any time there is the slightest intimation of Sodomite behaviour, and with the difference in your ages...'

I nodded with enthusiasm, knowing the matter had been resolved, and leaning forward, put in for good measure in a confessional tone, 'However, I must say, Father Abbot, I am still adjusting to life in a community with no women at all within it—not out of any great distress, but, still, it is a bit unnatural, yes? They are half of humanity, after all, and I miss their presence; I miss their wisdom and grace. Is it unusual to have such feelings, and can I have them and yet find purpose and even contentment in the monastic life?'

Father Abbot drank in the question—it was always edifying to see how, before speaking, he considered things put to him first—and said at last, 'Alas, Brother Johannes, you alone are the one who can answer that question. You will need to pray about it. Not all men are fit for the monastic life, not even someone like yourself, with such gifts in the discipline of Letters and knowledge. In my experience, many, if not most, of the men here, if you were to put to them that question, would answer the exclusion of women drew them here or was in some other wise a comfort to them. But that is a question each man must answer for himself. And you are still so young.'

I rose to go when it became clear he had nothing else he wished to say. My confident assurances to the Abbot aside, I did not visit Clovis at his room for the better part of two weeks, and we did not have sex for several more after that. More than anything else, going to sleep terrified me for a spell, wondering each night what pearls of knowledge I might let slip in my slumber, and why in creation I had said his name out loud on successive nights. Too, my curiosity had been aroused as to the identity of the monk who had lain awake at that hour on successive nights to hear me. Try as I might, I never saw evidence of anyone else in a wakeful state. I tried to convince myself before falling asleep not to talk aloud; I have no idea whether it worked, although I never heard from the Abbot or from anyone else on the subject again.

More and more, lay servants were being used for manual labour, fortunate indeed in my case, but there were occasions when I had to take a turn lifting or carrying heavy loads of wood, brick or stone, which would have been of no moment for a lad my size, but which my feminine physique made much more difficult.

In one instance, I had to summon Brother Achim for assistance, and when he helped me carry the load of quarry rock, I saw the surprise register in his face.

'Brother Johannes, are you ill today?' he offered. 'Do we need to speak to the Prior about reassigning your duties?'

I thought of how best to respond to this well-intentioned query, knowing a physical examination might well be the consequence of such a choice. 'No, thank you, Brother Achim; I appreciate your interest, but it is my arm that is giving me a problem. Some weeks back, I injured it in an accident, trying to break my fall, and now in the cold it is freezing up. I do not seem to have much use of it this day.'

'I understand.'

A much more serious development arose several weeks later, when I did fall ill that winter. After a few hours mending a fence on a cold and quite windy afternoon—bareheaded—I got sick within three days. The illness progressed to a state of misery, with a debilitating sore throat, sneezing and discharge. A day or so later, I developed terrible chills, and a vicious fever clamped its jaws upon me for four days, leading to unrelenting diarrhoea and lengthy bouts of vomiting, sending me rushing to the garderobe between fifteen and twenty times a day. Far from not permitting me to draw a bath, Prior Werinher insisted upon it. He also insisted on an attendant being in the tub room with me.

'Prior Werinher, begging your pardon, I must needs request I be permitted to take my bath in solitude, for personal but grave reasons.'

'I am afraid that would not be appropriate for someone in your condition; you could faint or otherwise injure yourself unattended. The bath will cause fatigue. You have a high fever, and with the mass exodus of fluids from your system, you are already in a weakened physical state.'

This would not be a simple or trivial matter. I hesitated, working myself up into an emotional state of mind but taking care to groom my voice within the proper range of a lad my age. 'Prior, when I was a small boy, my father raped me for many years and threatened terrible punishment'—here I struggled to maintain composure but then guided my voice into a breakdown—'if I ever told a soul.' I wiped my eyes, took a deep breath and pressed onwards. 'In coming here, I was given to understand nudity is not allowed and even bathing is not permitted for monks.' I looked up and gave the Prior my best face of twisted confusion, terror and betrayal. 'Now I must... now I must disrobe and suffer my helpless state in the presence of another man, some stranger to whom I have never spoken?'

Here I broke down again, and the Prior put his hand upon my shoulder, from which I recoiled in fright and alarm.

'I am sorry, Prior, it is just—'

'No, Brother, please do not concern yourself with this a moment longer,' he intoned in his most calming, accommodating voice. 'It appears you have had no episodes of syncope during your illness, so we will forgo the attendant in this instance. You shall be able to bathe in privacy. We do believe the cool bath is necessary to help drive out the daemons and fever which have you in their clutches, but in the interest of your well-being, we will not insist upon the attendant.'

'Thank you, Prior.'

These fabrications were most demoralising to me—and for more than the fact I had sinned and was in need of absolution. They also gave the Abbot and Prior an impression of me in key respects as to my private life not based in truth at all. It bothered me that for the balance of my time at Lorsch, they had before them a portrait of me as a fragile, damaged soul. On one or two occasions thereafter, I sensed a palpable shift in the tone of their instructions to me, just a bit more deliberation in choosing their words, though I hoped this was nothing more than my own imagination and guilt.

As for the sinful nature of my acts, that was beyond question. The lies I told were neither officious nor jocose but injurious in nature, inasmuch as they frustrated the abbey's interests—and those of the Church at large in line with her doctrine—in discerning and excluding women from its cloister. Under Augustine it is never lawful to tell a lie, as borne out through Scripture in countless places, and where the intent is to deceive with falsehood to benefit the speaker, this is malice, in particular where the interests of the other are harmed. My lies were told for the purpose of perpetuating the deception of Lorsch Abbey as to my true sex, and all I could do was ask God's forgiveness.

To this day, if I could undo all I have done so that I would never have ascended the papal throne, I would undo nothing. More than ever, I am resolute in my belief in the necessity for a pontiff of my sex. I find this all the more so at this precise juncture in the Church's history, when the male sex after Charlemagne has so distinguished itself by mediocrity and timidity. However suspect my moral choices were in those times, I believe the overwhelming good of their result has been to the true injury of none, save a doctrine whose relevance has long since passed, if indeed it ever was relevant. Moreover, I feel an obligation, yea, a duty to that entire race of the religious comprising the childbearing half of humanity to leave intact and unaltered that which has gone before, and would deem any such undoing, were it even possible, a criminal act against all mankind.

But in my years at Lorsch, there was no grand plan to vindicate such blatant falsehoods; they were told for the simple, naked purpose of preventing my ouster from the abbey and were thus indefensible. And so, as I acquired more skill and value in the eyes of the Abbot and Brother Dieter in the scriptorium, I became a woman of two minds. On the one hand, I grew ever more certain the monastic life was a natural fit for my inquisitive and intellectual nature, not to mention a certain preference for and comfort with precision and ritual in my daily life, which my duties in the scriptorium and even the Code—by and large—complemented. 835 turned into 836, and with each passing month, my faith in God and His guidance in my life redoubled in vigour. On the other hand, I fell ever more into despair over the status of my immortal soul, which at that point in time appeared cast into perdition by my many acts of deception and falsehood at the abbey's expense. I could not see a way out or identify any means by which to stem the ever-widening tide of these callous actions. I wept over it, I prayed to the Lord on it in silence as I lay in my pallet for an hour or more each night, to no avail. My sleep suffered because of it. Because I was raised in the Catholic faith, I do not ever remember not being Catholic and not believing in mortal sin and the host of condemnations and terrors it engendered. The whole of my young life to that point may not have stood for much, but at least I had lived it more or less free of sin—sin of the injurious type, that is. Most of my lies—or sins of omission—in childhood had been told to spare others rather than injure them or benefit myself. But my capacity for guilt was tremendous, and I recall now how sinful and unclean I felt before God when I prayed for poor Adolfo that one night at the foot of my bed after he had condemned my sheltered, privileged life. I had been guilty of nothing more than being born into a better family than his, yet in my own heart, it was as though I myself had condemned him to the life of a commoner: at that time, the most terrible feeling I had ever known involving another person. It bled into every image and perception I had of myself and my relation to the world, until it paralysed me.

But my present crisis was an hundredfold worse, because it involved actual sins I had repeated over and over against the house of the Lord. I even found I was starting to lose proper control over the use of my hands, which trembled on one occasion so much that my muscles were plunged into a kind of spasm, and I could not manipulate any tool or hold an object within them. And for some reason I could not fathom, terror so gripped me, I could not give voice to my fears even to my Beloved, as if doing so would somehow transform this conceptual struggle within my soul and with God into something real and present in the talking world, a situation I could not suffer, for I was still denying its existence. For several months, I went through the rituals of the day without a lone thought in my head, nothing but a constant, tremulous anxiety and voicelessness that clicked in my ears and blew through my teeth. I stopped breathing through my nose altogether, inhaling and exhaling through an open mouth without drawing in much air. This spirit exercised dominion over me; it dressed me, fed me, walked me about the grounds, used my arms to draw aside the sheet and slip into the pallet at night, plucked the strings in my head to initiate certain conversations with Clovis, my Beloved, while skirting others and used my eyes as instruments for transcribing the texts of Cicero, Justin Martyr and Boethius. But above all else, it decanted my own soul of all that was pleasurable and soothing, building into an anxiety of the unutterable, but I saw it not—until I was dumb, dumb to the queries of others and to my own—those asked and unasked—until, in the end, all that remained was unasked, unanswerable, nothing could be laid hold of, nothing could be thought of, nothing changed.

Late one night in the early fall of 836, quite late, about an hour before Matins, I drew back the sheet, after an eternity of listening for a single sound, and tiptoed past all the still, peaceful bodies to the kitchen with a candle until I found the tool I sought, hanging on the wall, and took it down and held it—long, cold, stiff and shining in the muted darkness—my heart pounding like a tortured animal, unaware of my own incantatory state until I heard the whispered words that had been repeating themselves over and over again, 'Forgive me forgive me forgive me forgive me forgive me, pray, forgive me forgive me,' grasping the strong, stiff arc of presence so tight that it cut into my fingers where I stood in the corner of the galley and stood and stood and stood and stood but could not do the thing. I saw the wood of the floor soaked in shining black; I saw my robes drenched in blood and heard the inhuman, perfect silence of an entire dorter calm and receiving the collapse of my expired body, unmoved by all my desperation and loneliness and the tears soaking my face. But God was nowhere in this vision where the world and nothingness converged over the moment of my extremity, because He was not there. He was in the dark beside me, yea, within me where I stood and could not do the thing.

Adolf Hitler announced the commencement of the state's building of the *Volkswagen* in a speech addressed to German industry on 15 February 1936. When Rahel read in the newspapers—all Nazi controlled—about the speech and the chancellor's ambitions for Germany behind it, it energised and excited her about what her future might look like, in ways she hadn't felt in years. Like so many of his speeches in the past, his words spoke of basic notions in terms that were revolutionary. If the people were to reshape the most vital sector of the nation's transport industry, their pursuit of the automobile could not be hindered by psychological considerations or restrictions. Hitler decreed that either the automobile would remain a luxury item for the wealthy few, with little to no effect upon the German economy, or it would transform the economy while transforming itself into an item in effect all citizens of the Third Reich would use. But for that to happen, the price of the automobile would need to come down to something anyone could afford. At these words, Rahel imagined a life for herself she had never thought possible before that moment.

The racism and persecution behind the rollout of this seductive figure, however, was nothing Rahel or the German people would have been at all aware of. Hitler appropriated the superb, populist moniker 'the people's car' from earlier efforts in private industry, starting with Béla Barényi's original prototype in the mid-1920s and Josef Ganz's Standard Superior, which Ganz even marketed as the *Deutsch Volkswagen*. In 1936, Hitler introduced the Third Reich's *Volkswagen*—remarkable in its similarity to Ganz's second prototype of the Standard Superior in 1934—to much fanfare, though Germany produced the cars in such limited numbers in following years, no one but German military personnel drove them. The Gestapo persecuted Ganz, a Hungarian Jew, and ruined his business, issuing threats on his life. Hitler's vision of 'the people's car', however, never came to fruition in his lifetime.

But the charisma and allure of his rhetoric drew in Rahel, as it did so many of her fellow countrymen, and for a period she remained smitten with the thought that, for a thousand marks or less, she too might be able to venture out into the German countryside on a fine summer day, into towns too far for her to travel to by other means.

The Führer's penchant for making electrifying speeches to the people, upon which they ceded absolute power to him based on the radical, innovative future they believed he would deliver to them, was still in its formative years and seemed destined to bring the bleak economic crisis in Germany to an end. Patek, on the other hand, harboured a deep distrust of the Führer's intentions and did not shy away from voicing the basis for that distrust. It also disturbed him to a profound degree that Rahel, suspicious by nature of so much else going on round her, could have such a positive impression of Hitler and his motives. They were sitting inside a café on a cold, blustery April day, a café owned by and patronised on the whole by Jews, where they felt more comfortable than they otherwise would in such conversation.

'Look at how he came to power,' he pointed out, counting out the dates on his fingers. 'The day after he is named chancellor, on the thirty-first of January, 1933, he promises the German people a parliamentary democracy. Yet the very next day, he dissolves Parliament. On the second of February, he forbids all meetings of the Kommunistische Partei Deutschlands and undertakes a systematic search and seizure of their munitions. Two days later, on the fourth of February, Hindenburg—no doubt at Hitler's bidding—restricts freedom of the press.

'Less than a week later, on the tenth of February, 1933, Hitler decrees the end of Marxism, and on the twenty-eighth of February, he disallows the KPD, one day after our Dutch Communist friend Mr van der Lubbe is arrested for trying to burn down the Reichstag—with the matches still smoking in his hand. Hitler has, in less than a month's time, dispatched the Socialist Party's primary voice of opposition and also silenced the most credible public mouthpiece for legitimate opposition to Hitler: the press.'

Rahel had listened with patience to all of this but at last spoke up in rebuttal. 'Because, dear Patek, the KPD has done such a fine job of fixing things and righting the economic collapse that has befallen us, have they not? And their comrade from the Netherlands showed just how trustworthy they are as a group. Why should Hitler's actions surprise you, given that? And the liberal press can be trusted too, of course, to support the chancellor's efforts and policies and paint him in the most flattering light possible, yes?'

Patek stared at her open mouthed, not knowing where to begin. 'All right, let's cede the point on the KPD, just for argument's sake. Fine. But since 1919, Germany has been a republic and a democracy, not a monarchy. A hallmark of democratic government is a free press; you don't have a democracy without one. I don't care how revolutionary or ameliorative an interim government is appointed; if you do away with the free press, you in essence gut a democracy of its checks and balances. There's just no other way to look at it.'

'But—' Rahel tried to respond, but he kept cutting her off.

'And that is not all, not by a long shot,' he continued. 'On the twenty-third of March, the Reichstag passes the Enabling Act, granting Hitler dictatorial powers, and those powers are conferred on him five days later on the twenty-eighth.' Patek shook his head. 'But this is not any enabling act like we have seen before. It grants Hitler these powers for a term of four years, not just a few months. Moreover, it gives the German government, which by that time *is* Adolf Hitler, unrestricted rights to enter into treaties and acts with other nations even in violation of the Weimar Constitution. The totality of these changes and the transfer of power to a single man is staggering when you consider he willed all this into reality in less than sixty days.'

Rahel opened her mouth to counter him but closed it. She knew how Patek was when he got like this; she would have to wait for him to finish. She drummed her fingers on the table.

'When Hitler can no longer expand his power any further under the statutory and legislative scheme, he unifies the powers of *Reichspräsident* and *Reichskanzler* under himself and appoints himself commander-in-chief of Germany. Again, he made all of this happen by the second of August, 1934. *Think of it.*' He stared with searching eyes into Rahel's face, hoping to see it flooding with understanding of the significance of all these arrogative acts.

Instead she folded her hands on her lap and shook her head. 'But nothing has worked for Germany under the old order, has it? Have we known anything but abject poverty over the past decade? Answer me that, Patek—have we?' He sighed long and deep without answering, and she continued: 'Right. Nothing has worked for us under Parliament in its present form—'

'But then why—'

'So, he abolished it.'

'Why did he promise us parliamentary democracy?' He seized at her shoulders. 'Why, Rahel? Why did he promise us what he then banned? Why did he not just say instead, "I am abolishing Parliament"? Perhaps because he knew the German people would not stand for it, so he just did what he wanted, with the "understanding" some "new" parliament—the SS—would be put in place later.'

But Patek had not accounted for the extent to which Rahel still held out hope prosperity might one day come to her as well, a sentiment Patek had abandoned long ago. With his engineering background, Patek was, for one thing, of a more elevated, skilled class of worker than Rahel, and as he was less dirt poor than she, the notion of being catapulted out of such a dire economy into a state of financial affluence superior to his present situation struck Patek as both implausible and without legitimate urgency. Rahel, meanwhile, lived from hand to mouth in an oppressive and small one-room *Appartement* with radiator heat that was almost nonfunctional and pounded out a cacophonous racket when it came on, roaches which nothing could get rid of and no fans. Moreover, from her building, she had to walk some eight blocks to the nearest tram stop (and the tramway lines were being shut down anyway) and over five blocks to the nearest trolley bus. Though Rahel had grown up in a not-quite-privileged household, she had nevertheless enjoyed an altogether respectable life. Her father's family came from old money, and although he had died when she was but a small child, he was much older than her mother and had left a substantial estate—and so Rahel had become accustomed to a certain level of comfort and affluence which had been lost to her now for a number of years, to her dismay. It had been her choice to major in music instead of studying something more lucrative or taking a husband, despite having more than her share of willing suitors, but the Depression had put an end to the music teaching positions she held to make life in Berlin more sustainable.

Patek, meanwhile, had grown up with a somewhat more philosophical approach to the boundaries between poverty and affluence. His father had done well for himself in the garment and trade industries through endless toil and long hours, more often than not six days a week with ten- to twelve-hour days, leaving his family with little more than an exhausted, somnolent shell on Sundays. An overweight chain-smoker with a weakness for drink, he had no relief from this grind, right up to the last day of his life, several years back, when he came home with tightness in his chest that turned in minutes to sharp pain and a fatal coronary. As a result, Patek saw his lot, even as an educated engineer, rooted in a life of hard work and long hours for modest wages and put little stock in anything Hitler had to say that claimed it could change that paradigm.

Rahel's sense of the economic, political and social upheavals over the past decade or so underlying the reduced opportunities in her own chosen field of endeavour was both less informed than Patek's and more prone to being influenced by the populist rhetoric and falsehoods Hitler promoted. Berlin in the 1920s, and in particular the vaunted Akademie der Künste, had become a world-class teaching centre for some of the greatest and most daring composers alive. Established traditionalists such as Hans Pfitzner, the self-declared anti-modernist and composer of the sublime *Palestrina*, and Georg Schumann taught master classes alongside *enfants terribles* Arnold Schoenberg, the creator of dodecaphony, and Ferruccio Busoni, artists for whom Rahel had far less affection but who drew ever larger numbers of students and lovers of music to the great city.

In the late 1920s and early 1930s, dissension among the visual artist contingency between more conservative factions and the Akademie's modernist interests as represented by President Max Liebermann precipitated the centre's foundering. Once again, however, Rahel understood the decline of the Akademie's influence as more related to the crippling of the economy from Germany's debts incurred from the Treaty of Versailles and leading into the Great Depression than from other issues. While she tried to stay informed about the Akademie from a professional perspective, she did not keep up well enough with it to know of and understand both the political and the anti-Semitic issues which led to its demise.

'I love you, Rahel, but for whatever reason, you seem to prefer skimming along the superficial level of what you read and hear about in the media—and, in these times, that is a dangerous practice indeed.' Patek grasped her hand and sat in closer. 'You must believe me when I say this: we are living in a time and in a place when being Jewish is as dangerous as being anything anywhere in the civilised world today.' He took a deep breath. 'Most of it is due to Hitler, but some of it… some of it is just Germany.

'Take the Akademie, for example,' he continued. 'Now, in 1932, before the socialists even came to power, Max Liebermann, a German Jew and president of the Akademie since 1920, was replaced with Max von Schillings, a known anti-Semite and reactionary. Since then, dozens of Jewish members have been terminated or have left of their own volition. Schoenberg, after Schillings laid him off, joined Einstein in moving to America in 1934. Others have joined them. It is impossible to otherwise explain why the most penetrating minds of our culture trapped in Jewish bodies would pick up and leave their homeland behind at the precise moment Hitler is, by all accounts, saving Germany—unless they knew it was no longer safe to be here.'

Rahel threw her head back in disbelief, closing her eyes, then opened them wide and stared at him with her mouth open. 'So, what—what do you think, are they going to round us all up and shoot us dead in the street, is that it? A couple men who happen to be Jewish and who are too marginal, too brilliant to fit in anywhere, decide to move to America, and we are all supposed to fear for our lives? Are you listening to yourself right now? Because you need to, so you can hear how crazy you sound.'

'Do you think because he's the head of our government, he won't kill people? Listen—' Patek was furious and started a sentence three different times before taking a breath and speaking with calm deliberation. 'You need to understand how this man looks at human beings, and Jewish human beings in particular. Have you read *Mein Kampf?*'

Rahel shook her head.

'Hitler categorises mankind into three groups: the founders of culture, the bearers of culture and the destroyers of culture. For him, the Aryan race is the sole member of the first group. The Japanese and Latins are examples of the second group, who are capable of maintaining a culture that has already been created but lack the nobility and genius to create one on their own initiative. Then we come to the third group: those who will destroy culture through their greed, malice, cowardice and ineptitude. In this class belong the Jews and the Negroes. It is in essence a subhuman classification, and the laws Hitler has put into place are the perfect logical, legal expression of such a status.'

Rahel sat up tall in her chair, leaning forward and speaking in a loud voice for the first time in the crowded café. 'Patek, this is Germany! This man can write what he wants and lump people into these categories, but—be truthful, now—what can he do with it? What kind of action do you think he can take against citizens of the world—'

'The Nuremberg Laws say that we are no longer German citizens on account of our ancestry. It's that simple, Rahel. You are Jewish, so you have no rights. You might be eighty and have paid taxes on your income to the German government for decades before Hitler ever nursed at his mother's bosom, but now, because of what these laws say, you are no longer entitled to any of the rights of German citizenship—you might as well be an American Negro. Just because you are a Jew, you are banned from serving in the army; you are even banned from sitting for doctoral exams at university. Legal opinions written by Jewish authors can no longer be considered by the German courts.

'But the laws go even further, dictating how you may and may not exercise your most personal, intimate right: the right to choose whom you may make love to or marry. If you want to have sex with me, that is fine, because we are both Jewish. But that Hugo fellow you told me about, the one who broke your heart? If you decided to have intercourse with him today, you would be breaking the law. The Nuremberg Laws define such mixed relations and marriages as racial defilement, punishable as treason—which in itself affords a glimpse of the level of psychosis we are dealing with, since Jews are not a race at all but an ethnicity.'

He paused for a second. 'If Hitler sees us as the destroyers of German culture, what role can reasonable minds expect us to play in his Germany—I mean, what would be his plans for us? I'm just asking...' Patek sat back, putting his hands on his thighs, and stared at her, refusing to speak, waiting for her reaction.

After looking down for several seconds, she raised her head and gazed into the distance with a wan expression. 'I grant you, these are horrible things you speak of.' She fell silent for a long spell afterwards. 'But I can't leave Germany. My family is here. And I have no idea where we'd go. It is terrible everywhere now. At least we speak the language here...'

They left the café and returned to Patek's flat, and she made love to him with both an emotional urgency and an animality he had never experienced with a woman before. No sooner had he closed the front door behind them than she slid her ample arms round his neck and pushed her tongue deep into his mouth, pinning him up against the wall in the hallway and grinding her groin against his. Her kissing so aroused him, he was erect standing in the hallway in less than a minute.

'I love you so much, Patek,' she cooed. 'I don't know what I'd do without you. Take me, my love, I need you.' He wanted to take her into the bedroom, but she muscled him down onto the bare floor and slipped her underpants down, undoing his belt buckle and his trousers until she found him and guided him between her thighs with moaning and ardent deep-kissing the entire time. The boldness and desperation with which she took him so intoxicated Patek, he felt as if he were on fire, and when they were finished, they slumped into one another in a sweaty pile on the hallway floor, where they lay for some time until they awoke with cramped necks and starving for food.

It was the most tender and unforgettable night of bonding they had ever enjoyed together, and after dinner they sat on the couch and listened to the entire Sabajno recording of the Verdi *Requiem* together by candlelight. To Rahel's astonishment and great satisfaction, Patek got tears in his eyes during the '*Ingemisco*' solo and the '*Hostias*'. But much more than just the music had moved his heart; it was all of it. For the first time, they talked in earnest about getting married, about what their life together would look like.

In a few months' time, on a bright, sunny afternoon in mid-June, 1936, while anti-Semitic sentiments in Berlin were at their lowest ebb as the nation prepared to host the Summer Olympic Games, they would marry each other without any family present in a quiet cere- mony at the *Standesamt*, the registrar's office in their district. But on this frosty April night, they went to sleep in his bed with their arms wrapped round one another after having made love a second time, but around two in the morning, Patek was awoken by a shaking sensation next to him. He turned sideways to find Rahel given over to quiet sob- bing where she lay, unable to stop, and shaking not just from the crying but from a kind of panic, as though she were overcome with fever.

'My sweet, what's the matter?' He put his hand round her shoulder and felt a convulsive trembling in her entire body. She couldn't speak and kept choking back her tears, until minutes had passed and not a single word had issued from her lips. 'Rahel, please, you're scaring me. What's going on?'

She lay on her back, still staring up at the ceiling, as if she were unable to move or turn her head. 'I'm so frightened. Please hold me, Patek. Please, please, don't ever let me go. I'm so scared.'

That moment of crisis in the small hours of the night in the kitchen initiated a turning point in my spiritual life, a resolution to the self-in- flicted torment I had been enduring those many months at Lorsch as regards my status as an irredeemable sinner in the eyes of God. For that extremity subjected me to an ordeal of two worlds at once: the first, the condign world I saw myself condemned to in death for my sins; and the second, the world in which I existed in that moment, and to which in the end I was returned, body and soul. In fact, I believed destiny would sentence me to all eternity in the first world, and of the two, it was the one most grounded in reality. But as I stood there par- alysed in fear and incapable of action, I realised our Lord God existed nowhere in the first world—and if I were to be cast into Hell for my sins against God, He would have been there, and I would have known the wrath of His condemnation. Therefore, the vivid world which appeared before me existed as a realm of my own making: not real. Not until that moment did I know where I was and my true destiny, that God was still there with me in the kitchen at that crucial intersection of my own judgement and His. In spite of all my misgivings, He had not abandoned me; yea, He had prevented me from doing the violence unto myself that I had come there to do.

In terms I could never explain to anyone, I knew beyond all doubt that God had given me this ordeal as a test of my faith: in Him, yes, but also in myself. Had I not seen and fathomed His absence and its significance within the nightmare vision of my death, it is certain I would have succeeded in my grim task. Instead I found new inspiration for the worthiness of my mission in the kingdom of the Lord. For whilst the fact that I had sinned and needed to be forgiven had not changed, in my heart I knew the Lord forgave me, and I understood at last that in His eyes the sin of disguise to enable good works because the Church would not allow women in monasteries did not constitute the sort of grave mortal sin that imperilled my immortal soul or for which I could not be forgiven. Forsooth, I felt with searing intensity that the greatest sin against God was the sin of believing one cannot be forgiven, a fundamental tenet we are taught early and often but which rings distant and abstract in the ears without a personal example of this doctrine in practice. My belief that night in the kitchen, that no way out, no salvation, existed for me save death, forged my personal experience in the bleakest terms of the profane thinking this doctrine condemns, and from this revelation I would never again turn away.

Confessing these events to my Beloved constituted the most difficult moment of my life in the talking world to that point. As I feared, my words cut Clovis so deep—most of all, of course, on account of his ignorance of the events they described—that he could not speak, weeping and moaning before me. In that conversation, I saw how profound and entire his investment in me this strong, proud, confident and brilliant man's soul was. In faithfulness to his selfless nature, his first griefs were all about me and the agony of my own situation that could have led me to such a dark and hopeless place. He could not get his mouth to work without breaking down, but his expressions and long embrace made this clear, and we held each other tight for some time without a single word between us. But he was cut to the quick by his ignorance of events so critical to me in my life—and in the gravest terms to his—and it became clear from the words that followed I had wreaked great damage upon him and his trust of me as well as to myself. The more he spoke, the more I feared I would be exiled to a life without him in it.

My throat closed, and my words were choking themselves. 'Are you—are you saying you cannot be with me, love?' I wiped the tears from my eyes.

He stared at me for a long time without speaking. 'I am saying that you were willing to leave me—to leave you—without giving me a chance to help you or even to know of it until the deed was done. I would have been left to ponder what part I played in your death for the rest of my life. I cannot think what to make of that—other than the bleakest, most obvious meaning. I fear it may well be blind folly to so invest myself in you again—which I had not allowed myself to do with another person in a very, very long time.'

'Clovis, my love, I promise you I shan't ever again take such a burden upon myself alone—I swear it.' I was crying. 'Please know I will honour these words—I would dishonour the world first—'

'That is what I would have thought,' he said in a soft, sombre voice, 'when we promised to share our lives with one another, no matter how trying or unpleasant.'

I took his hand in my hands, squeezing it with the ferocity of a soul left no recourse but desperation. 'Have I ever lied to you about the smallest thing? I have not. Yes, I should have shared my feelings about my sins with you—it had been building for months—and yes, I understand the gravity of the matter'—here I sat erect and banished the emotions welling up in me, so I could continue—'but in large part I was deceiving myself. How can I confide in you what I have denied to myself? I did not plan or know or have the slightest notion that I would walk into the galley that night with such a black heart. I went to bed feeling otherwise.'

'I know it. Alas, this weakens rather than strengthens my faith in your words. Were it deliberate deception or withholding of the truth on your part that you had chosen to end your life—if you knew you were going to kill yourself and concealed that fact from me anyway— we could at least agree you would promise not to be so deceitful in the future, and I could decide if such a promise were trustworthy. I wish it were that simple. Alas, as you have just admitted to me, this was not the case at all—quite the opposite. Instead it possessed you in ambush, without warning, and overtook your will. You might well find yourself as powerless to prevent such a catastrophic progression in the future should it happen again. In fact, I should expect it.'

'Damn you, Clovis!' I yelled, and punched him hard in the shoulder, caring not a whit where I was or what the consequences of my shouting might engender. I jumped on him and struck him with my fists as hard as I could, wherever I could land a blow. I was crying. 'I won't lose you—I won't allow it. I can't!' I fell off him onto the bed, collapsing into sobs that would not end. A hand reached out and touched me at my shoulder. I knocked it away. I turned round and faced him through my tears. 'I was never taught how to love. I was never loved. I was beaten; I was told what to want. I was a slave. When my father died, I was emancipated. I was happy, for a moment. But my mother picked up where he left off, so I left her. Today she is as dead to me as my father.' Clovis had tears in his eyes. He sat in silence and listened. 'I am sorry I am not better at this,' I said, choking back sobs, 'though I have never wanted it more. I doubt you will ever understand just how much I love you—because your love is all the love I have ever had: from anyone. I suppose—I suppose it is unfair to put so much responsibility on one man. Perhaps, forsooth, I will never learn to love as I should—' And here the hold on my emotions broke down in full as I saw my life laid out before me in an unending cavern of loneliness, ageless toil and regret. I could scarce form words through my sobs. I held up my hand in despair and looked up at the ceiling. 'But either way, you are my one chance in life.' I stared at him through flooded eyes, motionless.

'Then maybe that is our answer,' he said at last through his tears, 'because no one else will have us. For it is true, Joan; I may have loved before you but never like this—and most of all, I have never *been* loved until you, and to lose it would leave me deranged and in ruins for anyone else. And you are right; you do not love as you should, you love to your own peril. If your love were your blood, you would be drained of every drop and looking down on me now instead of up, for you love in glorious measure and give of it all.'

And so, through immense pain and tribulation, we came out of these events stronger than ever in our commitment to one another, and I was resolved as never before in my spiritual mission for God in the months that followed. But Clovis also grasped the gravity of my situation and insisted there were monasteries where each monk had his own cell rather than sleeping in a common dorter, so that the total lack of privacy need not be the defining aspect of monastic daily life. To him it was madness to remain at Lorsch when another, much safer option existed. In such an arrangement, the risk of detection as to my true sex would be reduced in great measure and would afford the two of us increased privacy as well. We therefore looked to the possibility of relocating to another monastery and moving far away from Lorsch. I voiced concern that he had already deeded his lands to Lorsch, but he assured me a small part of all his holdings had been gifted there, leaving substantial parcels available for elsewhere. Moreover, he had connexions through a contact at the king's court with monasteries in Greece. And again, Clovis had set certain events into motion back when he first deeded the lands, of which I had not known.

We were both taken with the mythos of Greece and its evocations of light, warmth and sea—not to mention his own familiarity with the theme of Hellas from his earlier years there—and we both welcomed the opportunity to get out from under King Louis' nose. We were already confounded by the alarming rate at which his intellectual lassitude was hastening the erosion of his father's advances, when we learnt he had with malice destroyed the entire collection of Germanic epics established by Charlemagne. We thus began to concentrate our efforts towards a move to Greece.

The term of my novitiate was also coming to a close. Upon completion, I would be required to take my solemn vows and would be a Benedictine monk for life, forswearing all property and even letters from family and friends. Marriage would be out of the question. The year was 837, and my 'twentieth' birthday (in fact, my twenty-third), the date upon which we agreed my novitiate would end, would be in one day short of six months' time, on the eighth of September. Neither of us wished to so surrender ourselves and our life together to Lorsch Abbey, and so Clovis shared with me for the first time some of what had transpired in the intervening months after he had first talked to Abbot Adelung and before he deeded the lands over to Lorsch.

As a consequence of his connexions in the king's court, Clovis was privy to information about Abbot Adelung that none of the Brothers could have known. Clovis had got word by messenger to his friend Fabian, many months before the signing, that he might be deeding lands to the abbey in exchange for residence and wished to know as much as he could about Abbot Adelung. As always, the tone of the note conveyed the most innocent and enthusiastic of requests in the event someone intercepted the note, and, as always, Fabian understood that Clovis's request, in asking to know 'as much as he could', was in reality limited to those facts which would be damaging or of great embarrassment to Adelung were they ever made public. As it turned out, Father Abbot had enriched himself through iniquitous means by a similar gifting of lands to Lorsch involving the West Frisian duke, no less, of the black summer truffles; Clovis did not share the full details with me then, in part, he said, to protect me, but the authenticity of what he did share left its impress upon me.

Through a connexion to the duke or someone in Father Abbot's circle, Fabian acquired this information using the considerable resources and influence of his position in the court, when the Brothers—and the bishop—could not. Fabian was a trusted man in Louis' court, as he had been in Charlemagne's before him, but, independent of his functions there, he brokered valuable information to interested parties if the price was right. Clovis always paid a handsome fee for such information, and Fabian's loyalty to him went beyond the many years of these transactions to a friendship between the two men which had begun in childhood. Clovis had obtained these details, knowing their disclosure to the Abbot might prove useful one day, although in what manner, he had not yet worked through.

I remember both my shock and deep disappointment in the Abbot upon learning of this. This man for whom there were no greys in life when it came to a monk's transgressions, and whose impersonal bearing in his dealings with others could be disconcerting, natheless stood as a beacon for me in my formative years of monastic life. This one man, at least, could be counted upon to uphold the most stringent standards in obedience to Scripture in the performance of God's works, regardless of the human cost and inconvenience. On occasion, when I found my own resolve wanting, I took spiritual succour in Father Abbot's example. To now discover the truth and see the Abbot's hypocrisy laid bare crushed my spirit. I remembered the earlier matter concerning the woman of dubious morals Adelung had secured for Archbishop Odgar's sensual pleasure whilst staying overnight at the abbey, and my heart fell even deeper into despair. If the most circumspect man I knew in the Church fell prey to such transgressions on multiple occasions, how egregious were the excesses committed by others less vigilant in nature?

Natheless, while in my pallet and alone with these thoughts later that night, I closed my eyes and sighed, putting my harsher judgments to the side as I imagined how Brother Dieter, Brother Tomas, Father Abbot and others would react to the news that Brother John the Angelic, so well thought of as to his gifts in Letters and his many valuable contributions to the abbey, in fact a woman, had deceived them all as to her sex for these many years. And so, to myself in silence, I prayed to the Lord to grant me forgiveness and the grace and humility to forgo harsh judgement against those whose sins were laid bare, when the sole difference between theirs and my own lay in the fact that mine were still concealed.

With preternatural timing, swiftness and unthinkable consequence, circumstances obliterated that gossamer distinction but three days hence, in a single moment on the path round the back of the abbey.

The Brothers walked this path during the temperate months as a way of clearing their thoughts, for it offered a beautiful, secluded walk, and also used it to take their shoes to the cobbler a few hundred metres down the path. Once in a way, the occasional villager came from or walked to the cobbler on the path as well. On that early March afternoon, one of unseasonable warmth, I walked with Brother Dieter, and while looking up at the bright sky and laughing at something he had just said, I heard, of a sudden, a single word close and loud: 'You!'

I looked up to see the tall dark-haired woman from the forest, the one who had come and spoken to Brother Peer so long ago, pointing her finger at me. *Six years* ago! *How could this be, in such a fleeting glance?* And yet there it was—and in the next moment I recognised her as well as she advanced upon me with the speed of fury. My stomach turned, the small space between us collapsing into nothing at her approach. She laid her hands upon me while Dieter looked on in mute astonishment. Then she tore my robes from me, pulled my tunic up at the collar with brute force towards the ground, ripping it entire, and exposed my left breast and belly in broad daylight.

I heard Dieter's gasp and felt the day spinning about me in lawless glee, all of it, my life ripped apart at the seams just like that garment, the sound of my assailant's hateful laughter, a toxic fount bubbling forth out into the open air, and my head careening towards Dieter, my mouth open and groaning as though I had been run through, while I shouted at her, though what I said I knew not in the least and did not hear. At some point, someone—Dieter—restrained me, held me back from my accuser while she retreated, still shouting accusations. 'I want her to be excommunicated, I want her jailed and I want my reward! She is a fraud and an evil, perverse, wicked soul!' As we reached the threshold of the entrance, Dieter said a few hushed words to her I could not hear but which had the distinct tone of assurance, and dismissed her.

The scene was a funereal one. I was grateful no one else had seen us, but Dieter led me without a word, with a solemn gait, into Lorsch Abbey, whereupon Abbot Adelung came forth at once. Overflowing at one and the same time with boundless rage and despair, feeling as though my life had already passed, I dared not utter a word as to how I had chanced upon that woman in the forest or why I had been out at all at that hour, lest I land myself and my beloved Clovis in even greater peril.

I stood before Father Abbot, my left breast and teat bared before him, my head down, unable to meet his eyes. I could not even cry and felt disconnected from the human realm as I stood before this man who had given me such responsibility, growth and praise over the last several years, who was in all likelihood the figure closest to a spiritual father I have ever known.

'It appears Brother Johannes… is *not*,' came the stiff voice, with a touch of irony but also hurt. 'And, pray, what is your real name?'

'Joan. Joan of Mainz.'

'I want you to look me in the eye, Joan of Mainz, and I want you to tell me what you have to say for yourself. I want to hear it from you now in your own words.'

I looked up at him, my face, my life a blank canvas on which I had no idea what to draw or in what hue. I breathed in, exhaled and trained my gaze upon him. 'Picture you,' I began in a quiet voice, but with distinct contention, 'the young boy in whatever neighbourhood you grew up in, the lad, the father's son, the young man and the path he found that led him to beauty and grace in life through the Word of God, who found his destiny in serving the Lord, who endeavoured with the full measure of his being to give voice to that noble mission.' Keeping my eyes fixed upon his, I cupped my breast in my hand and held it out into the open air. 'Now picture you with these.' As I watched, he coloured; I was silent for quite some time, and he fidgeted, his gaze darting about as though he were seeking an escape in his surroundings—to anywhere but the warm, naked, quaking thing in my hand, for I had begun to softly sob. 'Other than this, are we different in any way?'

'In the eyes of God, yes, we are,' he said, quiet but firm. 'And it is a mortal sin to deceive the Church as to your true sex.'

'And so, that is the simple end of the matter, is it? Not the slightest consideration as to the merits of my service and the countless good works I have rendered for the glory of God?'

'Nothing,' he said, shaking his head. 'Nothing whatsoever can be said. You know the verity of these words: It shaped the entirety of your deception, all these years here in this house of the Lord, amongst all these good men. It shaped each confidence you extracted from them, every good turn done you by each of them—all of it based on the baldest lie, all of it, the fruit of mortal sin.' They were powerful words.

Whenever I looked over at Brother Dieter, the expression on his face betrayed a man whose heart was breaking for me. As the impassivity of Father Abbot's response to my entreaties roused me out of my state of vulnerability and back into one of contempt and anger, I remembered something important, something no words by Abbot Adelung, however damning, could outstrip. It so steeped me in thought on the matter that for some time I missed what the Abbot was saying. Upon hearing the words 'pray for your soul', I spoke up, clearing my throat.

'Begging your pardon, Father Abbot; there is a compelling matter which commands your attention at this moment.' I fell silent, trying to order the next words in my mind. 'You must needs consult the nobleman Clovis to avail yourself of this issue. I urge you, before taking any further action in this matter, to seek him out forthwith.'

'I-I fail to understand what the nobleman has to do—'

'You will. Believe me, you will.'

'So… it is most curious how his name comes up yet again in these discussions. It appears there has been something with this man after all—another mistruth?'

'You will act to the detriment of your own interests by failing to seek him out.'

His hands behind his back, Abbot Adelung stept forward until his face was within a fraction of a metre of my own, his large greenish eyes searching mine. 'I do not care for the tone of your words, Joan of Mainz. You are to be gone from my sight and will gather your belongings together at once. You should be ready to leave the abbey by None, and not a moment later. These are heinous acts over a period of several years you have committed against God and against this abbey; I shall consult with the bishop as to whether the magistrate should be involved.' With that he turned round and walked out with Dieter, although I saw they were headed towards Clovis's room. The Abbot's last words did make my heart jump, but I closed my eyes, putting my trust in God and in Clovis, neither of whom had ever given me any reason to believe such faith was misplaced.

I went to the dorter and gathered up my belongings, but not long thereafter, the Abbot, accompanied by Clovis, strode into the large room and gestured for me to come to them. When I reached them, I studied the Abbot's face. His expression was pacific and unperturbed, but I suspected that in such a short time, Clovis would have been able to convey little of any substance.

'Your gentleman friend wishes us to speak in confidence—out of consideration for my own interests, he claims—so we shall retire to my office.' Again the words were clipped, but with a touch of amusement behind their coldness. He guided us into his office and closed the door behind us.

And so, on the twelfth of March, Anno Domini 837, Abbot Adelung of Lorsch Abbey, the most circumspect man I had ever known, discovered how little control one possesses over his own destiny, subject to the whims of others, once he has indulged but a single ill-advised liberty of his own. When he sat down, he opened by saying that I had committed mortal sin against God and against His servants in the house of the Lord, and that in addition to my immediate eviction, the magistrate would in all likelihood be contacted.

'I see,' Clovis replied, his hands folded in his lap. 'Alas, I am afraid we have some demands of our own.'

'Demands of your own?' The Abbot's eyes were wide. 'I'm not sure I follow—'

'You will enter into the abbey's official archives that I was your assistant abbot for the past three years here.'

The Abbot spluttered in uncontrolled laughter at this man who had stayed in a room by himself for some months and partook of the occasional menial chores undertaken by the Brothers.

'Also, of course, you will enter into the archives the services and the novitiate term of Johannes Angelicus and that he distinguished himself in the library and scriptorium; and it will never be known or mentioned by anyone—Brother Dieter, yourself or anyone else at Lorsch Abbey—that Johannes Angelicus was other than a boy of thirteen when he entered Lorsch Abbey and a young man of twenty upon his departure.'

'You can't be serious, my good man—this is sheer lunacy. Neither of those items have any place in the abbey's official archives. The abbey is, of course, most grateful for the generous grants of land you have deeded to us, but its complicity in such immoral conduct is not for sale, and I can't abide—I won't. The acts you speak of are more than sinful, they are criminal in nature, and moreover, seek to cover up the blasphemous and criminal conduct of this young lady over a span of six years' time. And you have attempted to bribe an abbot, an offence punishable by a sentence of no less—'

'Duke Volkert of West Frisia.' Clovis cut off the Abbot in a cheery voice, sitting forward in his chair and clapping his hands together. 'I believe you two know each other, do you not?'

Adelung stopped cold in his tracks, his face frozen for quite a spell. 'The duke is a major benefactor of the abbey, but I fail to see—'

'Four hundred librae. Paid to you by the duke in the late morning of the twenty-third of June, 833, in appreciation for the accommodations and special services you provided him. 'Twas not entered into the abbey's coffers, as is by custom done in the rare instances when such money is accepted, but pocketed by Abbot Adelung on that date for his own personal benefit.'

Clovis cleared his throat. 'Also, on the fourth of January, 830, the duke paid you three hundred librae under the same terms. Again unrecorded and kept for your own personal benefit.' He flashed a broad smile. 'I enjoyed reading the Rule of St Benedict but do not recall a section in it authorising such—what was the word you just used? Ah yes, *conduct*.' And then, in a very small voice, cocking his head to one side: 'Is there?'

I had to bite my lip to keep from laughing in front of them.

Abbot Adelung was crimson. 'I have no idea what you are speaking of—or from what sullied, ill-chosen corner of commerce you would ever have fetched such a blatant fabrication—'

'Oh. Very well then,' Clovis said, speaking fast, 'let me disabuse you of your conceit, as it were. An old professional acquaintance of mine, who is in fact often at the king's court, as he was with Charlemagne before him, secured the details of your transactions, and although he is no one you could ever identify or locate—else his inimitable value to Louis would be lost—he is one of the most powerful men in the realm on account of the company he keeps and the role he plays in our world. He has brokered the ascendancy of archbishops and princes and brought about the fall of cardinals and high-ranking nobles. An abbot would be little more than an acorn on the ground crushed underfoot, not enough even to stay the grumblings in his stomach on his walk to court.'

Adelung stared at Clovis, his mouth open but not moving, his eyes blinking several times. He had gone ashen.

Encountering no resistance, Clovis continued. 'And so, you see, I had knowledge of your first indiscretion before I ever set quill to parchment in deeding you my lands, for that is what astute people in my position do who wish to secure themselves every possible advantage when they become bedfellows with people who are otherwise strangers to them.' Here Clovis paused a moment, pressing his fingertips together. 'Perhaps you would like to change your answer and thereby continue in your capacity as Abbot of Lorsch Abbey. That sounds far more pleasant to me than whatever form of occupational or physical incarceration would befall you were I to report these improprieties to the bishop.

'As a professional courtesy, I will divulge to you that this gentleman of whom I speak has his ear to the ground at all times and in all corners, and if so much as a spider talks to an ant about "Joan of Mainz", he will know it. And when that happens, all your efforts to hold up your end of this bargain and preserve your good name will have gone for naught. Therefore, pray, acknowledge your understanding of and assent to all I have said here.'

The Abbot gave a grave nod. 'What of the girl? I have no hold over her. And she has asked for her reward again.' The Abbot had already resigned himself to an uneasy partnership with us.

'It is clear the remunerative aspect is central to her motivation in all of this, as it has been from the beginning. Satisfy her needs in this one aspect, and the battle is all but won. What is the reward you would give for this kind of information?'

The Abbot stroked his chin. 'I am not certain; in the neighbourhood of five to seven denarii?'

'Treble it. Twenty denarii. And with the reward, you give the same admonishment I gave you just now: that this generous reward is predicated upon her absolute secrecy as to the person in question. And—this next part is very important—you tell her you know the bad deed she perpetrated against this woman, and if she ever speaks of any woman who disguised herself as a monk to anyone, so long as she draws breath, you will make certain she is thrown in jail for what she did. That will be the end of anything you will ever hear out of that girl.'

Adelung furrowed his brow and hesitated before speaking his mind. 'But to the best of my knowledge, that young lady committed no crime, no bad act upon Joan of Mainz.'

'You are mistaken. But that is for us to know; it is no concern of yours. However, conveying you have knowledge of her guilt will be as powerful as if it came from Joan herself, yea, more so, given the authority of your position.

'As it so happens,' Clovis continued, 'we were on the verge of leaving Lorsch Abbey anyway, before the term of her novitiate came to an end, so we shall not be a burden on you beyond today. That should be convenient for all of us, should it not?'

The Abbot nodded with a faint smile, the enfeebled smile of a man whose last shred of dignity and autonomy has been stripped from him. Much as I imagined Dieter must have pitied me when I stood before him exposed as a woman, I was both hurt by Father Abbot and deep in mourning for him, and it pained me to sit and watch him for more than a few moments at a time. After Clovis secured from the Abbot in words an express understanding of all we had discussed, we arose and left.

Adelung told me to leave my habit and robes behind, so I changed in the empty dormitorium into the regular clothes I had brought with me to the abbey all those years ago; they were a bit tighter and shorter on me. We finished gathering my few possessions together and set out in discreet fashion through the back way for Clovis's estate a short while past None. He had brought Hannibal, and the two of us rode the brief distance to his property. I was lost in my own thoughts, and Clovis, in his infinite subtlety, understood I needed some time bereft of conversation. When we arrived at his estate, we had not spoken a word by the time we dismounted. The entire chain of events at Lorsch had left me stunned and contemplating my new status, although Clovis had astounded me with his mastery of the situation. Still, there were items in his demands of the Abbot I could not comprehend in the least.

When at last I spoke, I asked him, 'Pray, why on earth would you ask him to enter into the record your service to the abbey as an assistant abbot? You have not one day's experience in a monastery. Yea, I am more qualified for such a position than you are, and those are damning words indeed.'

'Why, dear Beloved, have you forgotten I took chores two days a week while in residence there? And as I said, I became quite familiar with the Rule in my spare time—of which, I remind you, I have had a great deal. How could one so young and nimble of spirit have such a faulty memory?'

'But... why—'

'It is simple. If I am an assistant abbot, I can bring you along as my assistant.'

Comprehension of his plan advanced at last upon my senses. If, as he had stated, Clovis had connexions in Greece, a post as assistant abbot for Clovis would allow us both to set up residence there and begin our life together anew without the slightest suspicion or drawing of attention to ourselves or our situation. For some reason he also felt compelled to point out my own status, still too tender in years myself to pass for a prior, which at that point in my life would have been equivalent to stating I lacked the requisite skills to serve as a joint commander of a division in Louis' army.

'Quite,' I snapped back. 'I am sure there is a point to this?'

'You don't see it, do you,' he said, laughing, shaking his head. 'That is all right; I will do the thinking for the both of us—'

'Thank you, no. I can think quite well enough for myself—and for the both of us. How dare you presume—'

But he cut me off with a raised finger. 'Begging your pardon, but you do not understand me.' He stood tall, clasping his hands together in front of himself, and stared down at the ground. 'All I am doing is pointing you in the direction—that is to say, making you aware of the direction in which you have already quite pointed yourself.' A brief pause. 'For that is what I do, you see.' Clovis looked at me, running his fingertip down my nose. 'I see grand prospects in your future. Bishop, cardinal—who knows?'

'In the Church? How?'

'By being you. That is all that is required. You are brilliant beyond this world. The rest will follow just as it has here. You will see soon enough.'

Ascending through the ranks of the Church was something I might have allowed myself to indulge thoughts of from time to time, but as the stuff of phantasy, and given the crises of recent events, not even then. I did not quite believe him, but natheless, he had been right about so much already that I trusted in and assented to his judgment, for the time being, at least. I was reeling from the turn of events which had transpired between Father Abbot's indiscretions and the predatory manner in which Clovis had both built this character flaw into the design of our future plans and used it against the Abbot at the precise, opportune moment. His talent for contrivance of events years in advance struck me as nothing short of terrifying, but in the times I had seen Clovis manifest this dark side of his soul, it had always been in the service of destroying far greater evil. On that day, I realised with finality that whilst the glory of God may triumph in the Hereafter, down on earth, prevailing in the world of men over evil souls in the *hic et nunc* often required waging the battle on their own terms to better effect. It had taken years to arrive at this point in my understanding, but I saw at last my struggles to assimilate into the monastic life as the product of a greater evil that prevented the induction of women into positions of leadership and teaching of Scripture within the Church. The Church's silence on this issue as one already decided and not warranting further discussion—both in the grander hierarchy and on the local level at Lorsch—left no available path of inquiry or discussion with which I might temper or otherwise refine my own conclusions. As a consequence, the utter despair and isolation of my status forged my conviction on this matter into a stronger alloy—with a blade which could not but sharpen with the passage of time.

A phone call woke Rahel up early Sunday morning on 11 April 1937, from her older and closest friend, Leah Abrams, a mother of two young children. At first Rahel had no idea who it was, as she heard uncontrolled sobbing on the other end of the line.

'Hello? Who is this?'

The sobbing continued unabated, as if Rahel had not spoken at all.

'Hello? Do you have the wrong number?' Rahel shouted into the telephone. 'I don't know who's calling—'

'Rahel, this… this is Leah, sorry, I've just found out my children can no longer attend school—'

'What? What do you mean?'

More sobbing. 'I mean, Mayor Lippert has just issued an order… all Jewish children are banned from public schools in Berlin.'

'He can't do that. He can't.'

'He can and he did.' Leah breathed in and out, struggling to collect herself. 'He is our mayor but he is also a member of the Nazi Party. The Nuremberg Laws say we are no longer German citizens.'

'Oh, Leah, I'm so sorry.' She thought back to when Patek had first told her this, on that wintry April day in 1936, and how reluctant she'd been to give any credence to his words. That day was a lifetime ago, and when she pictured herself then, sitting in the café prior to their contentious conversation, she saw a hopeful young woman dreaming of a future that would be distinguished by independence, prosperity, by her having the ability to motor to distant parts of her homeland. It was as inspiring a canvas of her future life as had ever been done, but since Patek had torn her dreams to shreds, she'd watched her world fail to brighten, and indeed darken and close in around her, tighter and tighter, until now it condemned her to iniquity, exclusion and the life of a second citizen—someone who, by dint of nothing else but her ancestry, was bereft of the most basic rights accorded human beings.

Rahel looked up to Leah, who had an advanced degree in the profession of psychology, where she had specialised as a graphologist, trained in the art of analysing a patient's (or on occasion a criminal suspect's) handwriting to assess their personality. In the medical profession, women were rare or unheard of in Germany, but Leah had been emboldened in her choice of graphology as a viable profession in researching the discipline years ago and uncovering the seminal work of a British woman, Rosa Braugham, back in the 1870s in the profession's infancy.

Leah was both an intellectual and possessed of powerful intuition in her understanding of human drive and personality, in the individual as well as in the collective, and they had engaged in illuminating if at times unsettling discussions of the recent events in Germany. Rahel felt at once great distress for her friend and a sinister foreboding of bleaker days to come.

'I don't know what I'm going to do.' Leah was sobbing. 'David and Sharon are both at the top of their classes, they're devoted to their studies.' After a brief silence, she started to regain control of her voice. 'This is profane. It will cripple their minds and their development for years if it goes on for a long time. What am I going to do, Rahel? I have no idea.'

Rahel was silent in thought for some time. 'David and Sharon are seven and nine, and both in the *Volksschule*.' This was more of a statement than a question.

'Yes, that's right.'

'At least Adam still has his job at the factory—do you think you could manage teaching them their subjects at home for a while, as simple as their studies would be at such young ages? Until this all blows over?'

'Blows over?' A sad, breathy laugh, followed by a long silence. 'And when do you think this will all "blow over", Rahel? In a few months?

Next year?' Leah was tearing up again. 'Once life was a feast, and we thought everything was pure shit.'

'I know, I know. Some days I wake up and it feels like I will never be the person I was in 1930 ever again. I still want to believe that someone will take the Nazis down, but that time seems far off now—and with each day it feels more and more like it will have to come from outside Germany.'

'It will. That's because all of Germany hates us now.' This was said without a touch of irony, in a flat, dead tone.

Rahel wanted to say something but started several times before she could bring herself to utter the words. She drew in a long breath. 'Patek says things are going to get much worse.'

'How much worse?'

'He thinks our lives are in danger.'

'You mean that Hitler will have us killed?'

'Yes, correct. Like he will just round us all up and—'

'Yes, of course. This is not a question. The question is when, not if.'

Rahel froze at these words. 'When' took her mind in its hand, as though it were a string, and pulled it taut towards itself, took it into the word, into its sound, into the picture that opened in front of her eyes: a black field of nothingness.

Her mouth opened, but there was no speech. Her friend said something else, but she didn't hear it, and a moment later goodbyes were somehow exchanged and Rahel hung up the phone.

In our first days back at his estate—to which I had not been since that afternoon years before in search of black summer truffles—we gloried in one another's company for most of two days, making love at all hours, perhaps in part because there had been a natural disinclination to indulge our desires in recent months, owing to those unfortunate events at Lorsch that drew more attention to my person and to our relationship than we wanted. This was not the fevered copulation of years past but something more gentle and simple in its pleasure, a kind of reckoning, I suppose, of the intense, hurtful conflict between us regarding my earlier crisis of which I had failed to apprise him and which almost rent us apart. We also feasted upon the divine luxury of being together in his private abode without any fear of prying eyes, to do and say whatever we wished, yea, even at times to sit about in silent satiety in the other's presence without needing to speak a word for long stretches of time. In those few days, I realised that this man understood me in all my ways like no one I had ever known, that we were alike in temperament and spirit, and that this made life an experience more perfect than anything I'd ever imagined I could have with another person.

Clovis and I had to decide how and when we were going to journey to Greece. Most of his connexions there were centred in Athens, but his most influential acquaintance for securing us assignments lived not in Athens at all but at Soumela, a Greek Orthodox monastery far east of Greece, one of the oldest and most spectacular monasteries in the world—but one which, owing to its being built into the side of a vertical cliff some twelve hundred metres up, found itself low on the list of places to which people wished to be sent or transferred. I myself had something of a fear of heights and did not consider this a desirable appointment in any wise. But Soumela had individual cells and a thriving intellectual centre with a commendable library and scriptorium. It was also home to one of the most miraculous series of events believed to have ever transpired in a house of God. It is accepted that a certain icon known as the Panagia Soumelá, or Παναγίας Σουμελά, an icon of the Virgin Mary, had been painted by the hand of Luke, and that he had carried the icon with him in his travels. This icon had been kept in a temple in Thebes after Luke's crucifixion at age eighty-four. In the fourth century, a young priest, Basil, was serving Divine Liturgy when the Virgin Mary directed him and his nephew Sotirichos to travel to Thebes and enter into monastic life. The two men visited the temple there, first advancing upon the *Panagia* icon and kissing it, then prostrating themselves before it with prayers of contrition and asking for direction. At that moment the church rang out with the singing of angels, and a dulcet voice emanated from the icon with assurances that she would lead them to their destination. The icon broke free from its shrine and, lifted up by angels, one on each side, was spirited away through an open window.

After journeying to the Meteora, then Agion Oros in Athos and after that to Maronia in Thrace, Basil and Sotirichos wound up in Trapezounta of Pontos, thousands of kilometres east of Thebes, where they were tonsured with the names Barnabas and Sophronios and learnt of Mount Melá and travelled there to find, to their astonishment, the sacred icon in a cave. Barnabas and Sophronios founded the Soumela monastery there in 386. The monastery had been pillaged throughout its history yet rebuilt after each sacking. In recent times, all the monks residing there had been slaughtered by Arab Hagarians in the seventh century, but the monastery had been rebuilt around 644.

Clovis assuaged my fears about Soumela's location, assuring me that after we had crossed the Alps, Mount Melá would be but one more summit, and a small one at that. Forsooth, his connexions informed him they would find something in Athens if we were unable to make the adjustment to Soumela. Because Clovis had a fluent command of both written and spoken Greek, the likelihood of his being awarded a post at Soumela—or at Athens if our stay did not work out there—was great. Owing to his prior experience in the trade route business and because the most viable routes to major cities like Athens and Rome had changed little in over 150 years, Clovis knew there were in truth but a couple ways to get there where we would not in all likelihood perish. No destination south of Germania can be reached without crossing the Alps, and the incidents of travellers freezing to death in the mountains are well documented. Hygeburg's *Hodoeporicon* on the life and travels of Bishop Willibald of Bavaria, as well as the journeys of Boniface and Aldhem, all chronicle passage by way of the Alps.

At first blush, I was terrified at the prospect of going through the mountains and enquired as to why we could not go by sea, be it even a circuitous route up north and down. But even for the English, that seafaring people, no treks by way of the Mediterranean were undertaken to or from Rome—or at least for which there is documentation—after Hadrian and Theodore, the archbishop of Canterbury, took that route in 668. Since then, except for Bede's mentor, Benedict Biscop, who seems to have crossed by way of the Little St Bernard Pass, all pilgrimages had gone through the Great St Bernard Pass, the pass of lowest elevation between the two highest summits in the Alps. Charlemagne brought his armies across the Alps from Francia into Italia in the invasion of Lombardy in 773 via the Great St Bernard Pass, even though he himself had journeyed to Rome by going through Mont Cenis with his main army. And indeed, Louis had already established a hospice there. A hospice had also been established in 831, however, on the Septimer Pass, east of the Great St Bernard Pass, and in general this route stood as the true and tested path of choice.

The St Gall Monastery, St Othmar's masterpiece for the Frankish vision of monastic life, had been founded in 719, and Charlemagne's uncle, Carloman, had journeyed to Rome by way of St Gall in 747, and this had been a favoured route to Rome ever since. For a few reasons, not the least of which was that we were travelling far east to Trebizond, that most distant outpost of the Roman Empire, and saw no reason to keep west going south, we chose to go to Great St Bernard through St Gall rather than down the Rhine. Once in Italia, we could cross over to Greece from Reggio rather than by Syracuse, as chosen by Bishop Willibald.

The more frightening and unknown part of the journey involved the long trek to Trebizond. Neither Charlemagne nor Louis had ever journeyed to the East. After his coronation by Pope Leo III in 800, Charlemagne harboured ambitions of ascending the throne in Constantinople and sent envoys there with overtures of marriage towards Empress Irene, who had arrogated the throne in the absence of an emperor. Salic law forbade a woman from ruling even under such circumstances, however, and the king's attempts came to naught when the people of Constantinople deposed her for failing to rebuke his offer with enough haste—although Theophanes the Confessor contends it was her *protospatharios* Aetios, eyeing the throne for his brother Leo, who foiled the union. Louis likewise had not made a pilgrimage to the East, but the firestorm of iconoclasm reached its zenith under his reign, further deepening the rift between the Eastern Church and the West and fostering a general instability between the two cultures, which would not relent until the Treaty of Verdun.

Starting in 829, in succession to his father, Eastern Roman Emperor Theophilos indulged in brutal methods of torture to effect the end of icon worship and painting, until just before the Treaty of Verdun. He flogged the monk Lazarus Zographos, the greatest painter of our time, within a whisker of death, leaving nothing but his bones and mere scraps of flesh on his back. Left in prison to die of his wounds, the monk, through the greatest of miracles, recovered and took to painting sacred images on panels, until Theophilos had red-hot horseshoes applied to Lazarus's hands, searing flesh into bone and rendering them unusable.

Another time, after whipping two monks who also happened to be brothers, Theophanes and Theodore, two hundred times, the emperor branded their faces with hot irons when they refused to recant. He also tortured Joseph, one of the most well-known hymn writers, amongst others. This precarious state of affairs between East and West reached its zenith by the summer of 837, and whilst Constantinople was a wealthy centre of culture, learning and nobility, we would be entering upon the lands round it as outsiders, and in truth we had no notion whatever of what we could expect to find there. All we knew for certain was that we would be met with infernal heat.

Timing was another critical element in our plans. We were in the third week of March, and Clovis insisted the single most essential prerequisite to the entire plan was the need to journey during the hottest months. We resolved to depart in late June. Even travel in mid-March or April carried a high risk of death, and for strong prospects of survival, warm temperatures were crucial to success. During the summer months, when the temperatures on the ground were blazing, the upper regions of the Alps were still cold enough to numb our faces and freeze our provisions into rocks, even if carried on our persons. In the summer, those temperatures were unpleasant but navigable; in the winter, the bitter cold could cause severe frostbite, paralyse and kill. Roman fever was another peril, although Alcuin recovered from it, as well as Willibald before him. Then there were the hazards of thieves and brigands, along with the occasional extortioner who would exact a crippling price for allowing passage or safe harbour. Armed with the knowledge of these sundry perils, we trekked back to Clovis's estate, where we worked out a detailed timeline of the entire journey as best as we were able, accounting for climate conditions and the number of days each leg of the voyage would consume. We took complete inventory of and packed up our provisions, weapons, maps, blankets, tools, cooking and climbing gear and other essentials.

Those two and a half months at his estate where we passed the time once our plans were worked out were the most luxurious, blissful months I have experienced, and came as close to the marital life of husband and wife as the two of us would ever know. It was within those spacious walls that, sharing all hours of the day and night with one another across a period of months, we became versed in the minute rhythms, moods, postures, gestures and silences that informed one another's bearing and being at each moment and in all situations. We seldom had a cross word, but over time the words themselves became less and less necessary; I learnt that the repeated flexion of his foot when crossed over the other knee meant he was becoming peckish; he came to understand that when I stood in the front room and looked out towards the land in front of the house, hands behind my back, it meant I was restless and in need of a walk. We settled into comfortable lovemaking: less frequent, less urgent, but more emotional, more grounded in our affections for one another. At long last the appointed day arrived, and we loaded up Hannibal and three other strong horses and, along with two of his best men for the journey, left on the eighteenth of June, 837.

I was to ride Hannibal because Clovis wanted the strongest, fastest horse under me were we to chance upon a hostile party in the course of our travels. In his unrelenting acumen, he loaded Hannibal up with less gear than the other horses but with the most essential items should I find myself separated from the others somehow. The other animals were strapped up with heavy loads, yet it had no effect upon them. The first leg of the journey, clear to the foothills, passed pleasant enough, with light breezes and temperate climes—a beautiful trek through the lower region of Germania, with frequent and unfettered stops along the way for picking fresh fruits and vegetables, although some were not quite ripened yet. When we came upon a church, we would tie up our horses, go inside and offer up prayers for safe passage across the mountains and for finding ourselves in the company of gentle souls in distant lands who would wish no ill upon us.

We rested for a day in St Gall to gather our strength and to discuss the Alps, with the easiest part of our journey behind us. The monastery was magnificent and in Abbot Gotzbert's last year at St Gall. We were the beneficiaries of peaceful times; since Louis had already decreed St Gall's independence, the monks no longer had to defend themselves against the bishopric of Constance, which had already seized the nearby Abbey of Reichenau under its jurisdiction. Under Gotzbert a beautiful church had been built and the library expanded. We stayed in the quarters for visiting monks and had a most welcome respite from riding.

Not even my fear had prepared me for the ordeal of crossing over the Alps. I adjusted to the altitude, the thinner air and my fear of heights with less trouble than I expected—but not the unbearable, paralysing wind and cold. The time of year and the lack of snow below the peaks made much of the journey pleasant, and we saw a good amount of verdure and wildflowers in the lower regions. Up in the highest summits, however, which were at times unavoidable, we bid farewell to the world, as distant and unreal as some scene painted behind us and in front of us, a realm unreachable and inconsequential to our travails. We were subsumed in a majesty and spectacle of boundless indifference to human life: an emotional and spiritual desolation I had never imagined before. At times the driving winds and snows obliterated all sense of actual motion and location, as if Hannibal were bearing me up and down some invisible stairway that hung suspended in air and led nowhere. Clovis and the others were close by, but on occasion they too disappeared into the tempest, and I feared never seeing any of them again. On one occasion, after an eternity of a quarter hour, I called out for Clovis at the top of my voice and heard nothing—not even my own words—in return, and despaired of having lost the others altogether, until the snows parted and we were reunited again. For much of this part of the journey, my ears ached in agony, froze, became overlarge and numb, and the same sensation spread down my cheeks and into my jawbone, while my lips seemed to swell to three times their size as well, tingling at first and then as numb and spastic as the rest of my face. I kept grimacing and smiling to keep my facial muscles moving, for fear they would freeze into an implacable mask. I could not chew or hold anything in my hands, which along with my feet felt as though they had been plunged into ice water and held there for hours on end; I had no idea that skin could feel such unendurable pain without ever being cut, and I threw up on two different occasions from the pain.

Nights in the tent were somewhat better, and Clovis and I held each other close for warmth; I've no idea what the men did. Alas, the ceilings of the tents were too low for fires without peril. Clovis had packed kindling for fires, and we had varying degrees of success with that, depending on the wind's direction and whether we were able to find any sort of natural alcove in which to build the fire. Often they were short-lived, and we would take turns shielding the fire while others warmed their hands over it and put their hands to their faces.

At last we descended one day from the highest summit at Mont Blanc to the Great St Bernard Pass. For the past couple miles, it had been getting warmer, and by the time we reached the pass, we encountered clear and wondrous moments, during which we were greeted with the sight of several cows grazing below. Small waterfalls of snowmelt ran past, and for a spell the low-lying clouds opened up overhead, the sun warming our faces as we came down onto the trail. Just below us lay the Aosta Valley, soaked in sunlight and bereft of cloud cover— one of the most beautiful sights I had ever beheld. We had made it! I dismounted, ran over to Clovis and bid him dismount as well, whereupon we embraced one another and rejoiced in unison with all in our loyal contingent, falling upon the ground to our knees as one, praising God and giving thanks.

As we advanced upon the town of Aosta, we came upon Italian men who wore their hair long like the Franks. Rugged men who farmed the land, and wealthier Italians in calf-length leather boots and bright-coloured tunics—both alike wore this hairstyle. The women also wore their hair long, although they often pinned it up and arranged it in striking ways. In the province of Rome alone, as it turns out, do men cut their hair at the neckline, though this may have been true in Sicily and southern Italia as well, following Emperor Theophilos's edict requiring that all male subjects wear their hair short. In most respects the townsfolk looked just like us. Their simple dress in these hot climes consisted of thin, light linen: short-sleeved tunics of a lighter colour with unadorned trim at the neck. These tunics came to the knees or sometimes to mid-calf for the women; over the tunic the women wore ankle- or floor-length gowns, often open in the front or with the familiar chains lifting the garment off the ground for walking, the same as our own. Peasants wore wooden shoes or were barefoot, whilst the upper class wore leather boots.

As for drink, if anything, wine was even more plentiful in Italia than in our homeland, and all the local inns and hostels sold it. Alas, ale was a rare find, and we were not pleased on the few occasions we did, owing to the fact the Italians still made it using gruel rather than hops, as our monasteries back home now used, and it therefore lacked the crisp or full-bodied taste to which we were accustomed. I had always found wine, even in its popular diluted form, to foster thirst more than slake it, and more so in hot weather, so the absence of ale there did not endear the Italians to me in that regard.

Whilst the mounting instability and erosion of the empire under Louis had not yet threatened the general conditions of peace and homage within the northern and central regions of Italia, other parts of the country had been less fortunate. The Sicilian governor and commander of the fleet of the Roman Empire, Euphemius, suffered initial defeat at the hands of an imperial army. In a move with grave, long-term consequences for the region, he enlisted the assistance of the Saracens, joining forces with the Amir, Ziyadat Allah, permitting Allah to rule Sicily in exchange for support and a generalship. But the Saracens manipulated Euphemius up until his death in battle. Then, in 830, Moorish invaders descended upon Sicily and seized Panormus, establishing Sicily as a de facto seat of the Amir.

Also in the 830s, the Duchy of Benevento in Lombardy had been a constant site of conflict. As in Sicily, Duke Andrew II of Naples enlisted the assistance of the Saracens against Prince Sicard of Benevento. Thus the Saracens, who before long would pose an imminent threat to Rome, did not come to Italian soil of their own accord but were invited there—multiple times. In 839, following unrest and civil war, the Saracens found this fracture of the greatest power in southern Italia not under Frankish control irresistible; now positioned on Italian soil, they endeavoured to make a feast of the table set before them.

For us, riding into Aosta in the late summer of 837, we were greeted with a peaceful, bucolic setting of great inspiration and relief to us after crossing over the Alps—but what we would find in southern Italia, we did not know. Frankish rule over northern and central Italia had established an extended period of continuous peacetime there, and Charlemagne's initiatives in placing persons who were literate in positions of administration and local government where possible had paid off in a seamless relationship with the Lombardy capital of Pavia. Royal commands to the cities were sent by way of the king's messengers, and appeals would come back to a centralised judicial apparatus in Pavia. This functioned well, notwithstanding the fact Louis himself never set foot in Italia. Few Franks, as it turned out, had settled in Italia—though most of those who did were nobles and, after Charlemagne's coronation in 800, had taken over the vast majority of countship appointments in Italia.

We stopped in the few churches we chanced upon as we made our way towards Reggio, giving thanks in prayer for our journey to this point and asking for protection the rest of the way. Where possible, we took lodging, but we came across few monasteries indeed after Pomposa Abbey, which happened to be on our path and far too significant to miss. Both its length and expansiveness took my breath away, and I remember on that day at None when we arrived being humbled by the grandeur set before me in that place and in my own heart by God.

But Clovis and I had both noticed in the past day or so that something was happening to Aldrich, one of the young men Clovis had taken on of late. A little over a week prior, we had spent several nights outside in the humidity, and so our thoughts turned to Roman fever as the possible reason for his downturn. We had been staying close to the

coast, and after some heavy rains, the temperature had cooled somewhat in the past few days, yet Aldrich remained diaphoretic, his hair
plastered against his forehead, and he began to complain of a fever as
well as fatigue and weakness in the muscles. The alertness in his eyes
had been replaced with a confused and glazed look, and we could see
in his face the effort it took to stay on pace with us.

Over the next several days, his condition worsened. We stopped at
a small abbey and were able to have the infirmarian dispense to him
some of the theriac Galene, long used since the time of Marcus Aure-
lius, when Galen himself first prescribed it for yellow fever. This cure-all
compound is made with over forty ingredients, including Falernian
wine, honey from the mountains of Greece, viper tissue, bitumen from
Judea, crocus from Cililia and opium from Anatolia. However, by then
Aldrich was vomiting every hour, racked with back pain, and the day
before we stopped, he discovered in horror his urine had turned red—
one of the deadliest developments in the progression of the disease. No
longer in any condition to travel, and despite Clovis's entreaties that
we stay with him at the abbey and support him in his recovery, Aldrich
already knew he was not long for this world and insisted, after a heated
exchange, that we go on ahead without him. 'God has punished me for
my sins,' he exclaimed, 'for I have been an insolent and ungrateful son
to my father and caused him no end of suffering. But let not my last
breaths be in vain and without consequence this day. By staying behind
here, there is still the chance, however small, that I may live to see
another sunrise, and you... you shall make it to Greece without being
further burdened with my condition, for there are more than enough
challenges to occupy your energies without it.' Each of us embraced
him in turn, knowing this was goodbye, and with heavy hearts we set
out again upon our journey and kept him in our prayers.

The temperatures were rising again, and although we had made
it into Italia, we had not made it out of the mountains by any means.
One of the most striking aspects of the northern Italian coast is how
high it sits above sea level. And whilst the northern towns were quite
small and rural, they were almost always set in the hills or on one side
or the other of a mountain.

Beyond Aldrich's loyalty and affable nature, we missed his physical vigour and strength, but his horse continued on with us, like all Clovis's animals were trained to do, relieving us of much added burden and the inconvenience of shifting our entire load to three horses. Worse still, he might have bolted altogether with all our gear on him. I found this behaviour extraordinary, but Clovis's affinity for the equine spirit simplified this mystery for me.

'Think of it this way. A horse is a herd animal and will always choose to live with a group of horses rather than as a rogue. And horses have been domesticated to serve men for God knows how long now. A horse sees a man like myself as another member of the herd but with a higher status than his own. He respects me at least as much as one of the other horses and has known and worked with these other men as well. Would he have stayed with us if we were all on foot? I don't know. But he never came to that choice; his one concern was whether to remain with the horses he already knows so well or to risk life on his own in the wild. That is not a choice at all but the most basic survival instinct.'

Italia was a country of rugged terrain, and the journey into central Italia, even near the eastern coast, punished my back with the constant jostling and steep inclines and declines. We had planned at first to go by way of Rome, but after poor Aldrich's fate, and not wishing to expose ourselves further to Roman fever, we revised that route, cutting southeast below Rome to Monte Cassino Monastery and then south, as chosen by Willibald on his return from the Holy Land. Founded by Benedict himself in 529, the monastery was one of the greatest in the realm, its library among the largest in all Europa, and a popular destination for pilgrimage. Whilst we knew Cassino lay between the Abruzzi and Aurunci Mountains, we underestimated the difficulties presented by those natural boundaries in reaching the abbey—a key reason for Benedict's choosing of the site. In addition to the jagged mountains, dense forestation intruded along many sections of the route, and at times even keeping our bearings required intense focus and continual observation. A few rudimentary paths looked as though they might just as well have been set into the hills by God Himself in a moment of brief diversion as by the hand—and foot—of Man.

One fine morning, as we closed in on the abbey, those thick forests followed us up on one side in our ascent. We rounded a bend in the mountain over the Liri Valley at a slow canter, still some distance from the monastery itself, catching a glimpse of its high walls rising into the piercing blue sky. At that moment, as I drank in this beautiful vision, my ears were assailed with the unmistakable squealing of a horse that had sustained serious injury. I turned forward to watch Clovis tumble onto the ground up ahead, blood spurting in a fountain from his steed's back leg as he rolled onto the ground almost on top of Clovis. Two brigands brandishing swords overhead descended upon Clovis as Ajax lay bleeding out in the dust. The three of us were spaced some twenty or so metres apart, which made the thieves' attack on Ajax from behind him and in front of me easier than it might otherwise have been. An instant later, Ewald's horse squealed behind me, and I turned round in time to see another brigand pull Ewald up from the ground and plunge a sword deep into his chest. I could hear words in a commanding tone being directed towards Clovis, but the wind carried them away; my heart was pounding and I could not discern whether they were speaking in Arabic or Latin or some other language, though I took that they were talking to him at all as a good sign. But they had Clovis in their clutches, and at that moment, as one of the men behind closed fast upon me, Clovis looked up at me, his eyes wide.

'Hannibal, away!' he yelled at the top of his voice, and without thinking—I was not even aware until later that I had done so—I kicked my legs hard twice into his barrel. The brigand could have been no more than two metres from me when Hannibal took off past the men in front of us with tremendous speed, faster than I had ever experienced a horse galloping before, and I was terrified, for we were high up and there were curves with a steep drop-off to the outer side, but he took them all in perfect stride, slowing down as little as necessary to prevent a mishap. Breathless, I kept checking behind me to see if they were in pursuit, but that never happened. After quite a distance had been covered, I was satisfied I had not been followed, and, not far from the monastery now, I went off the path a ways, brought Hannibal to a stop and fell off him in exhaustion and grief into the hillside, my body already convulsing in agony. I wept and screamed into the soundless air, pounding my fists against the ground and moaning as a procession of moments of my life with Clovis burnt through me like wildfire, ending in a vision of a girl moored to a hill, alone and rudderless, legs kicking like some insect, still alive but crushed into a place from whence it would never arise.

THREE

WHEN I AT LAST PICKED myself up off the hill, any concern for my own life had vanished with the hour. Indeed, I all but prayed for those hideous brigands' return to dispatch me forthwith from my inconsolable despair. This did not happen. Instead one hour bled into the next, then into days in the numbed, aimless meanderings of both my body and my spirit. For two days and nights, I did not eat or drink and slept under the stars, too weak and stunned to formulate a single thought or action. Even my anger was feeble and disjointed, as though some deeper sentiment were working in me that I could not bring to the surface, as if I had been damaged in some brute physical trauma I could not recall. I cursed God, I cursed those worthless, craven brigands for taking such a magnificent soul from this world—or at least from me, which amounted to the same thing—all for the sake of such transitory noughts as possessions and money. I knew Clovis was in all likelihood dead, but my heart and will, blind with shock and rage, refused to accept it. I grasped then more than ever how much I loved him, and not just out of my love for him. For, even were my own life never again to be graced with his presence, the thought he had been forever taken from this world was impossible; I rejected the possibility out of hand that God could be so unjust. But underneath it all, I was without purpose, without hope; I no longer wanted my life or life itself, which held interest for me no more. I had presumed I would spend the rest of my days with Clovis, and he had thought the same.

But of the two of us, he had anticipated this might not come to pass and manifested that perspective in countless subtle touches. I found, tucked into a small purse in one of the pockets of a bag Hannibal was carrying, the extraordinary sum of fifteen hundred librae—worth thirty thousand solidii, a king's sum. A note in Clovis's hand read:

> Most people have never seen a solidus, let alone a libra. Exchange in accordance. If someone tells you a libra is worth but 240 denarii, you should be offended.

In ancient Rome, solidii were either hoarded or used to pay soldiers—hence the origin of the word *soldier*, as they were paid in gold solidii—and to a large extent, this arcanity is still in force as regards the rarity of the solidus in the average citizen's life. Those monies were left me in expectation of this day. And as I have said, Clovis had loaded up much of the essential supplies and equipment I would need to survive on my own with Hannibal. Moreover, although I hoped it would never be necessary, Hannibal himself was a magnificent animal and would fetch a substantial sum at market.

On the morning of my third day, I awoke to the vivid memory of our first dalliance in the grasses, an experience nothing in my life before or since has succeeded in equalling, and of the later conversation at Lorsch after I had confessed to my breakdown that night in the kitchen. I relived the memory of his tender vulnerability, this man of such pride and strength, and the measure of power and autonomy he permitted me, forsooth, insisted upon—and not just in our relationship but in myself. Watching him again in the clutches of those thieves, and Ewald dying behind me, I saw, of a sudden, the world outside my body and fevered brain collapsing into disorder, as if the very trees rooted in the hillside, and the towns beyond them, were dropping away into the realm of apparition, into an antic disorder of physical reality in which nothing I saw or heard could ever again be counted upon as real and existing in three-dimensional space. I wept, but a trembling rage mounted within me that at long last erupted through the top of my head like a herd of horses galloping upside down. I raised myself up to my knees and lifted my arms to the heavens, pulling them out of their sockets to draw the skies down, and screaming in helpless fury until my voice gave out.

'All I needed was for this one man, my one love, not to die, not to leave me—for someone I loved not to abandon me! How does Jesus dying help me? With joy I would have taken my own sins, eaten them, licked them, slept with them, breathed them, shit them, been eaten by them and shit out by them, painted them on my eyeballs so I could see… nothing but my fucking sins for every moment of my days—if You had only left me my Clovis!'

There was no self-pity now, no searching for the sword on which to impale myself, nothing but wroth and murderous hate, and had God appeared before me in physical form, I would have plunged my sword as deep in Him as it would go; yea, I would have followed it down into my very death or worse if I thought it could hurt Him, into any irretrievable depth of atrocity.

Instead the wind blew, then stopped. Clouds passed, slowed, dissolved into still, azure sky. The livid noon fell across itself, it touched things where it was not; and a shimmering, brooding air returned with its source, a promise of light and mist too plangent to bear, a place far from this sweep of grass, drowned in the night but perfect in line and edge, its heart cut from rock and ray, wrapt about the great north, soaked in the ashen glow of dawn, voices, laughter, nervous kisses over the hedge, beck ringing off the main, a spreading-out over a long, forgetful path unwinding to naught but known by all—locals, artisans, drunks, wayfarers—and it was all beauty coming to its resting place, secret and pervasive—theirs, its, creatures in the stream's, the unborn's, time's. All but mine.

It drained my anger. I was a sorry, fallen thing without a place, cast to the edge, missed by no one, and the world mocked me from its vantage point. I wanted to destroy the mountain, sack the air—but my body was spoilt, without a hand or foot or finger I could bring under my dominion. Before me stood an ineffable mass of good and beauty that had no use of me, that had crushed Clovis like a powder into its crust: *Go home, little girl.*

A single tear, the most painful of my life, more heartrending than all which had gone before it, trickled out the corner of my left eye. Its sting mixed with the fluttering wind into the cerulean sky. Of everything, that moment's grief was the greatest, because I understood then that my life would go on, and Clovis would not be in it.

'I will never forgive You,' I whispered, my voice cracking, as I stared at the vacant sky. 'And I will never surrender.'

Patek and Rahel were sound asleep, intertwined in one another's arms sometime before nine in the evening, when a thunderous pounding upon their door awoke them the night of 27 October 1938. Then came the dreaded words through the door: '*Aufmachen! Polizei!*' The two of them spilled naked out of bed onto the wooden floor, when there was a loud cracking sound, and several SS officers burst into Patek's apartment. The first man in flipped the light switch, and Rahel, frantic, reached for a nightshirt to cover herself. The clanging of heavy boots advanced upon them and came within a couple metres of them in a matter of seconds. The SS officer in front, a tall, imposing Aryan with light skin and intense eyes, ordered them to retrieve their passports. Rahel stooped down behind the bed, slipping a leg into her pants.

'You! Stand and face front.'

'I'm trying to get dressed,' she said, gesturing and out of breath.

'Next time I lose sight of you, I shoot.'

When they were dressed, Patek walked over to the bureau, opened a drawer and took out their Polish passports. Rahel argued she was Patek's wife and German born, but the officer told her under the Nuremberg Laws and the 1913 German Citizenship Law, she was not a German citizen and would have to accompany him.

Infuriated, Patek turned away from the bureau. 'If I can just grab a bag—'

'You'll be right back,' the officer snapped.

Once they reached the street, Rahel and Patek were greeted with a nightmare scene: hundreds and hundreds of people in their pyjamas, robes and underthings, some naked under their coats, being escorted by the police to the local station. Hateful epithets were hurled after them: '*Juden raus! Geh zurück nach Palästina!*' On arrival they met a throng of thousands already there, fellow Berliners, a crush of people overflowing into the streets and parking lot. All round them they heard the wailing of women and children crying. They'd all been told to follow directions but without any explanation as to why.

'We've seen the last of our apartment,' Patek whispered in an icy voice. 'All these people were lured here on the pretext of a minor inconvenience; it was a lie.' Rahel saw the look in his eyes, and the light in them was dead. She felt sick to her stomach. 'That is, unless you regard the rest of our lives as a minor inconvenience,' he continued. 'Which is, after all, how they view us: as insects. Pests.'

After fifteen or twenty minutes, the two of them were loaded into a large police van along with many others and transported to the town hall. Once they got there, expulsion orders were shoved at them with the instruction that they must sign at the bottom.

'You are being deported and may not return home,' an officer said in a rapid, stern voice. 'You must leave Germany by the twenty-ninth of October, 1938.'

Patek protested he had lived in Germany since 1911 and was therefore a German citizen, but to no avail. Rahel argued that, as she was a German citizen herself, Patek had acquired citizenship by dint of being her husband. The officers cited the Nuremberg Laws and the German Citizenship Law of 1913. Although Rahel had been born in Germany, her father had not, and the officers would not listen to anything else. They asserted nothing had been presented to them to prove her citizenship.

'You wouldn't let us take anything—' she said.

The officer cut her off, stamping her expulsion order. The discussion had already consumed far more time than the officers would tolerate.

Rahel was exasperated, but Patek was her husband, and she had no desire to be separated from him regardless.

From a far corner came someone's voice raised in strident tones, followed by a loud, unmistakable sound, even in all the commotion.

Patek could see people backing away from where the man had been standing, and all at once the great room fell silent.

'There will be order.' The words were loud enough to be heard by all, but they were spoken in a slow, deliberate tone, calm and measured, without a trace of tension. In unison, all the officers raised their rifles and held them at the ready.

Patek wanted to resist, wanted to rouse the crowd into storming their captors, knowing in his heart if they did so, they would prevail by virtue of their sheer numbers. But he knew with greater certainty he would be one of the first to die, and Patek had no desire to give up his life or abandon his beloved Rahel. And so, like all the others in that massive throng, he stood in silent submission to the Nazis.

Rahel had tears in her eyes, but the sheer terror of what she imagined would come next prevented her from giving herself over to crying.

The armed officers detained the crowd there without food or water for the entire night and the next day. There was no real room to stand or sit, and the men and women of advanced age were unable to endure the pain even of sitting in one place for so long. People tried to move back to give the oldest people some room. One woman, who appeared about ninety, slumped to the floor in a moaning heap, unable to get up. An officer, offended at the sight of anyone lying on the floor, roused her to her feet and forced her to stand. When the officer saw she was about to fall down again, he withdrew a pack of matches, lit one and held it to her neck, jolting her into a standing position. When the officer left and she collapsed once again to the ground, people stood in a tight pack round her and over her to conceal her prone position.

Moving was out of the question; it was too crowded. The one bathroom towards the rear of the building was locked and accessible to none save the officers, who had a key. Rahel staved off the urge to void for several hours until she could no longer block out the pain.

Patek enquired of an officer where the bathroom facilities were located. The officer laughed, surveying the massive crowd as if in answer to the question. 'A joke, right?' He started to move off, but Patek grabbed his arm.

'*What do you propose we do*—piss and shit ourselves?'

The last word was not yet out when the butt of the officer's rifle came round, clipping him hard on the side of his mouth with sufficient force to knock him down. The officer put his foot on Patek's chest and pressed the rifle to his head while Rahel hyperventilated. 'Say just one more thing.'

In the course of the next several hours, the hall reeked with the stench of human waste and sweat, and the earlier energy of the crowd had been broken down into nothing more than a low hum of moans and physical exhaustion. Some people were starting to fall asleep standing up. Around ten that night, police wagons began transporting them in bunches of about twenty people each to a station, where they were hauled by train to a German border station at Neu Bentschen, a hub connecting trains coming in from all over Germany: Leipzig, Düsseldorf, Bremen, Hanover, Cologne. Somewhere between twelve and fifteen thousand Jews of Polish nationality who had been living in Germany all came by train around six in the morning on Saturday, 29 October 1938, to this place. Everyone detrained and was searched at the Germany-Poland border. Patek had forty-three marks in his billfold, and the officer confiscated all but ten.

'You had no more than this when you entered Germany, and you shall not take any more than that with you now. German law.'

With a derisive smile, the gaunt, bespectacled officer held the notes in his hand in front of Patek's face, took out his own billfold and, making sure Patek saw him, slipped them inside. This time Patek knew to keep his mouth shut. Eventually he looked round and saw human beings standing in the bracing autumn air for as far as he could see in all directions. At the most distant point, a two-metre-tall man appeared smaller in size than the head of the tiniest ant—a sea of humanity.

In time a stern yet precise voice came over a loudspeaker: 'You will walk two kilometres to Zbaszyn. This is where you will remain. There will be no talking. There will be no stopping. Anyone found eating, drinking or relieving themselves will be beaten and sentenced to hard labour. Anyone resisting German authority will be shot.'

The vast majority of those being deported were male, along with some wives such as Rahel and even whole families. The men were all ages and some were young boys, while quite a number were of old age. In front of Patek, two older men were unable to walk on their own and collapsed into the dirt. On the first occasion, the officers beat the men about their shoulders and torsos and forced them to resume their walk. The second time, the guard pulled up the one man by his hair and swung his club into the man's jaw and mouth right in front of Rahel, producing a sickening sound followed by a blood-curdling scream and spraying blood. Despite having not eaten in almost three days, she threw up what little was left in her system. A second blow delivered with even more force cracked his skull open, and the lifeless body fell into the dust and was left there. A guard, however, took custody of his bag.

Rahel stumbled into Patek's arms, crying with abandon for the first time now. 'I can't take this any more—I can't! This is inhuman!'

His heart broke for her and what she was going through, but he covered her mouth and pleaded in a close whisper for her to be quiet, reminding Rahel they could be beaten and sent to a labour camp for nothing more than her words and actions. One of the older men, a retired accountant named Hyam, drew her aside. 'We must survive to honour him, for if we die too, his death will have been without purpose. Remember that.'

These words were comforting to her. Espying a guard glaring in their direction, she recovered herself, resuming a brisk pace and standing erect, wiping the tears from her eyes.

Near the end of their journey, the guards must have determined the deportees were behind schedule, for without warning they ordered everyone to start running, when they were most depleted from the trek. Several of the elder men fell down in sheer exhaustion in front of Rahel and Patek, including Hyam, and the guards took their clubs to the men's feet and calves until they got up and resumed running. But soon after, Hyam clutched at his chest, his eyes wide, and fell to the ground again, while Rahel and others alerted the guard he was having a heart attack. The guard's response was swift and immediate in the form of crushing blows to Hyam's ribs and skull, which left him motionless and bleeding out into the road. The guard carried his bags away.

Hyam's younger brother, Jacob, had been travelling with him and wailed at the spectacle of his brother bleeding to death in front of him. He ran after the guard, pointing to Heaven and proclaiming for all to hear, 'HaShem will judge you in the Hereafter!'

The guard wheeled round and fired two shots into Jacob's chest and one into his head. 'There's your judgment,' he muttered, raising up his rifle and facing the others. 'Anyone else?'

All eyes looked straight ahead, and all feet marched at a brisk pace towards their destination. The crowd at last crossed the Polish border near Zbaszyn, a small village of six thousand, into which as many as fifteen thousand Polish-Jewish German residents were now to be added. The Poles residing there must have thought they were being invaded or attacked, and shot at the lines as they came over the border. It had started to rain, which made the travel even more arduous and resulted in many of the exiles getting sick. Before too much time had elapsed, a Polish general, accompanied by several officers, approached and demanded to examine their papers. The Jewish refugees all had with them their special passports, and after examining these documents, the military decided to allow them entry into Poland.

In spite of not having eaten since Thursday night and being sick with hunger, no one ate the German bread the guards passed out. The common thought was that the bread could be tainted or poisoned.

On Saturday night, they marched to a Polish military camp, and the guards directed them to horse stables littered with dung, because there was no room in the village anywhere else. Rahel clutched at Patek all night, fighting back convulsions from hunger or fear or both and prayed to HaShem for mercy, to deliver them from this unendurable situation. She had horrifying nightmares of watching her neighbours being butchered—first by the German guards and then by the Polish villagers—and eaten by the others around her for survival. She herself was sitting in a corner before Patek's corpse, contemplating whether she could take a knife in her hand and cut his arm from his shoulder, throwing up at the prospect of eating his flesh. She awoke in a cold sweat, with clammy skin and a sick heart.

While all the people went to bed starving that night, on Sunday a truck came from the nearby village of Poznán, and everyone rushed towards it, chasing after the thrown bread. Just a few managed to get the bread, but these souls called their comrades about them and broke the bread into small pieces so that many more got to eat something for nourishment. This bread had been baked by the Poles and was a welcome sight indeed. But all the deportees had been stunned into a state of disbelief and paralysis over how the German government had treated them and what this meant for Polish Jews going forward, beyond themselves and their families. These thoughts extended to the fate of Jews everywhere, not just Polish Jews. For most of the refugees their situation was unthinkable, like some bad dream the turning of the calendar page would rectify. But this was no dream, and there was no waking up from it either. The Nazis had shown less regard for them as human beings in these past four days than for the pets they kept in their houses. Short of a rabid animal threatening attack, Rahel could not think of any living creature she had seen treated with such brutality without provocation. And as Patek had remarked at one point earlier on, the conduct of the Nazis was not of the sort arising out of crisis and the anarchy of nature but occurred in the context of an elaborate, planned and organised paramilitary undertaking. Even just closing her eyes and seeing the helpless men bludgeoned to death on the road in front of her brought back the waves of nausea in full force. As soon as she had some privacy with Patek, she asked him, 'What does this mean? What is going on?'

Patek blinked several times, his mouth open as if he were unable to speak. For once, even the man never at a loss for words was stripped of the power of speech.

'Apocalypse. It's the beginning of the end.'

Being as I was less than a kilometre from Monte Cassino, I took the opportunity to collect myself there and rest my weary bones and spirit. They took good care of Hannibal—and of me—and in a couple weeks'

time, with the benefit of their caretaking and the invigorating mountain air, I had recovered my mettle and equilibrium enough to continue with my travels. Without Clovis, there was no place for me at Soumela—and the distance of such a journey on my own was a daunting challenge even with the prospect of a post there. But Greece in general and Athens in particular—now far less than half the distance to Trebizond—still beckoned with all its exotic seduction as a destination. Departing from Monte Cassino on Hannibal, I was located some one hundred kilometres north of Naples, which I covered in just over two pleasant and uneventful days, even with the rough terrain. Had we kept to the eastern coast, Brundisium, that timeless harbour of antiquity where Virgil took his last breath, and which had been resurrected as a thriving port by the Saracens, would have been the logical choice for passage to Greece across the Adriatic at a mere fraction of the distance from Reggio. Alas, then riding on the country's western side, I had a longer, more arduous trip across the mountains. Brundisium had been ambushed by pirates the year before, rendering the entire enterprise more perilous than I was comfortable with. Therefore, I continued down the western coast of the boot through Naples, Amalfi and smaller coastal villages to Reggio. By staying close to the coast, I avoided the mountains, but even then, riding through Naples, we were at an altitude of over 150 metres, with a straight drop to the Mediterranean—but with some of the most breathtaking views I have ever seen, as in the distance, faint and massive, loomed Mount Vesuvius.

As I came farther south, into Salerno, a landscape teeming with nobility and commerce greeted me, but set against a backdrop of brilliant, velvety green hills. The flourishing city had benefited much from the rule of the Lombards in recent years. Of late, this included the political subterfuge of Arechis II of Benevento, who, for the purpose of throwing off the scent of Charlemagne, transferred his seat of the Duchy of Benevento to Salerno, arrogating for himself dominion over the hub of Campania in the bargain. He ordered that the entire city be fortified, extending the walls and towers already in place at the castle upon Bonadies Mountain. I was able to stop along the way and partake of some hearty meals; for the most part, the people were hospitable and tried to make me feel at home in their country. Salerno's prosperity would continue in 839, when it declared itself independent of Benevento, transforming itself into the capital of an expanding and developed principality, but in 837, the city still enjoyed administrative unity with Benevento. Travel throughout the province was pleasant and an enticing indulgence of the senses, including the presence in abundance of local music at faires and meals. It would be several years yet before the Norsemen raids that were already bringing terror and anxiety to much of Francia would penetrate as far south as Italia—and also before the passing of Louis, which would further throw the realm into chaos. Given how the next several years would transform Italia on several fronts, it was a rather peaceful time in which to find myself as a woman travelling alone in the country—albeit one disguised as a young man decked out with the requisite accoutrements of self-defence.

I had already begun to enquire about passage to Greece from Reggio, and the local townsfolk told me the amplitude of merchants both providing and requiring such passage from that port would render such acquisition a trivial matter indeed. My arrival there confirmed this. I had not anticipated any real difficulty in securing passage for myself; Hannibal, however, was another matter. For every reason imaginable, I had become as attached to Hannibal as to any person I might have journeyed with. To begin with, he stood as my last real connexion to Clovis and reflected his master's strength and excellence in all ways. To some extent, notwithstanding the sentimentality of it, I felt as though my love's presence were not extinguished entire but persisted through those small touches in quadruped form. And like Clovis, Hannibal was my protector: it did not overstate the matter to say he had saved my life in the attack upon our party. Too, he made travel in certain parts not just bearable but possible at all. I could never have made it through the Alps on foot, carrying all the equipment and necessary supplies myself. And then, of course, there was my immeasurable fondness for him, and our bond was of a nature and breadth I had experienced with but two or three people in my life. Selling him to some stranger was unthinkable.

And so my conversations with the locals as to passage necessarily presumed Hannibal's passage as well as my own, for which I was more than willing to pay compensation with the understanding he would be treated well on the voyage and I would have some kind of access to him or at least be able to confirm his presence. I had been told by one helpful soul in Salerno that I should insist upon travelling in the same vessel as Hannibal, for he knew first-hand of an incident where the animals, which were transported in a separate vessel, somehow never shewed up at the port of destination—with the dubious explanation there had been some kind of mishap at sea. The merchant later confirmed all six horses had been sold at auction.

I inspected the vessel on which we were to travel, a somewhat larger modified Roman transport ship with a low but powerful sail, constructed with large doors that swung open, allowing passengers and equines to disembark ashore. Inside, towards the rear of the vessel, stood a series of stalls, sturdy and attached to one another, with supporting slings and devices for cross-tying and securing the animals within each stall. On the day of our departure, after I had paid the not-insignificant sum of eighty solidii, we were led on board. With some trepidation I watched Hannibal neigh with just a bit of resistance right at first, but soon thereafter his temperament was so calm, I imagined he must have made the voyage across water once or twice before, as he let the first handler lead him into the stall while the other secured the sling round his belly and the heavy chains at his feet. Stroking his long black nose with reassurances, I produced a lump of sugar and my eyes moistened as his lips brought the treat up into his mouth.

'You're all I have left; I'm not letting anything happen to you,' I whispered, the two men standing behind me, their hands behind their backs. They closed the door to the stall after me, locking it shut. I made my way to my seat on the ship and settled into thoughtful ruminations on Greece, of what kind of city awaited me in Athens, where I had decided I would take up residence. My life was at once more rootless, precarious and less worthy of pursuit with Clovis no longer in it—no matter how I tried to banish these thoughts. What had taken hold in me was something rather more vengeful in spirit; I resolved myself to fighting the evil Clovis had sacrificed himself to, of the iniquities in the Church at large and in society that forced women into the margins, into disguise, into the need of at least some monastic privacy, that had driven us from Lorsch. Clovis believed I was destined for greatness, and was willing to journey across the world to secure me a stake in that destiny—and he had died for it. I was not about to fail him now. For the first time, I came to view my life as being not about myself nor even God, but about honour. Clovis was in word and in deed a man of honour, through and through, and his honour alone made him the greatest man I had ever known. For me to do justice to his memory and the nobility of the sacrifice he had made for me meant honouring his vision for my life.

To my great relief, it was not a long journey; indeed, Reggio Calabria to Athens was one of the shortest voyages in distance one could take on the high seas. Moreover, the Ionian Sea was by and large a calm body of water this time of year, and the nights were cool and temperate. Athens is surrounded on all sides by mountains, so reaching it directly required sailing south of the ancient Achaean settlement of Pharai. The total voyage was about four days. Quarters were crowded, and the heat of our bodies intensified the torpor below decks, so the cool temperatures and gentle night breezes were merciful. Once we were off, the gentle rocking of the waves disoriented me at first, so peculiar was the sensation of being at once weighted down by something and yet lifted above it, but I became acclimated to it in a short time.

Then the second night came. There are no words for the placeless blindness, terror and isolation of travel in a ship's hold at night. Tossed about more than on the first eve, I slipt at last into slumber, but as a thing of feathers and little else cast upon a sky, nothing but a square of wood separating my bottom from the tops of continuous clouds, unseen and sinister. By intense concentration and optimism, I was able to resurrect the world of the land from whence I had come and the other to which I was headed. It was as though I had been abandoned to some powerless form, bereft of will or words or capacity for action. Late that second night, in the middle of the Ionian Sea, we hit a storm that jarred me out of the sleep into which I had fallen, tossing us about in a torrential and gusty rain which did not relent for hours. Lightning flashed with prodigious brilliance, and thunder boomed about the vessel with such force as to make the hull vibrate, and the more we were pitched about in unbound oblivion, the more my stomach and my will collapsed into a single, spiralling dread. I tried comforting myself with thoughts of my good fortune up to now, of how blessed I had been for the entire journey from Lorsch in being spared from mishap—even when placed in the direct path of tragedy, even as the vessel lay almost on its side at moments. My gaze travelled to the stalls, from which issued considerable commotion and squealing, though the horses were secured and slung in place. I prayed to God for mercy, pleading for Him not to let Clovis's death be in vain—for his sake, if not for mine. The rains trailed off at last around dawn, and I found out later that storms of this order were a common event and no real cause for concern. Natheless, I was exhausted and fell into a deep slumber not long after daybreak.

The remainder of the voyage passed in uneventful fashion, and we docked in Athens a couple days later. I was no longer in Francia. This was the Eastern Roman Empire, and the laws and customs under Louis had no place here. Not until I disembarked did I discover my money would not be accepted in this town, and thereafter found conveying my need for a money changer—let alone locating one—would not be a trivial task. They led Hannibal out—who looked no worse for wear—and both men engaged me in a laboured and protracted proposition for his purchase, which of course I had no interest in whatsoever. Their top offer was four hundred denarii, a handsome sum indeed, giving me a sense of just what Hannibal was worth in the open market to horse traders who were knowledgeable and versed in their trade. That notwithstanding, I was tempted to find some grounds independent of him on which to transact business, because it would have netted me some local currency and hence a voice of purchase in the theme of Hellas. All of us left disappointed, and when I enquired about a money changer, they both professed ignorance—a consequence, no doubt, of my rejection of their tender.

The spoken language in Athens was thick, hurried, glutted with consonants and incomprehensible. The ample but random store of Greek words I had accumulated from those years consulting the lexicons at Lorsch might as well have been in Frisian for all the use they were to me; not having Clovis and his facility with the mother tongue was fatal. My homeland and language were but a distant memory of no use to me. I struggled to convey my thoughts through gestures, connecting at last with a silver-haired merchant at a fruit stand by taking out a libra and indicating my inability to purchase any fruit from him. I made gestures of helplessness, then took out another coin, holding one in each hand and making them switch places, as one going from him to me and one from me to him, and his eyebrows arched upwards in recognition.

'Ahh—κερματιστής!' he exclaimed, flashing me a toothless smile.

He was explaining in his native language while gesturing with his hands how I would get there, and I stopped him at once. I took out a parchment (we had brought a generous amount of it with us) and a quill and asked him to draw it out for me, which he did. He drew an excellent picture, but it was rendered in large part worthless by a lapse in his memory, which set me upon the wrong route about halfway through. A couple enquiries to a soul blessed with fluency in Frengisk once I realised something was amiss got me back on the right path.

Uneasy about converting all my money into Greek solidii, I exchanged a little over a third of what I had, as I anticipated remaining in Athens for quite some time. I remembered Clovis's admonishment that an offer of 240 denarii for one libra should be treated with disdain, but this was in fact the going rate, and I was dealing not with a merchant but a money changer, a person forbidden by law to convert currency at anything other than the published rate of exchange. However, the solidus of Francia enjoyed a favourable exchange rate over the Greek one: 1.15 times greater, to be exact, which helped offset the low conversion rate of denarii to solidii. The Greek equivalent of the denier was a dull bronze thing called a follis, which had found its way into circulation in mass quantities in Athens the past couple years at Theophilos's bidding, in celebration of his military victories over the

Saracens. At any rate, I was now a woman of significant means, even if but a fraction of my monies were in usable form at present.

Athenian street life was not quite the dizzying array of commerce and humanity I had envisioned. I found a tattered sparseness and humility about the place, farmers selling fruits and vegetables, along with mendicants and the odd person of religious or philosophical learning, for the city had become something of a refuge for iconophile monks under Theophilos who were able to flee the monasteries for the caves of Mount Penteli. A few of the people were nobles, sporting bright-coloured linen and even silk tunics and leather boots, but they were more conspicuous here than in Italia, for example, for their scarcity. Natheless, Athens had been rebuilding over time out of the state into which it had been cast in the preceding centuries since the rise of Constantine and the closing of the Academy in 529 by Justinian. Many of its treasures had been looted, and, in infamy, the enormous eight-metre-high chryselephantine Athena Promachos of Pheidias perched atop the Acropolis had been removed to Constantinople in the mid-fifth century by Emperor Theodosius.

Beyond the human denizens lay a vista of piercing beauty, with a flawless dome of cerulean blue in perfect reflexion of the deep blue Aegean. Simple settlements in blinding white of temple, stone and crosses, soaked in the light of noonday sun, glowed off the rising hills as if carried skyward in the ecstasy of mass resurrection: a resurrection of hope, myth and the majesty of histories immemorial. For a long time, I stood with my back to the sea in a transfixed stupor, humbled beyond words or even thought by the divinity and mythic immortality of this place. All at once, however, the savagery, gravity and gruelling demands of the past many days caught up with me and were ushered in like a bad wind where I stood; I was in dire need of rest. Using basic, isolated words, like *where* and *inn*, I secured a room not far from the docks, where I could tie up Hannibal. Exhausted and not yet in command of my land legs, I wished more than anything else in the world to draw a door closed behind me in complete solitude. It was early in the day, but I was not equal to anything more than sleep and the silence of my own company. I lay down upon the bed, and my head spun in aimless flight, ensnared in a state neither wakeful nor the stuff of dreams, neither present in that room nor able to connect to my past, to my life with Clovis, to Lorsch—to anything meaningful with which I could construct a single image or thought from the torn and scattered parchments which had passed for my existence. From the revelations in Reggio Calabria, I knew in the back of my mind what I wanted to do, but I had no idea how to do it or where to begin. And for once, on that particular day, in this certain place, this was of no moment to me. I wanted to cry, but nothing inside remained to bring up, which I took as a good sign; was I at long last getting over Clovis? Before, there had been a residue of something altogether odd and disembodied, something passive, as of a shell being washed up on the shore by the tide. For that time, whatever was to become of me would be at the world's bidding and would have nothing of my own will in it. None of this came to me until I laid my head down to sleep, and in my last moment of consciousness, I thought, *I have much to do.*

I slept all day and arose for a few hours after Compline for a meal of roast lamb and a sweetish bread, with a rich, sanguine wine. Upon taking my fill, but still dogged by a flat foot and a thick tongue, I retired to my room and a bittersweet meditation on my time at Lorsch: of all the satisfying work I had done in the scriptorium and the praise I had garnered for it; of the vast works of early and contemporary Christian writings I had absorbed in my years there, and the conclusions, as well as the deep tensions and disappointments, they had accorded me of my faith; of the mishaps and final scandal of my revealed identity; and of the grim events which had led Clovis to decide in favour of our relocation to Greece and which had resulted in his death.

I teared up at this thought; forsooth, the beauty and exquisite bliss of my life while he was alive had vanished forever. I wished we could have shared a life together, but the forces of the outside world and that hateful woman had had other designs. At least Clovis, in his foresight, had set up arrangements with the Abbot to get us out of Lorsch unscathed. Once I resolved myself to these truths, I surrendered to sleep, which came with little effort not long after.

Monastic life in Greece had become a perilous calling under Theophilos and the persecutorial atmosphere surrounding iconoclasm. Icon worship was an integral aspect of Greek spirituality in Athens—as it was at Soumela—but was being rooted out wherever it existed. As a result, I despaired over yet another layer of subterfuge and displacement imposed upon my simple desire to practise my faith and service to God within the Christian Church—a faith which in practice seemed little more than an accumulation of false representations, disguises and omissions of my nature, my identity and my sex. Monks practising icon worship in these times were jailed, tortured and had their beards set on fire. Women disguising themselves as monks would fare worse.

The cultural and theological alterity of the Greek world, in itself a major aspect forming my fascination with and powerful attraction to Greece from the start, posed additional obstacles and perils to the prospect of my new life here. Icon worship embodied the most obvious but far from the lone departure from Christian beliefs and customs. In my initial studies at Lorsch, I traced my steps through the Eusebius translation in Latin back to ancient Greece, and then later through conversations I had with Clovis, whose penetrating mind devoured the writings of Herodotus, Plato, Plutarch, Diodorus, Euripides, Sophocles and many other Greek lights in the span of his five years in Athens. I discovered just how stunning those departures were in the theme of Hellas from the central tenets of the Church Fathers in the first couple centuries of Christianity. One of my most treasured memories with Clovis was a sumptuous dialogue between us in the calmer leg of our journey before the Alps, resting in a glade, when we exchanged on Greek practices of divination and spirituality, as well as figures of mythos and the death of real persons.

I had known of Plutarch in passing as a writer and a biographer, but Clovis had alluded to him in the context of Greek spiritual beliefs and practices, so I pursued the topic further with him.

'Did Plutarch author religious works as well?'

'Yes, though I would use the word *spirituality* or *divination* rather than *religion*. His God was grounded more in Plato, the way Socrates was associated with Apollo. Plutarch was a priest of the Temple of Apollo at Delphi, and in addition to his *Lives*, he also published a far-ranging work entitled *Moralia*, and three Pythian dialogues, including one entitled *De Defectu Oracularum*, or *The Obsolescence of Oracles*.

'In Plutarch's time the Pythia (Πυθία), or priestess of the temple, rendered the prophecies of Apollo, inspired by vapours or *pneuma* arising out of the ground. All Pythia were Delphic natives, and once they entered its service, they could never leave and were not allowed to marry.

'In the earliest times, all Pythia were young and required to be virgins, but there was a scandal in which one Echecrates, enamoured of the Pythia's beauty, seduced her and carried her off. From that point on, the Delphians required that the Pythia not be a virgin and be no less than fifty years of age.'

I couldn't suppress my laughter. 'That sounds more appropriate to their station, does it not? These Greeks... common sense only ever evolves out of catastrophe.'

Clovis laughed. 'Very true. At the height of its influence as the Greek world's preeminent oracle, three women served the temple as a triad, with two of the Pythia alternating turns in reciting prophecies while the third was kept in reserve. The oracle rendered prophecies during the nine warmest months of each year; in the winter, Apollo abandoned his temple.'

'So the temple was unattended the entire winter?'

'No, Apollo's immortal half brother, Dionysus, whose tomb was in the temple, assumed charge. Plutarch's friend Clea was priestess to both the rites of Apollo and the secret rites of Dionysus.'

This last fact perturbed me. 'That sounds a bit improper, to have a friend overseeing such sacred rites. Something in her office, her background in especial recommended this woman to such duties?'

Clovis flashed a broad smile. 'Indeed. She was Plutarch's friend. And he was a priest of the Temple of Apollo.'

'Ahh. Of course.' I shook my head.

'The ritual sacrifice of certain animals was required at the temple to bring the Pythia to the shrine for the telling of prophecies—'

'Do you know what I think?' I said, leaning into him, squeezing his wrist in my hand. 'I think the animals were sacrificed to feed the

Pythia. That was their wages. All the rest is mere mythos.' We both laughed.

'I love your perversity, Joan,' he said, taking my lips with his. 'Believe it or not, the Greek science of divination through reading the entrails of sacrificed animals was a serious art in those times. If the head of the liver was missing, this was a bad omen indeed. In *Electra*, Aegisthus declares his dismay at the incompleteness of the animal's liver, and right after, he is stabbed and killed by Orestes.

'Plutarch wrote on the Egyptian practices of animal worship in *On Isis and Osiris* and early on was contemptuous of their "superstition" and "atheistic and bestial reasoning", yet by the end he adopts a tone far closer in spirit to Marcus Antonius, shewing sympathy for such acts in spite of their error.

'His explanations of the symbolism guiding the Egyptians' iden-tification with certain animals are fascinating—as in, for instance, the sacredness of the crocodile on account of the fact it is the one animal lacking a tongue and therefore the incarnation of the divine, which does not require a voice to transmit it.'

This narrative from Clovis provided yet another link between the somewhat pagan, pre-Gnostic and non-Christian viewpoint of Plutarch and the budding Gnostic system of beliefs embodied in Valentinus which followed close behind. From an ecclesiastic perspective, this entire discussion would be a subject of ridicule. Any differences between the cultural worship of live animals as sacred and divination of the entrails of animals sacrificed to the gods in the service of prophecy would be insignificant save in terms of the fundamental flaws they shared.

Clovis also regaled me with an incredible anecdote from Herodo-tus's *Histories* concerning a miraculous poet known as Aristeas, who it was said dropt dead inside a fuller's shop. The fuller closed up his shop, going out and informing Aristeas's relations about the unfortunate mishap. Somehow, a Cyzicenian swore to having met and talked with Aristeas after his alleged death, and lo and behold, when the fuller opened his shop to allow the family access to the body, Aristeas was nowhere to be found inside.

According to Herodotus, some 240 years after Aristeas's death, he appeared in Metapontum, Magna Graecia, decreeing that a statue of himself be erected and a new altar to Apollo be dedicated. Aristeas claimed he had been journeying throughout the land with Apollo while taking the form of a sacred raven. This story, implausible on far too many fronts despite its entertaining twists and turns, left me wondering if Herodotus should by right be called the Father of History or the Father of Lies, as Plutarch intimated in an essay on Herodotus's malice. For not the first time, I pondered the question of just what constituted the task of history: to define the scope of our knowledge or the scope of our beliefs, and how could we tell which one was being invoked?

On top of all this, the Eastern view of the Trinity departed from Rome's and did not admit of the *Filioque* addition to the Nicene Creed mentioned earlier. And as bleak and oppressive as the Roman Christian view of women and their role in the Church was, it paled in comparison with the view of women in the theme of Hellas.

As if all this were not enough, there was also the language barrier. Life in a monastery here would be dangerous, and that peril would be magnified, given my limited capacities with the language.

At the very least, I would have to meet with an abbot and a prior and accord myself in their language in sufficient terms to convince them of my desire to serve God and the merits of taking me in as a member of their community, neither of which I could do at present. Moreover, to avoid the perils which befell me with such alarming frequency at Lorsch, I needed a monastery in which monks were housed in individual cells rather than in a dormitorium. I knew my lack of facility with the language would take away my strongest weapon of persuasion, drawing attention to the physical aspects and mannerisms native to my sex. Turning over these varied concerns in my mind, I arrived at the unsettling conclusion a fit within monastic life in Athens would not be available to me—at least not then.

In essence, the generosity and good intentions of others—the Polish government included—made possible the continuance of an intolerable situation in Zbaszyn. On 30 October 1938, even as Rahel and Patek pondered their new life of impossible squalor, assistance from Warsaw's Joint Distribution Committee arrived in Zbaszyn in the persons of Emanuel Ringelblum and Yitzhak Gitterman. Ringelblum, a man of singular cultural vision and perseverance, was one of the founders of the Young Historians Circle in the early 1920s, a group committed to the study of Jewish history as well as the right of Jews to live in Poland (Jews, for example, were banned under Polish law from living in Warsaw between 1527 and 1768). Ringelblum already had over a hundred academic articles on Jewish history, rights and culture published under his name.

Days after their arrival, the two men established a committee to aid Jewish refugees from Germany living in Poland, while a local Jewish flour mill owner, Grzybowski, set up another assistance committee providing for deportees to be domiciled in Polish army barracks and in various buildings on the mill's premises. But it was a filthy, crowded and savage existence, lacking dignity, privacy and any semblance of stability. Moreover, the Polish government allowed the overcrowded camp at Zbaszyn to continue unchecked in the hope the obscene environment and malaise at the border would pressure Germany into negotiating a return of the deportees to German soil. This, of course, never happened.

Another fifteen hundred refugees were put up with funds provided by Grzybowski's committee in private residences in Zbaszyn. Rahel and Patek were two of the lucky ones who garnered lodging through the latter, due in large part to Rahel's presence there. The family who took them in, the Szechters, were workers at the mill, Polish Jews from Kraków who had worked at a brewery until coming to Zbaszyn and joining the mill. The husband and father, Milosz, wore an eye patch from a permanent injury he had sustained in an accident at the brewery. Milosz liked to joke it was HaShem's way of punishing him for his roving eye. His wife, Katya, had mothered two boys and now worked part time at the mill. The younger of the boys, Mischa, had been recognised by two different music instructors as a prodigy on the violin, and the family struggled to earn enough money for the expensive schooling the ten-year-old was receiving on the instrument. The Szechters had lived in Zbaszyn since 1921 and in that time had witnessed and experienced first-hand the substantial erosion in the relationship between the town and its Jewish residents. More and more, the Jews of Zbaszyn, as elsewhere, had become more insular within their own culture and conducted their lives apart from the Polish majority.

In response to these conditions, the outspoken nationalist right-wing majority party, Endecja, called for a programme of forced 'ethnic assimilation', meaning the Jewish insistence on a separate culture and Hebrew or Yiddish as their dominant lingua franca was to come to an end. In Warsaw and elsewhere, 'ghetto benches' to which Jews were relegated were beginning to appear with increasing frequency in the back of lecture halls at universities. In smaller towns such as Zbaszyn, hostilities between Polish and Jewish youth were playing out on the athletic field and in the schoolyard. Mischa came home one day from school with his shirt and pants caked in dried mud, saying one of the largest older kids on the playground had pretended to talk to Mischa, pushing him back with his foot stuck out behind him so that he fell into a pool of muddy water, the boy laughing at Mischa and calling him a 'stupid Yid'. Mischa had to sit through two other classes while all the other children pointed and laughed at him.

Then on 7 November 1938, a shot was heard round the world which did not so much change the course of history as disclose the inevitable path upon which those in power had already set out. On that night, the Szechters and Rahel and Patek were all seated round the table at dinner with the radio on.

'A teenaged Jewish refugee, Herschel Grynszpan, an illegal in Paris, has shot that city's Nazi diplomat, Ernst vom Rath.' Rahel stared at Milosz's fork, which was frozen in his hand as the announcement continued. 'Grynszpan shot vom Rath five times in the abdomen, shouting, "In the name of twelve thousand persecuted Jews!" The diplomat was rushed to the hospital with life-threatening injuries. Grynszpan made no attempt to escape or resist the French police.'

Milosz exhaled a slow, heavy sigh. The fork still did not move. 'It has been learned that the assassin's family is living in the Polish town of Zbaszyn, where some twelve thousand Polish Jews were deported from Germany—'

'That's here, Father!' Mischa interrupted.

'Shh.'

'It remains to be seen where Grynszpan will be detained and tried, in France or in Germany, and vom Rath's condition is grave.'

Milosz sat back in his chair. '*Assassin.* We hear the tone of this, how it will play out in Germany. This will have horrific consequences for us all. Horrific.' Even Patek stared ahead with a blank expression, saying nothing. A prayer to HaShem was made, but it was of little use.

The diplomat died of his wounds two days later on 9 November, by coincidence the fifteenth anniversary of the 1923 Beer Hall Putsch. The leadership of the Nazi Party, assembled in Munich to commemorate the event, used the shooting death as a rallying point for unleashing its intended policies and objectives of terror and eradication upon the Jews. Minister of Propaganda Joseph Goebbels, speaking to the assembled Old Guard of the Nazi Party, said 'World Jewry' had conspired to commit the assassination. 'The Führer has decided that… demonstrations should not be prepared or organised by the Party, but insofar as they erupt spontaneously, they are not to be hampered.'

This curious incitement to unofficial, disorganised violence was construed to permit just that, and conforming instructions were typed up and distributed to local offices of the Party by the Old Guard leaders. Many of those in the rank and file of the local Sturmabteilung (SA) paramilitary units who carried out these assaults dressed in civilian clothes to promote the image of an insurrection fuelled by public outrage, not the Nazi Party's.

The radio brought news of these devastating events early morning at breakfast on 10 November 1938, following vom Rath's death from his injuries:

'Last night and continuing into this morning, thousands of Jewish businesses, interests and synagogues across Germany have been attacked, their glass storefronts shattered, and in the case of the synagogues, set on fire or demolished with sledgehammers. One young woman in Berlin witnessed her synagogue burning to the ground while firefighters smoked and laughed nearby.

'While we do not yet have reports of deaths, throughout the late-night hours, Jewish homes, orphanages and schools were ransacked, the orphanages emptied and the children led out into the freezing cold in their nightclothes, hospitals raided and their equipment destroyed and hundreds of Jewish men and women assaulted and beaten.'

All five of them sat in silence at the table, and no one could eat their food.

'Excuse me.' Katya pushed her chair out from the table and ran into the bathroom, retching into the toilet. Rahel's eyes were flooded with tears.

Patek stared at the table, his fists clenched, shaking his head and shuddering, speaking in a soft but firm voice. 'We know now we cannot sit in our chairs and pray that this will all end. There is but one end to this, the death of us all, unless we stand up to them. Any other response is madness.'

The broadcasts on the radio continued to present the events of these two days as the concerted uprisings of a public mob, as attacks on Jewish people and their property by German citizens. Streets were filled with shattered glass, leading to the moniker by which this livid moment which shocked the world's conscience would come to be known: Kristallnächt, or 'Night of the Broken Glass'. Upon hearing of the events of Kristallnächt, the former Kaiser, Wilhelm II, exclaimed 'For the first time, I am ashamed to be German.'

No fewer than ninety Jews died on 9-10 November 1938, but later figures put the death toll closer to two thousand. In spite of this, neither the extensive damage nor a single death was reported in the news under orders from the Nazi Party, which now controlled all news media. Not until rumours of widespread damage became rampant did the Third Reich permit the press to report that in fact some damage to property had occurred 'here and there'. Moreover, the German government issued a statement after the attacks, blaming the Jews for the damage and imposing an 'atonement' fine of one billion *Reichsmark* on German Jews as a whole. It also directed the press, at Hermann Göring's bidding, not to publish any information on the directors of insurance companies which otherwise would have been liable to the Jews for damage to their property. Instead, the Third Reich confiscated all insurance payouts to Jews, leaving the owners liable for the cost of all repairs. The pogrom of Kristallnächt was a testament to the priority the 'Jewish question' assumed for the Nazis, preceding Hitler's military initiation of World War II by almost a year.

The mounting conflicts after Kristallnächt came to Zbaszyn as well. Young Mischa was more and more often subject to ridicule and name calling; week after week, some incident or provocation initiated by his schoolmates sent the sensitive, introspective boy home in tears.

'I hate being Jewish!' he lashed out one day. His father tried to buoy his spirits with talk of how special their faith made him in HaShem's eyes. 'HaShem isn't the one getting mud kicked in His face and all over His shirt.'

'HaShem is the most just and wise of anyone you could ever imagine.' Milosz tried to explain how so much is unknowable, but once again his son cut him off through bitter tears, unable to listen to reason.

'If HaShem is so wise and great, why would He let me suffer these taunts—why would He make all the days of my life so terrible and full of dread? What is the sense of that?'

His father's attempts to explain again that not everything was meant to be known by mortals down on earth were met with more derision.

Rahel and Patek took to the boy right away, showering him with their love of music and admiration of his astonishing gift and introducing him to beautiful new compositions he had never heard before. Sometimes they sat listening to his playing in rapt attention for hours. For a few weeks, the two visitors felt very much at home and even sheltered somewhat from the ominous winds knocking at their doorstep. But in late November came the news that the Polish authorities had elected to close down the camp, after an entire town had been built by Ringelblum and others, replete with a hospital, a dental clinic, workshops for tradesmen, a post office, an emigration office, a welfare office, a commission of sanitation and even a court of arbitration. The

Szechters prized the tremendous improvement they had seen in young Mischa's demeanour since they had taken Patek and Rahel into their home, and had no wish to lose them now. 'We can hide you here, or we can talk to Mr Grzybowski,' Milosz said, but Patek had seen the writing on the wall and knew that with the mere possibility Germany could be taking them back, they needed to leave Zbaszyn as soon as possible. He also knew that the one place—other than the United States, with its language they could not speak—where they could be at all assured of safety was Warsaw, where his uncle Moszhe still lived.

As efforts at negotiations with Germany for return of the refugees continued in vain, the local authorities had been granting the deportees permits to leave the town for elsewhere in Poland. Many of them had reached out to family or friends in Warsaw, Kraków, Danzig and elsewhere. Patek and Rahel were filled with a sickening dread as fewer and fewer deportees remained in Zbaszyn. 'If the Nazis get their hands on us again, we won't be sent anywhere we can get to from this world,' Patek said. He and his uncle had stayed close since his father's passing six years back, and through their many correspondences and Patek's visit there three years ago, Patek knew his address by heart. There was no time to await a response in the *Post*; instead, he sent a brief letter ahead:

23 November 1938

Dearest Uncle:

I hope you will receive this in advance of our arrival. I am sure you are aware of the dire situation in Zbaszyn, where my wife Rahel and I have been sent after being deported along with all the others. The Polish government, having received no indication of interest from Germany in effecting our safe return there, has elected to dismantle the camp. While the authorities here are still in the practice of granting permits to depart for other cities within Poland, we must act fast to find safe harbour elsewhere. Since Kristallnächt, the prospect of falling into German hands again, as we are so close to the border, is not one we wish to entertain, for obvious reasons.

Therefore, having no other options before us, we are re-solved to come to Warsaw and impose upon your hospitality if that meets with your approval. I apologise, but everything is breaking down and happening at once, so that we must leave tomorrow latest without time to await your confirmation. We shall be setting out for Warsaw tomorrow, as soon as we are able to get the train. We look forward to seeing you soon.

All our thanks and much love,
Patek

He sealed and stamped the letter at the post office at two fifteen that afternoon. The permit was issued to them at eight forty-five the next morning on 24 November 1938, and by eleven thirty, they had packed their few humble belongings and set off on foot for the Zbaszyn train station. Following a three-mile walk from the camp, Rahel and Patek arrived at the station before one o'clock in the afternoon and stood another two hours waiting for the train to come.

Why did I come here, then? I pondered this question to the depths of my soul, and, after hours of impassioned contemplation, I arrived at nothing but emotional explanations of the simple-minded thought processes in my head which had governed my will: Clovis had decided it was the best course of action, and out of allegiance to him and his memory, I felt compelled to honour his judgment; the sheer inertia of the events already set into motion and the force of their author-ity, against which I could come up with no better course of action, demanded it; my curiosity for and desire to experience the Greek world I had heard about and imagined since my early youth urged it. All of these could explain why I did what I did, but none of them gave an adequate reason for doing so, now most of all. After Empress Irene of Athens' death in 803 and Saracen raids, Athens was a ragged mix: still an administrative centre, and made the seat of the theme of Hellas in recent times, Athens and life within it was confined to a small area surrounding the Acropolis.

I resolved to enquire into the prospect of teaching young boys: of teaching Latin or Frengisk, or Theodisc as it was known round these parts, to children of a young age, whose mastery of spoken Greek would be more rudimentary. I could also lecture on early Christian history at a high level of accomplishment and scholarship, but the audience would have to be fluent in Frengisk in addition to Greek. Finding lectures teaching conversational Greek to non-Greek-speaking persons also dominated my thinking at this juncture. These avenues of intellectual pursuit and instruction seemed far more probable in the Athens of centuries past than in the listless, agrarian society of the present-day city.

I decided to pay another visit to Elasus, the money changer with whom I had been able to exchange in Frengisk, a much smaller amount of monies in hand as the pretext for my return trip, in the hope he might be able to shed some light on these questions. To my great delight and relief, he was indeed well connected with some of the city's meagre intellectual circles and in particular with a few scholars who lectured on occasion at the Parthenon in religion, philosophy and spoken Greek.

After an unending procession of harrowing events and brutal outcomes ever since departing from Lorsch, this was the first small sign of mercy; in time, I might forge a new life out of ruin after all. After a short period, I secured a cell in a small nearby monastery, safe from persecution, with a room of respectable size, including a writing desk, a nightstand and a sturdy, larger and somewhat more comfortable pallet than what I had been used to. I made a significant donation of monies to the monastery, enabling me to live there and perform menial chores but come and go as I pleased. I received private instruction in spoken Greek for many months with a scholar of the redoubtable name Demosthenes, and with my affinity for languages and store of

Greek vocabulary, I progressed far beyond his wildest expectations. I had also acquired in my years at Lorsch more than a passing familiarity with the medicinal arts, and in Athens received further schooling in this discipline through a physician. I spent two years paying for these pursuits without any source of income, which I managed without difficulty given the substantial monies at my disposal. I settled into a life there with surprising ease, and as the weeks blurred into months, the long days of sun, sea and sky turned me golden brown and played up the light in my large, inquisitive eyes. In less than two years' time, I had already garnered with little effort the trust and comity of most of the people in the monastery and the town round me with whom I had intercourse, and was earning a reputation as a learned lecturer in the subjects of philosophy, early Christianity and the medicinal arts.

Life was simpler than it had ever been before. I devoted much effort to my lessons and my work in the monastery, which was more menial, but the rest of my time was a feast of chance experiences and encounters: with people, with nature, with the sea and with thoughts I had never permitted myself to have until then. As the months passed, in private moments, the woman who I had all along been becoming emerged and danced with storms in the dead of night or brought up the new day with a glorious, riotous sunrise. All the lies I had convinced myself were true, I crushed under my heel on the steps of the Acropolis. I found a secluded spot in a meadow far from the monastery, where no one else ever ventured, and lay naked and glistening in the hot sun for hours, armed with nothing more than my fingers and thoughts of Clovis. In the summer months of 840, I lost myself altogether, almost daring to be found out, my eyes closed, my mind flopping about outside my body like some prehistoric creature dredged up out of the depths of the Aegean and seeking the hardest rocks, the sharpest edge on which to be dashed and laid open.

One afternoon, something blotted out the sun as I lay in my favourite spot, and I opened my eyes, startled—nay, frightened—by the tall figure standing over me in place of the familiar, soothing etching of gilded clouds I had seen in my mind's eye. It was a woman, also naked, one hand on her hip, the other cradling a grapefruit-sized breast, a stunning vision of loveliness and sensuality—maybe the single most erotic and unexpected sight I have ever beheld.

'You seem to be enjoying yourself,' came the luscious voice, speaking the most tumescent, fecund Greek I have heard fall from mortal lips. Her words evoked exuberant laughter, without so much as a giggle or shudder within them. It was quite extraordinary. At any other time in my life, I would have been paralysed with embarrassment. Not then.

I opened my legs under her, looking up at her but shielding my eyes from the sun. 'I could well say the same of you,' I shot back, with more playfulness than rancour.

'Oh, you should,' she replied, and knelt down so I could see her without looking into the sun. She was a daunting, large woman, less than ten centimetres under two metres tall, with thick, dark, powerful thighs and broad shoulders, but possessed of a ravishing beauty as well, with huge eyes black as onyx and long, wavy hair as dark and purple-black as my own. She had a strong but beautiful nose and the most astonishing mouth I have ever beheld—mischievous and potent in its set and provocation but with a fullness that just withheld a deep, unknown wound I could not but guess at.

'My name is Joan,' I offered up without thinking.

'Call me Alcippe,' she whispered back. She lay down beside me, and we talked about things I cannot recall. The whole time, it was as if I were distracted by some distant yet pervasive drone or hum that captivated my soul entire and from which I could not turn my attention. She asked me questions and I answered them. Naked, truthful, without hesitation. On occasion I would ask a question back, and the answers were always mysterious puzzles that revealed nothing about the speaker.

'Where are you from?' I asked her.

'Where is anyone from?' she replied. 'What matters is not where I'm from but where I'm going.'

'All right, then,' I said. 'Where are you going?'

'You can perhaps answer that better than I.' I started to respond, but she cut me off. 'The question is, why do you need to know?'

'You are infuriating!'

With complete calm, she drew a finger with the lightest touch down my hip and the length of my thigh. 'A soul like yours is so seductive,' she whispered, 'drawn without effort to its boiling point, to that place where the flesh can barely house it before it ruptures from its own need to be unbound. Let me release you, Joan.' Her voice, her words, her cascading hair and her expertise in the most occult matters all overwhelmed me, and when she leaned over and took my lips, draping a heavy thigh over my slender waist, I yielded at once, opening my mouth and taking her tongue in the most incredible kissing I have ever known. Her tongue was huge, and she was fucking my soul with it the way Clovis had with his tarse, yet these sensations differed from what I had experienced with Clovis. Her power over me was one of pure eroticism, but with less of the emotional vulnerability I had felt from the beginning towards Clovis—yet the sensual allure and the doors she opened to my erotic being were unbearable in their intoxication. She asked me if I was hungry, and I replied I was. She had a small basket with her containing delicious creamy cheese and flavourful rye bread, which we both downed with some fruity red wine. After more kissing and caressing, we finished off with pears and figs, and as the sun approached its zenith and beat down on us in our verdant meadow, I began to feel nauseated to a most unpleasant degree for some time before needing to vomit. At first I attributed this to the intense heat and the haste with which I had gorged myself, but Alcippe was experiencing the same thing and before too long had vomited herself. Mild convulsions were also setting in, and I was starting to panic.

'What is happening to us? Have we eaten something poisonous?'

'You mustn't concern yourself,' she said, smiling with an odd calm, considering what was happening. 'I've been eating this same cheese and loaf of bread the past two days. Whatever is wrong, it's minor and will pass soon enough, I'm sure of it.' She handed me some chopped mint. 'Here, take this; it will help.'

'I don't understand,' I murmured, chewing the mint with the vague awareness I was asking this not just of Alcippe but also of myself, and the distinction between those two concepts was vanishing. I felt she would have heard me, even had I not voiced it aloud. I watched the light—and shadow—about Alcippe move on her face, on her strong, dark shoulders, into and out of the deep, glistening cleft between her breasts, like a numen composed of layers and folds. Countless silent motions crinkled and echoed between my ears in a thousand separate sounds: the turning of a leaf in a tree ten metres away, the rustling of the thick, twisted deposits of hair in her armpits, a bird winging overhead, the gentle soughing of the grass in the wind as a whole and the intricate, minute sounds of the individual blades rubbing against one another. I looked behind and above Alcippe and saw the trees resonating and vibrating about themselves in various states of light and shadow, their leaves and all their branches facing first in one direction, then the other, but moving not. Of a sudden I found I had been laughing for some time—laughing at the myriad sights and sounds which had been tinkering with my senses, a kind of involuntary laughter as random as the passing of gas. Tufts of cloud infused with light dipt towards the meadow and touched the grass in the distance, then withdrew into the sky. It was in that moment, watching the clouds touching the ground all round us, that I knew God was there in the meadow with us, letting all of this happen with His quiet assurance that all was right with the world and nothing need be feared. 'God's laughing with us,' I said, giggling in bliss. I looked back at Alcippe, and she was watching me and laughing also, her face shifting right in front of my eyes, her nose sliding down towards the right side of her mouth, an eye circling over one of her cheekbones, growing larger and then smaller as it turned. I should have been horrified, but the sight of it made me laugh harder. Over her shoulder I saw a cottony finger of cloud touching the grass and dancing about it before lifting again into the sky. 'Do-dee-do,' I sang, making dancing motions with my own fingers in front of her face. She burst out laughing so hard, she swallowed wrong, coughing up a terrible racket and making us both laugh even harder, and we fell into the grass doubled over in paroxysms of uncontrollable laughter while a wind, shaped into an enormous stone wheel of some kind with a wide, broad edge, rolled with the weight of concrete to and fro just over our heads. When we recovered, she slid herself on top of me, and at first I did not want to be touched—not just by her but by anything. But she lowered herself down until nothing but her tongue was touching me, dabbing at and suckling my nipple. She must have aroused my nipple for close to an hour until my legs opened and closed with increasing agitation. My desire and need for sexual release mounted more and more until I begged her to put her fingers inside me. In all this time not a word had been spoken between us, but with my eyes closed, the afternoon sky changed over hours into dusk and then into night, and into morning and daylight again, and into night once more, and whatever it was in my sex was awake in the light and asleep in the dark, but its dreams continued to arouse me, and as morning came, my own arousal wakened it anew, and by then the creature was part of me, it needed what I needed and I could no longer endure what I felt. My body and all my limbs were convulsing, and the tears were streaming down my face in bondage to an ineffable pleasure that either would not begin or would not end, I could not tell which. Something liquid but with the warmth of molten gold pulsed through my temples, my neck, my arms and all through my chest and chimed to the motion of the wind, shuttling in my ears as through vaults of eroded air and stone. 'Come kiss me, Alcippe,' I whimpered, 'kiss me and kiss me and kiss me, please, give me release—'

And with that I opened my eyes and saw it was still daylight; no time had passed, and even the same two thrushes were hopping about under the Aleppo pine nearby. I was softening into liquid form under Alcippe's fingers, lips and tongue until at last I throttled in a massive release, streams of images issuing out of me: close-ups of Clovis's face, his eyes, mouth, forehead, hair, his voice, the words 'I love you' over and over again, the rains soaking us the morning after our first tryst in the grasses, the bandits' assault on the open road, our horses squealing, the sword plunging into poor Ewald's chest and the crimson arc of his end, the brigand's arms round Clovis's neck, choking him—and then emptiness, nothingness, lodged in the black, suffocating folds of a boundless, heaving lung, a place starker than any I imagined my beloved Clovis to be in now, the most profane image I could ever conjure forth at the moment of my release.

At long last, a still calm, not a sound or motion as I lay spent and slippery with sweat in the grass. I let the colours of the meadow engulf me in my languor, holding each moment in time from one to the next until, without warning, the fluids ruptured, and I snapped awake—I had fallen asleep and knew it not, until I started up and opened my eyes. It had been in truth for no time at all—the sun was in the same position in the sky—but in my poisoned and delusional state, it took me a minute to perceive the odd difference: Alcippe was gone. I sat up and looked all about me, but she was nowhere to be found, and in that instant I knew beyond all doubt she was not coming back. Surveying the meadow and taking in the myriad sights and sounds surrounding me, I struggled to understand what I was feeling then. In one sense I was abandoned by this seductive creature who had done so many things to me—by ambush, no less—and then left me there alone and taken apart on every possible level, and yet in another I was relieved beyond words because, for reasons I could not, forsooth, fathom, she terrified me. What persists to this day is a memory of one of the most predatory, lawless and irresistible souls I have ever encountered in a woman of more staggering beauty, power and charisma than I have ever beheld. Indeed, a compelling attraction to my assistant, the young and innocent Rafaela from Verona, in a woman otherwise immune to the charms of the female form, is inexplicable save the fact Rafaela's face and her mouth most of all are shocking in their resemblance to Alcippe's. But in that hour, alone in the meadow with all the terrors she had set loose in me, I cursed Alcippe and declared good riddance all in the same breath. I swore if I ever saw her again, I would pound her into a pile of bloodied flesh and bone, but she was over twice my size and far more dangerous, and I knew it to be the folly of a madwoman.

My fragmented experience of the world and myself still in full thrall, with no one else to bounce these sensations off of, the effect of all this upon my spirit and senses was many-fold magnified. As I sat in the grass, it undulated and rose up under my bare haunches in a trillion fingers reaching towards the heavens and threatening to seize me up in their grasp, and so I stood—for what seemed the first time in days. Never had walking erect felt so alien and unnatural. My feet plopped one in front of the other as if I might fall to the ground out of the absurdity of my body in vertical form, my shoulders veering from one direction to the next. My arms were more or less at my sides, but they radiated out like wooden spindles several metres in length from my trunk. The wind coursed through me like the gaping maw of a gigantic beast, with a stentorian bellows-breath to match. The scale of nature about me was vast and elephantine. I was as a small, feeble critter, stumbling about in a world of towering forces and living things, amongst which there was little differentiation between one and the other. The wind was as possessed of long, cavernous teeth and heaving ribs as any living animal, and for a period of time, I swore it gave chase to me as its quarry. A bird wavered in the air overhead as a silent witness, as if keeping a certain distance from the violence it knew was about to befall me. Horrific images passed in front of my eyes, of my body being torn apart by mammoth teeth and cast about in long, glistening pieces, and when the wind shrieked, I would fall into the grass, shivering and pallid as though on the verge of being sick again. More and more clouds moved in, and the sway and pitch of the land deepened before me and dropt away, as it were, from my feet, a continent in collapse. Even the sky was perched on the brink of some destructive bottoming out, and immense boomings hundreds of kilometres across propelled the landscape in somersaults up and over itself, as if I might leave the earth altogether and fall up into the roof of Heaven. I was exhausted from what appeared to be many hours of heightened panic, when perhaps half an hour of real time in all had passed. And, for reasons I could not fathom, just as these terrifying onslaughts on my senses and equilibrium relented, I became fixated on God as an object of desire: sexual desire. Roaming lost in the land of Homer and Aeschylus, I was overtaken with images of Leda and the Swan, of that mythical coupling and the sensations of a young girl's flesh quivering in waves of pleasure and feathers as she moaned in the clutches of Zeus's sovereignty; but these images progressed to more familiar images in human form of so obscene and pleasurable a nature, I dare not speak of them even now. For this was no longer Zeus but God Himself embracing me and, yes, ravishing me with the most primaeval, penetrating acts a woman can suffer. But *suffering* is not at all the right word, let me be quite clear, and as I was pinned down into the grass, I could no longer tell who had done the seducing, and I remember shouting out in the meadow, 'Good God, can I really be this vain?' But in those moments in the grass just before the winds began to presage rain, I took a form outside myself—in measure and substance eternal, not real: *the essence of a beauty He could not leave, like the one creation He must always have about Him.* I dared not look upon Him, for His sounds were monstrous with agony and a great commotion of wind and congress pulling me out of myself and up into the air, His eye in me, my form and His locked in worship, the very atoms of His Being flashing worlds apart at the seams. At last the rolling, thunderous union fell away, and coursing waters lit by fire over distant provinces hardened and sank into iron banks and moored me to my verdant bed. I was blind with mortal hubris and degradation where I lay, and for days and days afterwards, a massive drone pressed me into my place in the grass until the skies darkened and the rains rained over me, my life, my approaching death, until towards dusk the spell dissipated and went down with the old sun in a riotous blur of departure, and I was cradled in the hidden light of all matter and took my leave back to the monastery.

The bearded, olive-skinned subdeacon of the papal curia under Gregory IV made his way in the brilliant heat and Aegean-fuelled light of Athens towards the Parthenon. Weightless yet mindful birds floated overhead, never wandering far from the commerce below. The year was 841. The Saracens, having conquered Sicily, were now in Calabria, and Greece lay in the throes of a second iconoclasm under Theophilos. Athens was no longer the glorious centre of culture and learning it had been in centuries past, but the subdeacon was grateful natheless for any excuse to land upon its shores—in this case, a visit with an old friend, well placed in the Church of the Eastern Roman Empire in the theme of Hellas, to discuss the current state of iconoclasm. The pontiff wanted an assessment of the Orthodox Church's response in light of recent stories involving the burning of monks' beards and even isolated killings. Gregory was concerned about the stray Western monasteries within Greece which were not practising icon worship. The subdeacon's friend could not receive him until tomorrow, leaving him the day to spend in Athens at his leisure.

He had decided to attend a lecture at the Parthenon after first stopping at a stand for a flagon of wine with fruit slices and roast lamb. One of the locals there told him about some interesting lectures on Christianity in the early centuries, which he presumed might well be illuminating from a Greek Orthodox perspective in the time of Theophilos. This could give a window into the nature of doctrinal teachings upheld by the emperor in these parts in response to the iconophiles.

Upon finding a comfortable seat, he sat in on the lecture of a young cleric who was speaking with passion about the importance of Christian unification between East and West, and the critical aspect of reciprocity and full participation in the formulation of all doctrinal amendments. He spoke in complex sentence structures, yet his Greek was at times halting, as if he'd just come to it within the past year or so.

'The unilateral decision of the Third Council of Toledo in 589 in adding the word *Filioque* to the Nicene Creed is a penetrating example of what happens when this practice of full representation and consent is not embraced,' the lecturer was saying. 'The Orthodox faith has always included the Father alone in its recitation of the Creed:

"'We believe in one God, the Father almighty, maker of heaven and earth, of all things visible and invisible; and in one Lord, Jesus Christ, the only begotten son of God, begotten from the Father before all ages, light from light, true God from true God, begotten not made...

And ascended to heaven, and sits on the right hand of the *Father...*"

'That is because in Orthodox doctrine, the Father alone comes from nothing, and because the wording in Scripture, John 15:26, contains the very language taken by the Council of Constantinople in fashioning its Creed: "But when the Comforter is come, whom I will send unto you from the Father, even the Spirit of truth, which proceedeth from the Father, he shall testify of me."'

Many heads in the assembly were nodding.

'This is always how the Creed has been worded in the Orthodox Church, and to state, as Epiphanius of Salamis did in the year 403 in *Ankyrotos* and as St Augustine of Hippo did around the same time in *De Trinitas*, that God the Holy Spirit proceeds from a double procession of the Father and the Son, is heresy in the Orthodox faith.' Here he paused for some time in silence. Looking out over the crowd before him, he raised his hand. 'I'd like to put this to a vote, if I may. Would all those who do not agree such a representation is heresy, please raise your hand?' He waited for a long time, but not a single hand was raised.

'Yet this is what the addition of *Filioque* does,' he continued. 'The Third Council was composed in full of bishops of the Western Christian Church, so its adoption of *Filioque* into the Nicene text is twice blasphemous: first for its content and second for the council's action of amending the Creed without the permission or representation of the Eastern Christian Church at the council.' The lecturer turned to another section of the volume in front of him on the lectern but first looked up.

'Doctrinal unity and the lack of full representation are contradictory concepts,' he said, laughing, shaking his head. 'Before Church leaders ever take any action, they must needs consider whether representation of all factions and their participation in the process are secured. Otherwise the doctrinal authority of any measure or amendment they pass is illusory.'

The subdeacon raised his hand. 'You are aware that at the time of the Third Council, a profound and divisive crisis as regards Adoptionism and the heretical views of Arius held the Church in full thrall, requiring immediate action to forestall the real and imminent possibility those evil doctrines would prevail?'

'Of course,' the young man replied, smiling. 'And it would, no doubt, have taken many weeks, if not months, to convene a council in which both East and West would have had full representation.' He paused for effect. 'But there was all of history afterwards for the word to be withdrawn, for such a council to be convened—yet this was never done.' Here he locked eyes with his questioner.

The subdeacon nodded in approval.

'Once the immediate crisis passed, ample time existed for revisiting this issue within the entire Church, but the East continued to be denied a final doctrinal resolution, and this action—or, if you prefer, this continued inaction—was in itself divisive in its arrogance, just as Charlemagne's coronation in 800 was divisive in its arrogance,'—and here he paused again, looking down at the volume on the lectern before resuming—'and just as the imposition of silence upon women in the Church and their exclusion from roles of leadership is divisive, when the writings of Paul in Romans 16 acknowledge in clear terms, give thanks to and exalt the contributions of women, even as apostles.' Here there was a general flutter of restiveness and shifting of bodies in their seats, an unspoken yet palpable resistance to these last words.

The subdeacon sat in silence, knowing others would take up the response. This was Greece, after all, where women were accorded far less of a voice even than in Rome.

And indeed, a much older man raised his voice in objection without asking permission to speak. 'Women have no place in the Orthodox

Church beyond silent obeisance to the Word. All the trouble begins with women.'

For the first time, the lecturer appeared to stiffen, standing erect with his hands gripping the corners of the lectern. There were murmurs in the crowd of apparent approval of the man's words. 'And, pray, what is meant by "all the trouble begins with women"?' he offered with just an edge of tension in his voice, speaking to the white-haired man in his seat.

The old man laughed and glanced about the assembly, holding his hands up as if to say, 'Does he not understand?' Facing front and folding his hands together in front of himself, he began: 'Look at it this way. Whenever the Church has had women in leadership roles, she has foundered. In the first centuries, elder women were permitted to be deaconesses, and these were mere lay positions. They assisted the priests. That was all. Jesus could have chosen His mother, the Virgin Mary, or Mary Magdalene or some other woman worthy of such a position to be one of the Twelve Apostles of His ministry here on earth, but He did not. Instead, He chose twelve men. And after that, seventy more disciples were chosen to spread the Word, and these too were men—all of them.'

'What about Romans 16?' the young man asked in response. 'In that passage, Paul mentions an apostle—a Greek, no less—named Iounian, or Junia, who was almost for certain a woman. Paul greets and pays tribute to Andronicus and Junia, "who are of note among the apostles". Even those who would insist these two were noted by the apostles rather than being apostles themselves cannot deny Paul admits they have "been in Christ before me". How then can one sustain the insistence upon women's silence in the Church?'

His adversary dismissed the lecturer's question with a wave of his hand and a guffaw. 'That means less than nothing. Paul never identifies the person you speak of as a woman. Indeed, it was almost certain that both of them were men, in especial if they were both apostles.'

Many of the others spoke up in support of his words.

'I see,' the young man said with a nod and a furrowed brow, fingering his chin and starting to stroll across the stage. 'So, because Paul omitted to identify Junia as a woman, although the name, in and of itself, creates the clear presumption it is female, it would be irrational to presume Junia is female and not male, is that what you're saying?'

The older gentleman nodded with an air of parental relief, as though he'd at last gotten his child to do something the child had been refusing to do or see.

But the lecturer halted and turned back towards the old man, holding up a single finger. 'But if that is the case, and omission of a word that would defeat what is otherwise an outright presumption in Scripture does in fact defeat that presumption, by pure virtue of its omission, then, pray, which is the word in John 15:26 confirming the Holy Spirit proceeds from the Father and not the Son?'

The old man opened his mouth with a muffled bark, followed by helpless silence, his hand gesturing at empty air. 'I—the passage says that—the Holy Spirit "proceedeth from the Father"—'

'Not "the Father alone" and not "from the Father and not the Son". It never says that He proceedeth from the Father alone,' the lecturer said.

'No, that is different, it is not the same thing at all—'

The subdeacon, florid with admiration and grinning from ear to ear at the young man's mastery, stood up. 'No, in fact, it is the same. You haven't an argument you can make in your defence. You cannot decree that scriptural omission is identical to outright denial or exclusion in one instance, and dismiss such an omission as irrelevant in another for mere ideological convenience. You would reduce the Bible to a chameleonic document with no real, enduring meaning beyond the personal biases and predispositions of its most recent reader.'

The man was fidgeting in his seat but robbed in that moment of the power of speech.

Turning his gaze from the old man and surveying the assembly, the subdeacon shrugged his shoulders. 'I am the subdeacon of the papal curia under His Holiness Gregory IV, and I believe I may speak with some authority on these matters.'

The lecturer bowed his head towards the subdeacon. 'We are honoured—and blessed—to have you in our midst this day. And we thank you for your sage observations.'

The subdeacon bowed back in subtle acknowledgement. 'However,' he cautioned, 'I would not on that account make the mistake of presuming my words allow for the inclusion of women in pastoral roles any more than they permit of a deduction the Holy Spirit proceeds from the Father alone and not the Son. Indeed, the Western Church and His Holiness deny in the strongest terms both notions, and, borrowing from principles of statutory construction, the burden is on you as a proponent of each to prove those omissions are meaningless.'

The lecturer pondered this for a moment. 'Begging your pardon, subdeacon—' He fumbled for what to say without a name.

'Leo.'

'Thank you, Leo. But, if I may, whilst I understand your assertion as to the former as regards the sex of Junia, I am at a loss to see how the burden is upon us to disprove the inclusion of the Son in the Nicene Creed.' Here he folded his hands together in front of himself and trained his eyes on the subdeacon. 'After all, the textual omission of the Son in John 15:26 creates the very presumption of its exclusion which you speak of, does it not?'

Leo pursed his lips at this response but smiled within himself. 'Well done. But we must needs recall that what has been adopted as Church doctrine creates its own presumption.'

Here the lecturer adopted a relaxed stance, speaking in his most conciliatory tone to soften the words which came next. 'Quite. Natheless, I would point out that the verse in Scripture omits the Son in entirety, and as you yourself admitted but a moment ago, the addition of *Filioque* to the Creed is grounded neither in Scripture nor in Church doctrine but rather was added to foreclose the doctrines of Adoptionism and Arius from further incorporation. It was itself the product of human concerns alone and is to that end an artefact of administrative purposes.'

Leo was nodding. 'Again, well said. Forsooth, I cannot dispute in full the earlier point that, in the interest of Christian unity, the amendment should be revisited.'

'My purpose here today in this lecture is twofold,' the young man continued, turning towards the audience. 'First, I wanted to shew how the exclusion of certain factions or voices from important decisions by the Church inhibits rather than fosters unity. When these divisions occur along doctrinal lines—as in the addition of *Filioque* to the Nicene Creed or in the exclusion of women from pastoral roles—they tend to fragment and isolate individual groups, even from other groups in similar circumstances of oppression by the majority view within the Church.

'As a group, for example, you appeared to dismiss out of hand the notion women could participate in pastoral care in the Church, based on Church authority at fundamental variance with Scripture. And yet, this is the same method by which the Western Church excluded your Church from its decision to include *Filioque* in the Nicene Creed—a method I presume all or a substantial majority of you would deem invalid.'

Subdeacon Leo was shaking his head in wonderment, unable to suppress a gentle laugh at the young scholar's mental adroitness.

'As we can see, the doctrinal status of the group being excluded is far less important in practice than the mere fact any such exclusion erodes unity in and of itself amongst the entire Christian community. This is an effective method of control the Gnostics used often in the early centuries of Christianity.

'My second purpose was to illustrate by way of these examples how people employ consistent methods of logic through inconstant means to arrive at contradictory, even absurd, conclusions based on personal convenience. You will recall I took a poll of this audience as to the doctrinal heresy of the double procession maintained by the Western Church. All of you were in agreement, yet not a shred of textual evidence beyond that of omission exists to support the conclusion the Son is excluded based on the text of John 15:26. Moreover, the evidence in Romans 16 supporting the conclusion Junia was not a woman is at least as weak as—and perhaps weaker than—the evidence in John 15:26 demonstrating the Holy Spirit proceeds from the Father alone and not the Son. Yet the overwhelming tenor of the group is that Junia was a man. This distinction, it seems to me, makes sense from the sole perspective of personal convenience rather than from any position of doctrinal authority.'

A blond young man raised his hand. 'Begging your pardon, but just because you have cited two examples in which a conclusion was reached without irrefutable support, you may not on that account conclude neither conclusion is valid, nor even that one of them is invalid, yes? There may, after all, turn out to be support for the truth of both.'

The lecturer smiled, pointing at the speaker. 'I wondered when someone was going to get to that,' he said. 'And you are quite correct. However, proving or disproving the impropriety of these conclusions was not my intent here. Rather, I wished to illustrate how faulty logic drives conclusions when they are grounded not in reason but in personal preferences and biases towards or away from certain groups or beliefs and their place within the Church.' Noting he was at the end of his time for the day, he concluded, but the subdeacon sought him out as people were leaving, extending his hand.

'Leo of Rome. I thought it would be a pity not to make a formal introduction after so rich and nuanced an exchange was had on such penetrating matters.'

'Johannes Angelicus of Mainz,' the young scholar returned, taking the subdeacon's hand with warmth and firmness between his own, but colouring. 'Thank you for your praise.'

'The name fits you well. *Brother* Johannes?'

'Yes, though I never took my vows.'

'Where was that?'

'Lorsch Abbey in—'

'Yes, I know,' Leo said, laughing. 'You needn't say anything else after "Lorsch Abbey"; it would be almost provincial to say more.'

Johannes coloured even deeper. Leo found this man's sincerity and self-consciousness refreshing in one so learned. 'Do not concern yourself with your vows,' the subdeacon continued. 'You are more erudite than many bishops I know.' Leo folded his hands together, putting both forefingers to his lips in a deep, reflective silence. 'Your views are somewhat more liberal than my own but not in any egregious way— and I could use someone to keep me honest.' Another pause. 'I am seeing an old friend tomorrow afternoon, an abbot well connected here in Athens, to discuss the iconoclasm problem and how Theophilos is responding to it. There have been ugly rumours. His Holiness is concerned as to the safety of Western monks in the theme of Hellas. I could use someone to transcribe, and I will want to hear your own impressions beforehand.'

Johannes was taken aback by the unexpected overture but both flattered and elated at such a prospect. 'It would be my honour to accompany you, subdeacon.'

'Leo,' he said. 'If all goes well, I would consider having you accompany me back to Rome in a more permanent capacity if that were of interest to you.'

Johannes did not have to think. 'Then I will hope this may come to pass,' he replied, and added, 'I would need to have my horse with me, though—he is like an older brother to me now.'

'Consider it done.'

Johannes conducted himself with ease and composure at the meeting and provided Leo with observations prior to their visit, which helped shape and direct the focus of the subdeacon's questions to his friend and colleague. In particular, Johannes supplied first-hand confirmation of the lack of oppressive or otherwise untoward conduct by the local ecclesiastical authority towards the non-Orthodox monastery where Johannes had resided for some three years, or towards any of the Brothers in service there.

However, when Leo's friend stated in unequivocal terms no inappropriate or inhumane treatment of monks practising icon worship, beyond excommunication and dismissal, had taken place in the theme of Hellas—at least none he knew of—Johannes spoke up in direct response for the first time.

'Do you, then, have no knowledge or opinion of the treatment of one Brother Demetrios, an Athenian icon worshipper, whose beard was set afire, whereupon the unfortunate Brother suffered permanent facial burns and disfigurement on that account?'

Abbot Thanos sat up and stiffened in his chair, bristling at this suggestion, and with a tone of evasiveness said, 'Myself, I am unaware of any such incident, and the name you mention is not a familiar one.'

Johannes sat forward, smiling. 'Brother Demetrios has been serving the Lord here in Athens for some thirty years; the events I speak of unfolded but a few weeks ago, and he mentioned you by name.'

Leo's heart fell at the sight of his old friend and confidant denying all knowledge of or responsibility for events he in all likelihood knew well, given Thanos's direct ties to Athens and the long service of the monk in question to the city. Johannes's knowledge of Brother Demetrios both as a fellow monk and friend—for he had seen the old man after his disfigurement—sealed the verdict on this issue. Forsooth, Demetrios had complained of Abbot Thanos by name, amongst others who had failed to speak up against the barbaric practices being followed by zealous fanatics, rumour had it, at Theophilos's bidding.

After expressing disappointment and scorn on the part of the Holy See, for the brutal mistreatment of pious Christians but also for Thanos's straight-faced duplicity in forswearing all knowledge of these events, Leo took his leave, refusing the Abbot's hand and setting to the side once and for all a friendship of some twenty-plus years.

As they were leaving, Leo halted at the end of the hallway and turned to Johannes with a vexed expression. 'I am curious why, in our briefings, you never thought to mention anything to me whatever of Demetrios.'

Johannes met the subdeacon's focused gaze. 'Would you have mentioned it in some way at the outset and provided him an opportunity to defend himself, given the long history of your friendship with the abbot?'

Leo stared at the floor. 'I suppose I might have.'

'For that very reason, I thought it best, in the interest of enquiry and the truth of the matter, to exclude it. It is natural to want to help out an old friend, but it might well have mitigated your perception of the true nature of the situation and the full measure of his deception.'

A bitter smile formed on Leo's face, his eyes narrowing. 'Let us take our leave of this land,' he said in a hollow voice, and the two of them stopped at Johannes's monastery, took charge of Hannibal and proceeded to Rome together.

Uncle Moszhe had not yet received the letter when Patek and Rahel showed up at his door, and although he was home at the time, given current developments, he was reluctant to answer the door when not expecting visitors. After several failed attempts, Patek pounded on the door with full force, yelling, 'Uncle? Uncle Moszhe! It's Patek!' at the top of his voice through the door, which brought his uncle face to face with him.

'My goodness, Patek, Rahel, what brings you here? You look terrible.'

'Thank you, Uncle,' Patek said, knowing his uncle's propensity for innocent gracelessness but too exhausted to address the comment with tact. 'I guess this means you didn't receive the letter.' After Patek explained the situation to Moszhe, his uncle gave both of them a hug, fighting back tears and cursing Hitler. Between Patek's father and uncle, Moszhe had always been the more emotional of the two. For that reason, Moszhe reflected more sympathy for Rahel's state of diffuse helplessness than his nephew's more action-based approach to the conflict.

'We need to arm ourselves and raise an army,' Patek said in response to Moszhe's flood of pronouncements that the worst was over now the two of them had left Germany. 'Uncle, be honest now, do you think Hitler will be content with ruling Germany? He has already annexed Austria and Sudetenland. What makes you think he will stop there? And what on earth moves you to believe he will be satisfied exterminating Jews in Germany? He has already identified the Jew as the enemy of Europe, not just the enemy of Germany. He can do anything he pleases at home, but if the Jew is allowed to flourish and proliferate elsewhere, the same bad end will still come to Germany—and the rest of humanity, that is, *his* nation-state, because that is how Hitler views the rest of the world.'

'Always so headstrong.' Moszhe scoffed, shaking his head and talking to Rahel as if her husband were not there. 'Patek always knew better than his dad what needed to be done; that was all I ever heard from my brother, he of blessed memory, even when his son was but a boy of ten.'

But Rahel spoke up in defence of her husband. 'I thank HaShem for men like Patek. If we were all like me—so trusting, so willing to always see nothing but the good in people—where would we be now?' she asked. 'I put complete trust in Hitler; everyone did. I thought he was our saviour. But Patek knew better. You should salute him instead of ridiculing him.'

Moszhe's eyes widened at her pluck in addressing a male elder. 'A woman who supports her husband, that is all to the good,' he said with a smile. 'But you'd better be sure what the husband is saying is worth standing behind,' he added, shaking a finger at her. 'The Nazis are very powerful and organised. How are a few thousand Jews going to stand up against the Third Reich? We'd be obliterated.'

'Obliteration is what is already happening to us,' Patek snapped. He told his uncle of the thoughts that had been taking hold in his mind: that there were still many wealthy and powerful Jews, both in Germany and abroad, with the means and the connections to fund an army; that enlisting these people now was critical, before Hitler succeeded in liquidating all Jewish capital and commerce; and that people needed to be educated on the evil, duplicitous nature of the ego behind Germany's ascension, of its insatiable appetite for power and dominion and most of all of its single-mindedness of purpose in ridding the world of every Jewish person. Patek was confident that once people understood the monstrous and merciless nature they were dealing with—and the certainty of their own extinction if they did nothing—they would shrink from confrontation no more.

These debates continued among the three of them over the next many months as the world became ever more dangerous. With lightning speed following Kristallnächt, the Nazi Propaganda Ministry transferred its hatred towards Jews from the subjective domain of the public arena to the 'objective' one of legislative enactments. With surgical precision, these laws stripped Jewish people of their rights one by one. This legislation promoted a general policy of Aryanisation: the transfer of Jewish-owned interests and property to Aryans for a pittance of their actual value.

Jews, already barred from employment in the public sector, were now forbidden from practice in the private sector of most occupations. Jewish academics were no longer permitted to use libraries. On 15 November 1938, the week before Patek and Rahel left Zbaszyn, the Reich Education Ministry expelled all Jews from German schools. On 29 November, Jews were no longer allowed to keep carrier pigeons, disabling at least in part their ability to communicate. On 3 December, SS Chief Heinrich Himmler revoked the rights of Jews to own or operate an automobile or truck. On 5 December, the Reich Economics Ministry froze all Jewish assets and property. Then, on 20 January 1939, Adolf Hitler delivered a public speech to the German Reichstag in which he stated the following:

> The peoples [of the earth] will soon realise that Germany under National Socialism does not desire the enmity of other peoples. I want once again to be a prophet. If the international Finance-Jewry inside and outside of Europe should succeed in plunging the peoples of the earth once again into a world war, the result will be not the Bolshevisation of earth, and thus a Jewish victory, but the annihilation of the Jewish race in Europe.

But a peculiar brew of events involving German diplomacy with its neighbours—Poland in particular—was taking shape. German Foreign Minister Joachim von Ribbentrop had met with French Minister for Foreign Affairs Georges Bonnet in 1938, and based on his understanding of Bonnet's statements at that time, Ribbentrop assured Hitler in 1939 that France would not come to Poland's aid if attacked. Germany signed a non-aggression pact with the Soviet Union on 23 August 1939, in which each nation pledged neutrality in the event either was attacked by a third party. Under the secret terms of the treaty, however, the two nations agreed to divide Poland between them, with Germany taking the western part and the Soviet Union taking the eastern part.

One week later, Patek, Rahel and Moszhe, after staying up late and drinking the last of Moszhe's beer and vodka the night before, were rocked awake just after nine on 1 September 1939, by the thunderous sound of bombs exploding in nearby parts of the city. One of the blasts felt but a few blocks away and shook their building. As they and the rest of Poland were about to discover, the German Luftwaffe had bombed the southern central Polish town of Wieluń in the hours before dawn without a declaration of war, all but obliterating the town and killing over thirteen hundred civilians. No Polish military presence existed there at the time. Germany followed this up within hours with aerial raids of major cities throughout Poland, including Katowice, Kraków, Tunel and Tczew before hitting Warsaw.

On 3 September, the nations of Britain, France and Canada declared war on Germany, which still had issued no declaration of war in spite of unabated bombing. Hitler, having posited himself with artifice as a reluctant witness to the hypothetical global conflict outlined in his 20 January speech to the Reichstag, now had his world war into which International Jewry had 'plunged the peoples of the earth'. He had chosen as his target the nation with the highest concentration of Jews in all Europe. In fact, as early as June of 1939, Hitler had already fantasised the destruction of Poland's proud capital, Warsaw, and had drawn up architectural plans for its conversion into a bucolic German town of less than a tenth of its 1.5 million inhabitants. The royal castle alone would be spared—to serve as Hitler's retreat. The Führer was drawn to the ideas of one Friedrich Pabst, a German military architect who conceived of crushing a nation's cultural identity by first destroying its physical monuments and symbols.

In the first week of September, 1939, it was clear Germany had but one objective: the capture and total subjugation of Warsaw and with it the entirety of Poland. Devastating and unrelenting artillery fire and aerial bombing of the city continued day and night for many days, driving hundreds of thousands into the streets and out of the city. Moszhe, Rahel and Patek huddled together in the hall of Moszhe's apartment under the biggest doorway in prayer, hoping to be spared the unthinkable, as blast after deafening blast shook the building to its foundation, the sound of plaster breaking off and falling all about them, as the stentorian explosions grew louder and closer. One night, after a series of terrifying salvos came one upon the next and struck the fear of death into them all, after the bombing at last trailed off sometime well past midnight, they ventured out into the street to survey the damage. Their neighbourhood was unrecognisable, alien: mountains of gigantic rock slabs and stone in the street, motorcars crushed under massive debris, the air choking and thick with dust, the eerie plainsong of the sirens echoing throughout the empty streets and then, bodies, some cut open or chopped in half, others crushed into a stew of ground-up flesh and bone—and somewhere in the distant night, the moans and screams of a few souls in agony, still clinging to life. At first the trio tried to walk towards the sounds they heard, but even after arduous and peril-ous walking for blocks through the rubble, the sounds were no closer—or even farther away. The earlier aerial raids over the past several days had already driven out most of the city's population, creating a ghost town. The combination of night and the thick, oppressive dust floating off Warsaw's ruins cut visibility down to nothing and cast a pall over the world, as if all hope of life had been drawn out of the air, leaving noth-ing but a dead, dry, elaborate prison of collapsed being, stretching out in all directions and frozen in time and space. Moszhe stood before the smouldering wreckage and stared, his mouth open and silent. The worst possibilities he could ever imagine—atrocity, the end of the world—were coming to pass right before his eyes. His head, his shoulders, his old and fragile ribs had been spared—for now. His nephew Patek and Patek's young wife, thanks be to HaShem, had also been spared—but nothing was guaranteed. How much longer would this good fortune hold true for the three of them? Weeks? Days? Hours? Wherever aerial attacks commenced, ground forces were sure to follow.

One lone line of four street lamps still burned overhead at the end of their street; beyond them lay a realm submerged in darkness. Rahel looked down and saw a woman's legs sticking out of a pile of rubble, covered in blood. Looking closer at something strange, she knelt down to the sight of the tiniest hand she had ever seen, perhaps three cen-timetres wide, protruding at a right angle to the plane of the woman's legs—was this her baby? The hand was motionless, unreal, its fingers all spread out in perfect symmetry, like something done by a sculptor with an extraordinary feel for the mortal form after death. In its perfection it looked more like a doll's hand, something manufactured or produced, save the gash at the wrist to which it was attached. Its fragility and the state of her own mind in willing it into something fake overwhelmed Rahel, and she fell down into the street, sobbing and screaming in convulsions. Patek held her in his arms and let her sob, saying nothing until she had cried herself out, consoling her as best he could, stroking her hair in the plastery light of the overhead lamps.

Returning to the apartment in silence, all three of them were thunderstruck by the sobering reality that whatever they were going to live on would have to be already in the house. By sheer luck, Moszhe had sizeable stores of grain and other staples he had bought a few days ago, which would allow them to survive for a time, but gas and water mains had been cut by the bombing, requiring more primitive means of preparation and cooking. Rice cooked in boiled milk in a shallow pot using flint and petrol on kindling and newspaper was a curious, sticky concoction, but it would keep them alive.

The next night, watching his nephew doting on Rahel, even under such harrowing conditions, Moszhe was moved by the affection and respect between them. 'These are different times to be living in, my friends,' he said, and, glancing at Rahel, went on: 'The kind of spunk and assertiveness you show, towards your husband, yes, but also towards your male elders, would have been judged with disdain in my time.' He shook his head and smiled at her. 'But it has made me fond of you.' And both Patek and Rahel gave a nervous laugh. 'In these times, I believe it may be more useful than blind obedience and feminine passivity.'

'It is in truth what drew me to her from the start,' Patek offered. 'I can't imagine how I would have survived this without her by my side,' he said, adding, 'or without you taking us in, Uncle.'

'Still…' she began, 'I thought Hitler was the answer to our prayers, just like the rest of Germany. Only Patek—'

'Yes, but that is not what I mean,' said Moszhe, cutting her off. 'I mean, the two of you bring the best, most genuine essences of who you are to one another, and you receive it with grace—and, and it works.' The two of them stared with blank faces at him, not knowing what to say.

Moszhe looked at the floor. 'My Elena, she left me because I was never there for her, because, well, I was too busy being the important man who expected her to be there for me because, you know, I was the man; that's how it worked.' They sat listening in awkward silence. 'Elena was the one who fixed our meals, prepared my clothes, kept the house, did the shopping, had dinner waiting for me even on all those long nights when I did not return home until nine o'clock in the evening—but I did not know her mind, I did not engage with her about the events of this world the way you two do, and when I did, it was to express my opinion, not to be subjected to hers, which could not have mattered in the least…' His voice was breaking, and he left off.

Moszhe reached over and stroked the back of Patek's head. 'You are a good man, nephew, and you are married to a passionate, wonderful woman, and HaShem has given each of you great blessings with the other.' He leaned forward and fixed his gaze on them both. 'And you are going to need all of it.'

The residue of resentment Patek and Rahel had harboured towards Moszhe for his old-world views of women and marriage melted away after his confessions of that night. Moszhe had understood too late his era and his own personality had predestined him for the loveless life to which he was now condemned, a life haunted by remembrance of how ungrateful he had been to the woman who made her life with him and how little he had taken account of her within their marriage as a person with her own feelings and perspectives. It was clear he approved of Patek and Rahel's relationship; with sadness, they also realised he envied it.

Figuring their sector had been destroyed, the three of them surmised the Germans would not waste more munitions on rebombing the area. They were wrong. Three nights later, on 12 September 1939, not long before midnight, silence yielded to a sudden din of aerial bombings, brief but closer than anything they had experienced before. A massive blast tore off their hearing and brought the ceiling down into collapse all round them. A huge broken beam came crashing down upon Moszhe and ran through his abdomen below his sternum, all but cutting him in half. It happened in an instant, so Patek missed it. Moszhe died in seconds, blood gurgling up round and out of his mouth. He had tried to

speak, but Patek's ears were ringing from the intensity of the blast, and he couldn't hear anything. When Patek took his uncle's hand and stared into the faraway despair behind his eyes, Moszhe was already gone. Patek's eyes filled up with tears, blurring his vision. For the first time, something beyond the abstract, ideological concerns of this conflict had reached in and put its touch of death to his own heart and taken away someone he loved. He laid his head down on Moszhe's chest and said goodbye to his uncle, thanking him for opening up his home and his heart to them, before the vibrations—for he still could not hear them—of more bombs jerked his head up, reconnecting him to the present. He looked up to the startling unobstructed view of the night sky through what just a moment before had been the centre of the ceiling of their living room.

'Rahel!' he shouted, taking her by the arm and pointing to the ceiling, where a portion of the adjoining wall near them was about to come down—and certainly would with the next blast. 'We've got to get out of here!' But she could not hear him and did not understand. He pulled her to leave.

She refused to budge, her eyes wide with terror, her arms raised in frantic gestures. 'Where in creation do we go?' All he could hear were muffled sounds, but he understood what she was saying; he saw the resistance in her eyes, and he saw her lips forming 'where' and 'go'.

'Anywhere but here!' he yelled, seizing at her shoulders and shaking them as if to startle her out of a trance. 'Where do you want to go—to dinner, seated round the table? That life is gone! And there's no way back to it—except through the end of this world as we know it. Where do we go? Wherever we can!' He pulled her again, and before they left, he found a large canister of rolled oats and brought it with them.

After stumbling out of their decimated building, the two of them made their way as best they could past and through the piles of concrete and stone that was once their street—towards where, they had no idea. They were looking back and all round them, for they knew ground forces were closing in on the city, but they could not hear. Their deafness magnified the sepulchral unreality of the world through which they were journeying. For blocks and blocks they walked through wreckage without encountering a single soul or even one standing structure that could have afforded protection. In time their hearing returned, but it brought nothing but bad news: the sounds of gunfire in the distance and orders being shouted in German, the voices of German officers growing louder and advancing upon them.

THE END